Evolution

The Wasteland Chronicles, Volume 3

by Kyle West

Published by Kyle West, 2013.

EVOLUTION

First edition. August 4, 2013.

Copyright © 2013 Kyle West.

Written by Kyle West.

10 9 8 7 6 5 4 3 2 1

Also by Kyle West

The Wasteland Chronicles
Apocalypse
Origins
Evolution
Revelation

Watch for more at kylewestwriter.wordpress.com.

To those who have read from the beginning: thanks for your continued support. Your encouragement has kept me going.

Chapter 1

Two months later, and none of what I'd lived felt real. My dad would always be dead. Khloe would always be dead. Bunker 108, along with most every other Bunker, was offline and gone. The United States, along with the rest of the world's governments, no longer existed except as an idea. In their wake were the new players – the Raiders, the gangs, and the empires fueled by slavery, bullets, and blood. In the end, they wouldn't matter, either. After all, this world wasn't ours anymore. This world belonged to *them* – the Xenos. Samuel and Ashton called them that.

When we returned to Earth, it wouldn't be just survival this time. Our mission was to save a planet doomed to die. We needed to take what we'd learned from the Black Files and utilize it. The people of the Old World believed global warming, war, or famine would be our undoing. They were wrong. The Xenos pulled the plug before we ever could – and we were madly trying to plug it back in.

The break from action was nice for the first two weeks, but I was starting to get bored. I filled the time by working out. Samuel was training me in hand-to-hand combat, and Anna was training me in the katana. However, there was only so much I could learn before heading back. I feared not being ready in time.

The coming mission was the only thing I could focus on. In a weird way, it was an escape. Maybe saving the world was the delusion that kept me going. The four of us were caught in it, each in our separate ways and for our separate reasons. It had become our focus, our obsession. Everything else was on hold until our mission reached its conclusion, whatever that conclusion happened to be.

Samuel said Ragnarok was only the beginning. I had come to realize what that beginning actually entailed. Everything would become twisted by the Blights, preparing the way for the Xenos. No one knew when they were coming, or what they were like. But we knew that they were advanced enough to have sent an asteroid hurtling toward Earth, and were probably capable of interstellar travel.

Why they didn't come when we were so weak, no one knew. It was one thing to be grateful for. It gave us time to find a solution.

It was only a matter of time until everything was controlled by the xenovirus, and through the xenovirus, the Voice. Stopping it meant going after the Voice itself. Ashton and Samuel conferred for hour after hour, trying to hash out a plan that would succeed in destroying the Voice while keeping everyone alive. If Bunker One was any indication of what Ragnarok Crater would be like, we were in for the fight of our lives. Even with backup, the Voice wouldn't go down easily.

It wasn't as if Ragnarok Crater was a small thing. It was over a hundred miles wide. The Voice, or whatever controlled the Voice, was located somewhere in that huge area. We had to find a better way of locating its exact point of origin. Ashton said he was working on a solution to that problem.

The bottom line was: we didn't know enough yet. Finding those Black Files had opened a Pandora's Box of questions when we expected answers. We knew the Voice was coming from Ragnarok Crater in a series of low-frequency sound waves, and that the xenofungus transmitted these waves, communicating with all life-forms under its spell. Anything infected with the xenovirus would listen to the Voice's directives. All xenolife behaved as if of one mind. *Something* was controlling it. If we killed that something, it could spell the end of the invasion.

Well, this part of the invasion, anyway. The Black Files stated the Xenos were still coming – I assumed on some sort of ship – or maybe a whole interstellar armada. When they arrived, they were probably expecting to have a planet tailor-made for them, covered with the Blights and all resistance dead. Assuming we *did* kill off the Voice, we still had to deal with Xenofall. We didn't know when Xenofall was coming. It could be tomorrow, one year, or ten years or more from now. We might even all be *dead* by the time Xenofall happened.

Samuel kept telling me to take it one step at a time, so that was what I was trying to do. The first step was preparing myself as much as possible – not just getting my strength back, but getting stronger besides. I ran along the Outer Ring an hour each day. I was improving my speed. I had sprinted more in the past few months than at any other point in my life. I did pushups, pull-ups, and crunches in addition to my martial training with Samuel and Anna. I wanted to be ready for anything.

By the end of the day, I was so tired that I usually fell right asleep. There were times, though, when I couldn't turn off my brain. So much had happened that it was impossible to process. I was constantly stressed. I suffered nightmares. I dreamt of Khloe, buried alive in the dry, red sand. I dreamt of the night when it all went to hell. And the monsters were always there, surrounding me, chasing me over bleak plains and jagged mountains.

The Blights were growing, festering like open sores on the surface. When I looked down at Earth, I could see the Blights when the blood-red clouds weren't so thick. They were only in North America, but according to Ashton and Samuel, that would change over the next ten years. The planet looked *sick*, for lack of a better word. It was as if it were a living thing being poisoned from the inside out.

Then there was the rest of the world, too. The entire planet was depopulated to the same extent as America – or worse. Ashton called the ten years following Ragnarok the Chaos Years – a time when the world's population dropped from 8.4 billion to mere millions. In China, city-states and proto-empires fought amongst the ruins of civilization. In Europe, extreme cold had completely hampered population regrowth. In equatorial regions, people were faring little better. War over limited resources still consumed most of the world. Wars would exist as long as there were enough people to fight them.

None of these people knew about the xenovirus or Xenofall, and trying to communicate that through language barriers seemed impossible. In his first years in Skyhome, Ashton had visited different parts of the world – China, India, Russia, Japan, Africa – but always found one of two things: either no one had survived, or there were so many survivors fighting that making contact was too dangerous. Maybe the Chaos Years ended in 2040 for the United States, but the rest of the world was still living them.

If we didn't succeed in stopping the xenovirus, all of humanity was as good as dead – and not just humanity, but every life-form that had managed to evolve in our planet's tumultuous, 4.6 billion-year history. As unimaginable as that length of time was, I *knew* Earth had never experienced anything like this. A new form of life had invaded. When I left Bunker 108, I never imagined something like the xenovirus could exist. All I wanted was a community to live in, another Bunker, somewhere to be safe.

Well, I had found my community; but now, we were the ones trying to keep the world safe.

***

"Hold still."

Anna grabbed my hands, giving me a stern expression. She twisted my clenched fists roughly on the hilt of her katana, forcing them vertical.

"Keep your grip loose, yet firm."

I tried to do what she told me. I looked into her hazel eyes, which she promptly rolled.

"Stop looking at me and focus. Make your mind blank. I imagine a black plane, a void. Have you been practicing that?"

"Yes," I lied.

"No, you haven't. I can tell." She sighed. "That's the most important part."

"Where did you get this void thing, anyway?"

"I don't know. I made it up, but it works."

I smiled, holding the katana as steady as I could. "So when do I get to swing this thing?"

Anna raised an eyebrow. "Would you quit being perverted and pay attention for once?"

"I'm trying."

She sighed again, but it was forced. The beginnings of a smile played on her lips.

"Seriously. You need to practice meditating. Once you get the hang of it, you can make your mind completely blank. I always do it before a fight. It helps my concentration." She looked at me. "Do you understand?"

"Yeah. Makes sense."

"Good. You really need to practice it. I can't stress that enough." She looked at my arm, touching my left biceps. "You're getting stronger. You've been working out still?"

"Yeah, of course. I didn't realize you were such a fan."

"I'm just commenting on your physique," she said. Despite this comment, her face flushed slightly red. "I can actually see you when you stand sideways. You were so rail-thin before."

"Ouch." I set her katana gently on her bed. "My 'physique,' huh?"

She ignored my comment. "When you go to your hab today, I want you to do the mediation. I mean it."

"Alright. I get it." I turned for the door. "I'm going to grab dinner, if you want to come."

She shook her head. "I still need to practice myself. Thanks, though."

"You've already practiced this morning."

"I practice twice a day. If you can wait a couple hours...maybe. We'll see."

My stomach growled in protest. Between my hunger and her playing hard to get, my stomach was probably going to win. "No, I probably can't wait that long. So you want to meet at the same time tomorrow?"

Anna took up her blade, staring intently ahead. "Works for me."

I left her room and made my way back to my hab. After two months in Skyhome, I finally got the chance to see Anna a little more. Nothing had happened between us. At least, not yet. Even if I thought I was picking up some flirtatious vibes from her, it always looked as if she was doing her best to suppress them. Which made sense; after all, we were all here for the mission. But when you spend a lot of time with someone, you can't help but think about them.

So far, Anna had only agreed to help train me to use the katana. I wanted a backup, in case I somehow couldn't use my gun, but I think we both knew that I was just using training as an excuse to get to know her. I had learned a lot, but I was still a long way from being even semi-competent. All the same, I appreciated everything I was learning, and it was nice to see her.

Still, after two months, I was hoping that things could have progressed a little more with Anna. And I wasn't just crazy. After all, it was *my hand* she decided to grab down there on Earth, when the crawlers had been coming for us on the runway, and it was *me* she had snuggled with on the plane. And the way she looked at me sometimes, when she thought I wasn't looking...well, let's just say there *had* to be something there.

Hopefully, the right opportunity would present itself.

Chapter 2

Back in my hab, I practiced the meditation Anna taught me. I was failing miserably. No matter how much I tried, my thoughts kept spinning out of control. I'd always been a sufferer of the disease known as "thinking too much."

I was grateful when a knock came at the door. Hoping it was Anna, I went to answer. I pressed the exit button, causing the metal door to slide open. I couldn't help but be slightly disappointed when it was Samuel, standing in his characteristic muscle shirt and camo pants. His head, as usual, was shaved bald, and his facial features were sharp and toned. Even after all the R&R, he had been working out. That was Samuel's way – everything he did was for the purpose of succeeding in our mission.

"We're all meeting in Ashton's office to go over the final phase of the mission at 19:30."

"Alright. I need to eat still."

"Make it quick. You have fifteen. Anna and Makara are already waiting."

"What are we going over?"

"We're leaving tomorrow."

"Tomorrow?" I asked. "I thought we still had a couple weeks."

"It's go time, kid," he said. "My arm's healed, and if we stay up here any longer, we'll go soft. Besides, the xenovirus isn't taking any breaks."

I guessed that much was true. "Alright. I'll head over."

As Samuel walked away, a surge of energy rushed through me. Tomorrow, we'd be back on the planet, doing something that mattered. I was already starting to feel more alive. Makara had been training to pilot the *Odin*. Ashton himself had been teaching her, in the mornings, and they had run some test atmosphere re-entries, and even some landings. Basically, anything she'd have to do during the mission, Ashton had taught her. He had told me that she was a natural. That made sense, because she drove the Recon like a pro on our way to Bunker One. It didn't surprise me that she also had an affinity for piloting the *Odin*.

I left my hab, entering the main corridor of the Mid Ring. It was time to head to the commons for a bite.

The Mid Ring's main corridor was hard to get used to. It curved slightly upward along its entire length. The whole thing made a circle, and was always spinning to supply Skyhome with artificial gravity. The Mid Ring was divided into four Quadrants – Alpha, Bravo, Charlie, and Delta. Charlie Quadrant contained the commons, the clinic, and an archive, where there were computers. In Charlie was a rec room with a large screen used for movies. The rest of the Quadrants were dedicated to habs, mostly. My hab, along with Anna's, was in Delta Quadrant. Makara's and Samuel's were each in Alpha.

Then there were the two other Rings – the Outer Ring and the Inner Ring. The Outer was where all food was grown hydroponically. The Outer also contained recycling tanks and water reclamation units, or WRUs. Most of the water was dedicated to watering crops in the Outer Ring, but every molecule of it was saved and recycled with near 100 percent efficiency. Any time there was a shortfall, which only happened once every few years, *Gilgamesh* returned to Earth, filled up, and made up the difference.

For power, solar collectors were attached to the outside of the Outer Ring. Altogether, they took in more energy than the station would ever need. There was also a backup fusion generator, the same kind that ran the spaceships, in Skyhome's central nexus. In the event of a massive solar flare, the solar collectors would probably be blown out, rendering them useless until they could be replaced.

The crops of the Outer Ring provided oxygen, and Skyhome's citizens provided carbon dioxide. State-of-the-art filtration and monitoring technology made sure the air composition maintained a proper balance. In addition to the food grown in the Ring, chickens were also raised. They provided eggs and the occasional meat. Most Skyhome citizens had a full-time job growing crops and raising chickens. There were also specialized technicians and engineers who kept the orbiting city maintained and made repairs when needed. Dr. Ashton doubled as the station's medical practitioner, even if biological research was his main field of expertise.

Of the three Rings, the Inner was the smallest. It contained administrative offices, including Ashton's, and the inner workings of Skyhome, called the Central Nexus. The Nexus turned all three rings of the station, and consumed the most energy.

Connecting all of the Rings were the four tunnels (also named Alpha, Bravo, Charlie, and Delta, depending on what Quadrant they were located in). The tunnels were arranged like the spokes of a wheel. Along Alpha Tunnel, between the Mid and Inner Rings, was the hangar, where both *Gilgamesh* and *Odin* were docked.

Skyhome's construction in the 2020s had pushed experts and engineers to the limits. It was no wonder they had only constructed one Skyhome when the original plan had called for six. All the same, Skyhome's operations were fascinating. It amazed me that the United States pulled off its construction; it was also amazing that Ashton and others had been able to utilize it following the fall of both Bunker One and Bunker Six.

When I reached the commons, I grabbed a bowl of vegetable stew from one of the kitchen staff and sat down to eat. Once done,

I headed over to Ashton's office in the Inner Ring. I stood before the metal door before pressing the entrance button. The door hissed open, allowing me to walk in.

I had only been in Ashton's office a few times. Rather large, the office contained his built-in metal desk, lines of file cabinets along one wall, and a large workbench on the opposite wall. The workbench was filled with tools and objects of Ashton's mechanical tinkering. The office was rectangular in shape, and at the end of it, three large ports looked out onto the surface of Earth, a vibrant green and violet and red.

Ashton sat behind his desk, regarding me with sharp blue eyes as I walked forward. The others were already here. I went to stand between Anna and Makara, as Samuel stood to the right of Ashton's desk, arms folded. On Ashton's desk rested a thin monitor, and on a corner several binders were neatly stacked. The surface of the planet spun slowly beyond the port, due to the Inner Ring's rotation.

"Let's get started," Ashton said brusquely.

Ashton's accent was hard to pin down. He had been born before Ragnarok; his voice carried a hint of southeastern regionalism that was most likely all but gone from the world. My only way of determining his accent was from movies I had seen back in Bunker 108 – which, admittedly, wasn't a perfect measure.

"The purpose of this meeting is to give you an update on the situation, and what we're going to do about it. As it stands, you all will be heading down to Earth tomorrow to resume the next phase of your mission. You will be heading to the Nova Roma Empire to speak with Augustus – make him agree to lay down arms and join us in the fight against Ragnarok. Meanwhile, my job is to monitor your mission from afar while trying to pin down the exact location of the Voice."

"Have you figured anything out on that front?" Anna asked.

"Some," Ashton said. "Makara and I have taken *Odin* on a few flybys of Ragnarok Crater, in hopes of securing more accurate measurements. It has helped, and we have pinpointed the origin of the Voice within twenty miles. I need to get a more accurate measure, however. When our assault on the Crater begins, you must be able to find the Voice quickly, and destroy it, before you are overwhelmed. I still need more information, and if I do two more flybys of the Crater, I will be able to triangulate the point of origin of the Voice. That's what I'll be doing while you are on the surface. I'm confident that with another few months, I'll know the exact location of the Voice."

"Alright," I said. "What's our job until then?"

"There are four major powers in North America. There is the Nova Roma Empire, by far the strongest, and the one who should be approached first. There are also the Los Angeles gangs and Vegas gangs, both of which are quite sizeable. Last of all are Bunkers 76 and 88. Neither have responded to my radio calls, but that doesn't mean they are not there. Both have weapons and supplies that would be invaluable in the attack."

"Why Nova Roma first?" I asked.

"They are the most powerful. If Emperor Augustus can be convinced to help us, it will make the other Wasteland leaders fall into line. There is also the matter of the war between the Empire and Raider Bluff. That must be stopped before it can even begin. That involves speaking to Augustus in person."

"It just seems like a very difficult thing to do," I said.

Ashton looked at me sternly. "Nonetheless, it must be done. Do you think I would send you in there if I didn't think you were capable of it? If not you, who else?"

I didn't have an answer for that, so I didn't say anything.

"It will be difficult," Samuel said. "But it is absolutely necessary. The Wasteland cannot be caught up in a war at a time like this. We need to lay down the facts for Augustus before he does anything stupid."

"So," Anna said, "do we just walk into his house or something? That sounds like a risky maneuver."

"Yes, that is the plan," Ashton said. "Soon you will know everything. But before I get to the how, it's useful to give you all a little bit of background." Ashton looked at me. "The story I have to tell relates to your father, Alex."

I was surprised. What could my father and Cornelius Ashton have in common?

"You knew my father?"

Ashton smiled. "I met him, long ago. He was still a boy. Eight, nine years old perhaps."

I did that math in my head. My dad had been thirty-eight when he died.

"You met him before Ragnarok?"

Ashton nodded. "I did. There was a summit for all the highest-ranking officials of Bunker One, about two weeks before we were put underground. That was where I met your grandfather, Lorin."

"Bunker One?" I frowned. "He entered Bunker 108, though."

"Yes, that is so," Ashton said. "But he almost didn't enter any Bunker at all. His wife, your grandmother, was stuck in Europe at the time, with your father. At the summit, he refused his berth until both your grandmother and father, then a child, could be brought safely home. President Garland refused that request. He and your grandfather were old rivals. Regardless, that is how your grandfather lost his spot in Bunker One. He did, by the way, find a way to get to Europe and rescue your grandmother and father in all that madness. He was able to bring them both back home. Only by that time, the doors of Bunker One had closed. The spots for Lorin and his family had been filled. He was refused entry."

I was shocked at this story. Never, in all my life, had my father told it to me. It made me feel a little betrayed, in a way. Why had he wanted to keep it from me?

"It was likely a very traumatic time in your father's life," Ashton said. "He probably witnessed horrors in those last days of the Old World that he never wanted to speak of again. You shouldn't hold that against him."

Of course, that had to be the reason why. Part of me wondered, though...had my dad even planned on telling me?

"What happened after my grandfather got back to America?" I asked.

"With Ragnarok's impact just days away, Lorin was directed to Bunker 108, in the San Bernardino Mountains. It was the only one that had enough room for three people. He survived a harrowing journey cross-country that was likely as dangerous as yours. Those days were awful, and some might say the world ended long before Ragnarok fell. He did end up making it to Bunker 108, somehow, because we received a transmission from him a week following Ragnarok's impact."

"Do you know anything else?"

"After that, I'm afraid not much. I buried myself in my work. I had my own wife, and two children. All three perished in 2048 with the fall of Bunker One."

"I'm sorry," I said.

"It was long ago," Ashton said.

The room was quiet for a bit. It occurred to me that Anna, Makara, Samuel, and I all had one thing in common: we had all lost our parents. Such was the case for many people – perhaps most people – in the world. It was all because of Ragnarok, and what it carried.

"I tried everything I could to rescue my wife and kids, but the dorms were the first hit by the crawlers. I couldn't have made it even if I had tried." Ashton paused, as if it pained him to speak. "They swarmed everything. Everyone was rushing to the runway, to get out however they could. I headed to the motor bay instead. I could only hope my wife and children made it. To this day, I don't know if they ever got out. They would have touched down in L.A. with the others."

"I don't know, either," Makara said. "Samuel and I were in two separate whirlybirds that took off. If they were among the refugees, they didn't say. It was so long ago."

"I don't remember anything, either," Samuel said. "I think three copters got out. One crashed – the one Makara was on. She was the only survivor. The other two formed a community on the east side. If they were among them, I'm afraid the news isn't good. They were acquired by the Black Reapers years ago."

Ashton nodded. "I have lived as if they were gone for the past twelve years. I wasn't expecting any miracles. No scientist should."

Something chilled me about those words. Cornelius Ashton was a cold and distant man, but it seemed as if he hadn't always been so. After losing everything, all that remained was his life's work of studying the virus that had destroyed his family.

I gave Anna a sidelong glance. Her hazel eyes met mine. I looked back at Ashton.

"I found myself escaping with two others. One was a mechanic named Dustin Cornell, and the other a pilot named Preston Yates. Cornell has since passed, but we all made it to Bunker Six, not too far north of Bunker One. The Bunker had been evacuated in the face of the coming storm, and was still largely untouched – the crawlers had completely ignored it. We acquired *Gilgamesh,* not really sure where we were going. But, Yates noticed a destination already programmed into the ship, called Skyhome. I knew the U.S. had created a large space station in the 2020s as yet another failsafe –a place the President could retreat to if conditions on Earth became absolutely intolerable. But, until I finally saw it when we left the atmosphere, I did not know Skyhome's true scope. It was massive – so much so that it is a wonder the U.S. could ever hide it. Nothing about it was published during the Dark Decade as far as I know, but during the time of the Dictatorship, the press could only report what the government allowed it to. We all assumed that anything sent to space had something to do with stopping Ragnarok, and that was all we were ever let known. The majority of those missions had to have been for building Skyhome."

Ashton frowned, then gave an embarrassed smile, as if cognizant of the fact that he was rambling.

"Forgive me. I came to Skyhome in 2048, and have lived here ever since. When we first came, there was already a community of survivors from Bunker Six, who had used *Odin* to get here – which surprised me, because Skyhome's existence was supposedly only known to the highest-ranking officials in the U.S. government – namely, the President and top military people. Apparently, though, a few residents from Bunker Six found out about Skyhome and came here rather than going to Bunker One. Bunker Six, you see, was attacked first."

"What about our mission?" Anna pressed. "It's helpful to know our history, and where we came from. But if we leave tomorrow, we have to know what to do."

"Of course," Ashton said. "But I think it is important to remind ourselves why we fight. If you do not know why you fight, you cannot go on. I want you all to ask yourselves what you are fighting for. Let the question haunt you, press you onward toward your goal."

Ashton paused a moment. He lifted a glass of water, and took a drink. After clearing his throat, he continued.

"Forgive me, Anna, but it is time for another history lesson. Not one that relates to me, or my past, but to Emperor Augustus himself. You will want to listen closely, because this information is key if you are ever to get an audience with him."

"What is this information?" I asked.

"It was not only Alex's father and grandfather I met at the summit in 2030."

Chapter 3

All of us stood in stunned silence at Ashton's announcement.

"You've met him?" I asked.

"The Empire did not arise in a vacuum," Ashton said. "It was controlled by a drug cartel called the Legion in the Dark Decade. It was not called Nova Roma, then. The Emperor did not call himself Augustus, nor was he yet an emperor for that matter. He was born Miguel Santos, to impoverished parents, and his life before Ragnarok could fill books. From our conversations at the summit, this is what I learned, or at least what he told me. He turned to business as a youth. By business, I'm sure he meant his drug dealings, for which he was infamous. Because of his daring and cunning, he rose in the ranks in the Legion, the gang to which he committed himself. The Legion was one of the most powerful drug cartels in Latin America, and during the Dark Decade became even more so. Mexico became embroiled in civil war with the resurgence of the drug wars in the 2020s. In 2024, when Legion leader Osbaldo Banderas died in a gunfight, Miguel Santos, now known as Augustus, stepped in and took charge."

"Alright," I said. "What does an Old World drug cartel have to do with the Empire, or anything for that matter?"

"He's getting to that," Makara said.

"Santos, a very wealthy man, envisioned a bold new plan – a new country separated from the mess that Mexico had become. After hiring thousands of mercenaries, he carved out some territory along Mexico's western coast – in roughly the same area the Empire holds today, stretching from the old Mexican states of Jalisco to Oaxaca. This area includes Acapulco and other coastal cities. He called this area *El Territorio de la Legión* – or Legion Territory. Despite the violence of the Dark Decade, Legion Territory, ironically, became the safest place in Mexico. Out of need, the United States recognized its legitimacy."

"Why?" I asked. "What need?"

"Because Miguel Santos became one of the chief financiers of the Bunker Program. That was why he was invited to the summit. He was hoping to secure a spot inside Bunker One."

The pieces were starting to come together.

"So did he ever get inside?" Makara asked.

Ashton shook his head. "No. I was, in fact, the one responsible for his not getting in. Because, Alex, he was hoping to take your grandfather's spot."

"What?" I asked. "That's insane."

"When your grandfather refused his berth, he made me promise to do all I could to keep it safe. I complied. While your grandfather was gone, I publicly condemned Santos in front of the entire conference. Though everyone knew his dealings, no one was brave enough to point them out. People who did such things ended up dead. But his crimes could not be ignored. President Garland could not give Santos his spot – but he also did not save it for Keener, as much as I tried to convince him to do so."

"Who got in?" I asked.

"In accordance with law, the berth was assigned by lottery. This was where it gets more amazing, because the berth was given to a Khmer couple and their young son."

We all looked at each other, amazed. It had to be someone related to Samuel and Makara.

"What was the father's name?" Samuel asked.

"The father's name was Pram. The mother, Lakhina. And their son...Samuel."

"Alright," Makara said. "That is *beyond* belief. Samuel was our dad. How many people were in that lottery?"

"Millions," Ashton said.

"Maybe there is some sort of plan, after all," Makara said. "Those are my grandparents and my father, as a kid. How is that even possible?"

"It is an incredible coincidence," Ashton said. "But a coincidence all the same."

"Say what you want," Makara said. "*That* is a miracle right there."

"Why would you keep this to yourself?" Samuel asked, the shock still on his face. "You must have made the connection when I told you my story."

"Though a scientist," Ashton said, with a smile, "I do have a flair for the dramatic. I wanted you all to realize how incredible this opportunity it is – how minuscule the chance that we were all put here, together, and how we should never, for one second, take that for granted."

Imagine the odds of that happening – that *my* grandfather's refusal to be put in Bunker One led to Makara and Samuel's father being saved. It made me feel as if there *was* a plan, that we *had* been preserved for a reason. Even more, the fact that Santos did not get the berth led to the creation of the Empire itself. So many things, including my very existence, hinged on the single event of my grandfather's refusal to go into Bunker One while my grandmother and dad were stuck overseas. It made me proud for a moment. Awed, in a way.

"Let's get back to Santos," Ashton said. "He was refused entry to Bunker One, and his public embarrassment made me his enemy." He smiled ruefully. "I didn't think it mattered at the time. I thought I would never see him again. Santos left the summit, enraged. He declared war on the United States upon returning to his villa in Mexico. Not that it mattered, anyway. There was but

... weeks left until Ragnarok's impact. Despite his money and connections, it seemed that Santos was doomed to die like the rest."

"Only he didn't die," Anna said.

"No," Ashton said. "That he did not. Mexico was not as hard hit by Ragnarok as the United States. Mexico is more southerly, making it warmer. There is evidence to suggest that global wind currents keep its southern portions fallout free, though I've never visited the Empire, so I cannot confirm this. Satellite imagery shows many settlements are scattered throughout Mexico, their density greatest in regions that were once controlled by the Legion. Post-Ragnarok, the Legion transformed from gang to government. Santos, a longtime fanatic of Roman history, had the opportunity to incorporate its values and ideals into his own country. He branded himself Emperor Augustus, and renamed his territory Nova Roma – or New Rome. Nova can be translated from Latin to mean 'new,' but the word itself creates the image of a nova, or a new star. This lends insight into Augustus's mindset. He sees his Empire as an incarnation of light in the darkness, something that shines brightly in a dark world. He created a capital, also called Nova Roma, from the ground up – where he found the labor for such a feat, I do not know, but satellite images show large building projects all throughout the Empire."

"They must be using slaves," Makara said. "Imperials would sometimes come into the Wasteland, from the south. They never attacked us Raiders, but when the Raiders found people, they often brought them back to Raider Bluff to be sold to the Southerners – which is what we called the Imperials. We never knew where they went – but they paid in batts, and that was all that mattered."

Ashton nodded. "I don't know what awaits you all in the Empire. Even though the Blights have yet to infect it, it is still a very dangerous place. After all, Augustus is a dangerous man."

"He wants to acquire Raider Bluff," Samuel said. "That much was made clear by his emissary, Rex, who spoke to Char while we were there. They are officially at war with Bluff, and if it hasn't already, the Empire will be sending an army there soon."

"That must be stopped," Ashton said. "Augustus *cannot* be allowed to conquer Raider Bluff, or any other city in the Wasteland, for that matter. This is a critical time in which all people must band together against the Xenos – even former enemies."

"Yes, but how do we convince Augustus of that?" I asked.

"Augustus is surely aware of the Blights," Ashton said. "You've said it yourself, Samuel – you met an Empire patrol that was also after the Black Files in Bunker One. I don't know the Empire's motive for wanting the Black Files, or how they even knew about them. The only way they *could* know is if someone in Bunker One is in Augustus's circle. Such a person might be dead now. It has been twelve years since that attack, after all. Regardless, *that* might be our way in."

It made sense. But if someone from Bunker One was in Augustus's circle, they would obviously also know Ashton, and maybe even be interested in stopping the spread of Blights.

"Likely, it's not someone who is acting against us on purpose," Ashton said. "If they are in the Empire, they may have been there for a while. They may believe the Empire is the only thing standing against the Blights and total annihilation. As such, they may have told Augustus about the Black Files, hoping that Augustus would want to find and use them. If all that is true, it is very likely that Augustus is taking the threat of the xenovirus seriously, and is interested in stopping it."

"I hope all of that is the case," Makara said. "If not, it makes our job that much harder."

"And that is why you must hurry," Ashton said. "You must make Augustus change his mind about invading Raider Bluff before he has the chance. And I think if you can make it to Nova Roma and find him, he may yet be convinced."

"But he is dangerous," I said. "And unpredictable. This is a man who has murdered hundreds, maybe thousands, of people. He is probably a complete tyrant. How do you expect us to do this?"

Ashton sighed, as if expecting that protest. But I needed to know an answer. I needed one that didn't involve our running to our own deaths.

"I've thought this over for the last two months," Ashton said. "I can see no other way. It will be dangerous, but you are the only ones I know who have survived dangerous situations like this. The Empire will live up to its promise to conquer Raider Bluff, if what you've told me is true. How else are they to be stopped, unless Augustus is given all the facts?"

I didn't have an answer for that. I wished I did, but I didn't. We were going to have to risk it all again.

***

Samuel looked at me, not saying anything. I couldn't tell what was going through his mind, but it felt as if he was trying to communicate something.

"Tomorrow you will start," Ashton said. "Get all the rest you can tonight. I want *Odin* out of the bay by 0900. Remember...Augustus will be forced to take you seriously when you drop my name."

We all turned to leave, but Ashton stopped me.

"Alex, Samuel...stay behind a moment. Makara, Anna, wait outside. I'll go over the landing procedure with you both one last time."

The women nodded, leaving Samuel and me with Ashton.

"Anna is training as Makara's copilot," Ashton said. "She'll need a backup."

Anna hadn't told me a thing about that. People's keeping things from me was starting to become more than a little annoying. I had to talk to her about that.

"What did you need me for?" I asked.

Ashton nodded, urging Samuel to continue.

"Alex," Samuel said, "in case anything happens to me down there, I need to know you have my back."

"What do you mean? I've got your back already."

"I know that. Sometimes, everything goes to hell and there is nothing you can do about it. That shot with Brux...we were lucky it was just my shoulder. Just a few inches and it would been my chest."

"What are you saying?"

"I could die out there. Any of us could. If it's me, I need to know...are you good to lead the crew?"

Me, lead the crew? I had expected someone like Makara, or even Anna, to be a better first choice. They were both better fighters than me. I could tell Samuel saw that question in my eyes, unasked.

"We're all here because of the xenovirus," Samuel said. "Out of the crew, I think it's you and I who understand the heart of this mission the best. It's more than just survival. It's saving the world, nothing less. We've both seen firsthand what the xenovirus can do. Not that Anna and Makara haven't. They're both great fighters. But I want you to run things if I die down there."

"You're not going to die."

"I hope I don't. But it's a possibility we must be prepared for."

"Why me?"

"You have a level head. You are in it for the mission. You want to avenge your father, and to do that, you must stop the xenovirus. That's all true, isn't it?"

It was true. But the mission had grown into more than that. I was fighting for my friends. And yes, I was fighting for the memory of my father and Khloe, who both died because of the xenovirus.

"I don't know if I'm ready for that kind of responsibility," I said.

"The xenovirus didn't ask if we were ready," Ashton said.

"I hope you never have to do it, Alex," Samuel said. "But you don't have the luxury of being yourself anymore. You have to always be tough, putting yourself on the line day after day, keeping everyone focused on the goal. I want nothing more than to find a place to rest and call home. I can't have that, not yet. But I'm fighting for that future, and for the future of everyone else. We all are."

He paused, letting me soak that in.

"I need you to step up if anything happens to me. It can't be Makara. It can't be Anna. It has to be you."

"I can't imagine someone like Makara ever following me."

Samuel nodded. "She's stubborn, but you've changed. She'd be a fool not to follow you. I don't think you see it yet, but you have yet to reach your full potential. You don't realize what I see in you. When we go down there, something in you is going to flip. You're going to feel it. It might happen instantly, like a switch, or it may be more gradual. I don't know. You'll become who you were always meant to be, and everything will be different."

I sighed. There was no getting out of this.

"I don't pretend to know exactly what you're talking about," I said. "But I'll do it."

Samuel nodded, and turned to Ashton.

"You won't be alone, Alex," Ashton said. "I'll be up here, letting you know the latest information. If anything changes, you'll be the first to know. Right now, it's just Samuel and I, trying to figure out everything and make sure we make the right moves. We'll let you guys know as soon as we discover anything. We just want to be ready for any possibility."

"I'm not easily killed," Samuel said.

"I guess all that's settled," I said.

"Get some rest," Ashton said. "We'll see you all off in the morning."

Samuel and I walked out of Ashton's office. Makara and Anna waited against the wall. Their eyes questioned; they could sense something was different, even if they didn't know exactly what it was. Anna gave me one last glance before going into the office. The door hissed shut behind her.

Samuel and I walked quietly back to our habs. His hab was close to Alpha Tunnel. He turned off, and pressed his hand to the entrance button.

"You alright?" I asked.

He forced a smile. "As good as I can be. I know it isn't easy, but nothing is."

He looked tired. Even after two months, he hadn't really been resting. He and Ashton had been planning everything while the rest of us got to relax. I think it was then that I realized just how much responsibility being a leader was.

"We have a big day tomorrow," Samuel said. "Everything changes."

Samuel shut the door behind him, and I headed back to my own hab – about as far from Alpha Tunnel and the hangar as you could possibly get in Skyhome. I looked a couple doors down, to where Anna stayed. I considered waiting for her to come back. For some reason, I decided against it. I went inside, and shut the door behind me.

Chapter 4

"Do you believe in God, Alex?"

Khloe and I were lying on her bed. Her parents were out. When she had invited me to her apartment, I had not expected a discussion of the metaphysical. The question hung in the air a moment before I answered.

"No."

"Why?"

I sighed, thinking. "If there is a God, he wouldn't have let Ragnarok happen."

Khloe did not respond for a moment. "You think so?"

"I don't know. What do you think?"

Again, she was quiet, as if deep in thought.

"I keep thinking of what Father Nielsen used to say, before he died. How God let it happen because we let ourselves go too far, you know? We forgot about Him because we loved things more. And...Ragnarok was his way to take away all the things that kept us far from Him. Now, we need Him more."

"Couldn't he have taken the things, and left the people alone? Was having all the machines, all the computers, all the money, really so bad?"

"Of course it was," Khloe said. "That's why Ragnarok happened. We're in the Last of Days."

"Well, I can agree with you on that point, at least."

We lay there for a while longer. It was a bit awkward, as it always got when Khloe and I discussed religion. I had stopped going to chapel years ago. My dad never went, and when my mom died when I was seven, that was when I stopped going, too. I stayed out of there as much as I could. Father Nielsen was a nice man, but for some reason, his words never sat right with me. I was tired of hearing about how *bad* we all were, so bad that God wiped us out with a meteor. I didn't know *why* Ragnarok came. No one did. When people didn't have a reason for something, they made one up. That was what happened with Ragnarok. People couldn't stand random chance. They had to have a reason for the pain, even if there wasn't one.

That was what my dad said, anyway, and I was inclined to agree. Then again, Dad hadn't really been the same since Mom died. That was a while ago, but he had smiled more, back then. He hadn't been so harsh about life.

"You need to have faith in something," Khloe said, pulling me from my thoughts. "Otherwise, what's the point of anything?"

I shrugged. "I don't know. I feel like I have plenty to live for."

"Like what?"

"Live for life?"

Khloe rolled over to face me, her face framed by her black hair. Her blue eyes were young, bright, and beautiful. Full of hope. Even at sixteen, I already felt that I had lost a bit of that.

"Well, I hope He's there, and I hope He's listening. I hope there's *someone* listening. I hate to think we're left to ourselves, because we need someone to protect us."

I wanted to tell her that I was listening, and that my listening was enough, but somehow, the words never made it out.

***

A siren wailed, piercing my hab in Skyhome. I shot up in my bed, remembering that horrible night almost three months ago, where a similar siren in Bunker 108 had marked the end of my old life, and the beginning of the new.

I was covered in a cold sweat as the emergency red lights flashed on and off. The sirens continued to shriek like banshees.

Proximity alert! Foreign mass incoming, velocity: four kilometers per second. All inhabitants, take shelter in an airlock or escape pod. Impact in one minute, thirty-seven seconds...

I rushed out of bed, throwing on my clothes. I grabbed my Beretta from the nightstand, and threw on my backpack. It was always packed and ready to go. Outside my door came panicked screams and running feet.

My first thought was of going to Anna, and making sure she was safely out of her hab.

As the emergency warning blared again, I rushed out the door into the Mid Ring, running straight for Anna's room. While every other hab door was wide open, Anna's had remained closed. It was supposed to open automatically in an emergency.

I felt panic clench my chest.

"Anna!"

I pounded on the door. From within, I heard her scream. I could not decipher the words, but she was terrified and the goddamned door wouldn't open.

"Hold on!"

I mashed the open button on the control panel. It didn't respond. It was as good as dead. And Anna was too, unless she could open it from the inside.

58 seconds...

I drew my Beretta and pointed it at the control panel. I had no idea if this would work or not. Shooting a gun in a space station was an incredibly stupid idea, but I had nothing else. Anna was going to die, trapped in her room, if I didn't at least try. I pointed, aiming right for the panel, and fired.

In a shower of sparks, the bullet entered the panel. Immediately, the door hissed open. I couldn't believe my luck.

Anna ran out, falling into my arms. I held her shoulders and looked into her face.

"There's no time! We need to get to the Inner Ring."

Proximity alert, the warning system began again.

"There's no way we can make it to the Inner Ring before the blast doors close," Anna said.

"We have to try to make it." I grabbed her hand. "Come on!"

We ran around the circle of the Mid Ring. Everyone was out of sight.

45 seconds...

"Shit, we'll never make it!" Anna said.

We ran on, about halfway to Alpha Tunnel. Lines of doors rushed past us in a blur as we sprinted full speed around the curve of the Ring.

20 seconds...

At last we reached Alpha Tunnel, turning into its long, straight path. On either side were windows that showed the spinning stars as Skyhome continued its rotation. The entrance to the Inner Ring lay at the end of the tunnel. Standing on the other side of the blast doors were Samuel and Makara, screaming at us. Distance and noise masked their words. In less than twenty seconds, the blast doors to the Inner Ring would close.

We were clearly not going to make it in time.

"Come on," I said. "The hangar's this way!"

"What?" Anna asked. "We'll die there!"

"We need to get to *Odin*. Come on!"

We ran partway down the tunnel and turned into the hatch that led to the hangar. Once inside, we gunned it for *Odin*, the nearer of the two ships docked side by side. If Anna and I could get inside the ship and close it off, we might be okay.

That is, if the incoming foreign mass didn't hit the hangar or the ship.

I saw no other choice, though. I pulled Anna along, sprinting for the ship.

10 seconds...

We ran up *Odin's* boarding ramp. Anna mashed the code into the keypad.

5 seconds...4...3...

The titanium alloy door opened with a hiss. I pushed Anna inside, following after her. As I pressed the button to shut the door, the voice sounded again.

2...1...

***

The ship skidded across the hangar when the foreign mass impacted Skyhome. Anna and I crashed to the floor, toppling into one another. It felt as if the entire station had been flipped on its side. For a moment, I was terrified that Skyhome might fall off its orbital path and get pulled down to Earth.

I felt myself float upward. The Mid Ring was slowing from loss of power. The ring would soon be at a complete standstill, meaning there would be nothing to keep our feet on the ground. My back banged into the ceiling, just enough to cause some pain. The ship's interior was lit by a dim red lighting. A stainless steel container shot past my face and crashed into a cabinet. From the cabinet spilled silverware that did a crazy zero-G dance. Somehow, Anna and I had both been thrown into the ship's galley.

The red lights blinked off and on, flickering a few times before remaining steady. The room spun around us. In a dizzying revelation, I realized that *I* was the one spinning. Pots and pans floated before me as if on strings, doing their own crazy spins as they clanged into one another.

"Grab onto a wall," Anna said.

I reached for the wall, stopping myself from spinning. I stayed still, willing my rising nausea to go away.

"You alright?" Anna asked.

"Not sure. I think I'm going to be sick."

"You should be alright in a second," she said. "The ship is anchored to the floor with struts, so it's not going anywhere."

That was good to know. I already felt better. I let go and Anna pulled me away from the wall.

"We need to get to the cockpit," Anna said. "There's a transceiver and we can see if the others made it."

Samuel and Makara probably had, because I had seen them at the end of the Alpha Tunnel, in the Inner Ring. Unless that part had taken a direct hit, they were probably okay.

I pushed myself along cabinets and walls to get to *Odin's* main corridor. I turned to the cockpit, clawing along the smooth walls to propel myself. Upon entering, I pulled myself toward the captain's chair, and strapped myself in. Outside the forward window I could only see darkness. The lights in the hangar were all out, and for all we knew, all of the air was gone as well.

"That's not good," I said.

"Here," Anna said, flicking a few buttons on the dash.

Odin hummed, powering on. I could hear the fusion drive in the ship's stern firing up.

"What are you doing?" I asked.

"Powering on the ship to get life support running," Anna said.

"We need that," I said.

"Thanks, Captain Obvious."

"Hey."

"Sorry," Anna said. "You're sitting in the captain's chair, and you made an obvious statement. It had to be said."

Anna flipped the transceiver on, finding the frequency to communicate with Skyhome.

"Skyhome, this is Anna Bliss. Alex and I are on *Odin*. What is your status, over?"

Anna's voice would be spilling out of every speaker connected to the Skyhome network. Dr. Ashton or the others could be anywhere.

To my relief, the radio crackled to life.

"Anna, this is Ashton. Samuel and Makara are both with me in my office. Something hit the habs, and all of Delta Quadrant depressurized. Thankfully, everyone made it out in time. It only affected the Mid Ring. The blast doors kept the air in everywhere else. We were lucky. I guess those monthly drills were good for something."

Those drills had been my bane. Getting up randomly at 2:30 or 3:30 in the morning and sprinting for the Inner Ring was no fun, but it least it had trained me on what to do in a situation like this. However, Anna's hab door malfunctioning had not been part of any drill. Usually the drills gave us three minutes to get to the Inner Ring. This time, we had half that, and it was for real. I was just glad I'd remembered the *Odin*.

"Glad to hear you guys made it," I said. "But how do we make it out of here? We're stuck on *Odin* if the entire Mid Ring is depressurized."

"The whole Mid Ring isn't," Ashton said. "Just Delta Quadrant. But we have no idea what the hangar is like, so *don't go outside*. I need to assemble a team to do an EVA and see if we can get that puncture sealed. It will take hours to find that hole and seal it, and pressurizing and heating Delta Quadrant could take even longer."

"So there's literally nothing we can do?" Anna asked.

"Affirmative," Ashton said. "As soon as the atmosphere's back up, getting the Ring rotating again should be no issue, granted that there was no damage to the mechanics of the station. If there is damage, you guys could be stuck in there longer."

I heard someone else take up the microphone.

"Alex." It was Makara. "Why the hell didn't you make it?"

"Anna's door didn't open. I had to improvise."

"Wouldn't open?" Ashton said.

"Yeah. It stayed closed."

"Our techs will take a look at that," Ashton said. "That it would not work at a time like this…"

"Well, I'm fine now," Anna said. "Thanks to Alex."

Samuel was next to speak. "Keep your heads in the game. The Mid Ring should be online soon, though I expect there will be a hell of a mess to clean up. Until then, sit tight, and *don't open that door.*"

"Copy that," I said.

The radio cut out, leaving Anna and me alone on the bridge.

"I'm sorry I didn't get out in time," she said.

"For what? It's not your fault."

"It might be," she said.

I paused. "What do you mean?"

"I honestly didn't realize the door was shut. I was looking for my katana. It wasn't where it normally was. I was searching for a good fifteen seconds until I turned around and saw that my door wasn't open. That's when I started to panic, and when you came along and got it open."

"Could you have opened it from the inside?"

"I don't know," Anna said. "I didn't have time to try it."

"Anna…"

I stopped myself. There was no point in getting upset about something that was over and done with. Anna seemed to guess my inclination toward anger. She unstrapped herself from her seat, angling herself away from me and toward the aft of the ship.

"Hey," I said.

I unstrapped myself as she pushed herself away. I grabbed her boot. Instead of stopping her, as I thought it would, it pulled us both together. Her head bonked into mine.

"Ouch!" she said.

We were face to face. She stared at me a moment, her eyes at first angry. Gradually, they softened.

"I'm glad you're alright," I said. "That's what matters."

Realizing I was still holding her, I let go, even if part of me didn't want to. Well, maybe most of me.

She smiled. "I can't believe you shot open the door."

"I'm glad that worked out, too.

She sighed, turning slightly away. "I don't like playing the part of the damsel in distress. But maybe just this once."

"It's not that bad," I said. "I know you saved my ass more times than I can count."

"Well, we both know that's true."

We looked at each other for another moment. Something softened in her eyes, and for a moment, I thought we were going to kiss.

Anna turned aside. "Since we're here, we might as well get some rest. There are bunks in the back."

I nodded, unable to push down my disappointment. "Might as well."

Despite the scare the impact had caused, sleep did not elude me. As soon as I lay down and strapped into my bunk, I was out.

Chapter 5

After twenty-four hours, we were out of there. The EVA team sealed up the hole within a couple of hours, but pressuring the Ring took a while, nearly depleting the station's oxygen and nitrogen reserves. The techs restarted the Ring's rotation. Finally, when the Ring hit that happy 1G, its rotation steadied.

The stuff we had left in our habs was safe. Each hab's door automatically shut upon detecting a sharp pressure drop. The lack of gravity for hours straight had made a huge mess of things. Ashton dedicated the entire day to cleanup – anyone who could be spared was set to putting things back in order. It was amazing what a few seconds of chaos could do.

Skyhome's techs later found the foreign object that had nearly sent us all to our deaths; a thin titanium rod, a few centimeters long and half a centimeter in diameter. It looked as if it could have been part of a satellite. I could hardly believe it had caused such a scare. Skyhome's tracking system had a lot of objects to keep up with, and it was amazing that it could predict such a small incoming object with such accuracy.

Just as I finished reordering my room, Samuel stepped in the doorway.

"We're all meeting in Ashton's office at 1930 hours."

"What for?"

"One last briefing before we leave tomorrow morning. Also, can you find Makara and let her know? Can't seem to find her anywhere."

"I know just where to look," I said.

Samuel nodded and left.

My mind was set racing. In the two months I had been up here, it was starting to feel a bit like home. No, it wasn't Earth, but Skyhome had all the amenities that I had grown up with and sorely missed. There was plenty of food and water, warm showers, soft beds to sleep in, and people to talk to. There was routine in Skyhome, outside of the odd titanium rod clobbering it. Maybe that part wasn't so great, but it was safer than the surface, with its monsters, Raiders, and dust storms.

I was always shifting between hating this place and loving it. It was hard to argue with safety, a full belly, and a community to support you. It was strange that you could hate something like that, but I guessed you could if it kept you from doing what you needed to be done – in my case, going back to Earth to finish what we had started. If no one did that, this community up here would come to an end.

I remembered something else Ashton had told me. People could not live up here forever. There could be another impact that might be much worse. There could be solar flares frying all the electronics. It was only a matter of time; a question of when, not if. Everyone in Skyhome had to return to Earth, someday. It was all the more reason to continue fighting.

I headed out the door, making my way to the Outer Ring to find Makara. That was where she would most likely be. I liked to go to the Outer Ring to watch Earth below. The Outer Ring spun at a rate of one full rotation every four minutes, fifteen per hour. Every time, it afforded a slightly different view of our world. I always tried to catch a glimpse of California and America, but of course, most of the time they were not there. When they were, half the time they were dark with night. And if they *did* happen to be there, the cloud cover was so thick that it was hard to make out anything at all. Everything appeared all dusty and red, an effect that cast a violet hue over the oceans.

I entered the glass automatic sliding doors that led into the Outer Ring. These doors helped keep the Ring warm and humid. The thick aroma of plants and produce tickled my nostrils. The Outer Ring was the freshest part of Skyhome, and anytime the chill of space became too much, going here was a sure solution. All the crops were kept in neat rows on the floor, and metal tiers supported by struts added additional space.

I climbed some steps to one of these tiers, and walked along it. A small catwalk branched from the tier, leading to a large set of ports perfect for Earth watching.

When I reached the ports, my suspicions were confirmed. Makara sat against the wall, staring outside. Earth entered Skyhome's field of view. As I went to stand beside her, she continued staring outside, taciturn.

"Makara?"

She tensed at my voice, but did not stop looking out.

I sat down next to her. For a moment, we watched Earth pass by in silence.

"Are you alright?" I asked.

She didn't answer for a moment. She seemed drained.

"It's freaky, isn't it?"

Her voice was dull, monotonous, as if all life had been stripped from it. Now more than ever, I was worried about her state. None of us had known Lisa the way Makara had. Instead of improving over the past two months, she had withdrawn into herself more than ever. I didn't know what it would take to bring her out.

Looking down at the planet below, I saw what Makara was talking about. It was a rare, cloudless day, and the dust was mostly absent from Earth's atmosphere. On the surface, the sun might have even been strong enough to mostly break through the dust. It took me a moment to recognize that we were passing over the central United States.

That was when I saw it. There were no words to describe the horror of seeing that massive scar defacing what was once Wyoming and Nebraska. It dug deep into the Earth, and alien pink, orange, and purple bled from it like blood, spreading in all directions across the plains, creeping up the mountains, coating valleys, painting the surface a sickly pink and purple. At the edge of the western deserts, the Great Blight ceased its landward crawl. In the east, it extended all the way to the dark line of night that was rushing to cover the land. Somewhere in that Crater was the Voice, the thing we were trying to stop.

"We'll be there before too long," Makara said. "Count on it."

"Hard to believe."

I looked at her face – still beautiful, though sad. She didn't meet my eyes. Her long black hair fell over her shoulder in waves. She gathered the hair and clenched it, as if it were a neck she was trying to choke.

"Whether I'm alright, I don't know," Makara said, answering my original question. "I'm just trying not to think about it. I'm just hoping there's a happy ending and a reason for all this madness. I'm trying to figure out what I'm fighting for. Ashton talked about that, at the meeting. I don't know what that is yet."

"You can fight for Lisa."

"I need more than the dead to fight for. I need someone here. Only I don't think I will get that. Not until it's too late, anyway."

Outside, the Earth was nearing the edge of our vision. When it fully disappeared, Makara spoke.

"I think I will only be alright when we succeed," she said. "When I find my place in this world. The Angels gave me that, but it was taken away. The Raiders gave me that, to an extent."

"Your place is here," I said.

"Yes. But how long will that last?"

Her harshness took me aback. "As long as we are together. As long as we fight. We go on, because that's who we are."

Makara gave a short laugh. "Inspiring."

"You said it yourself, down on Earth."

"Yeah, I know. I wish I still believed it." She sighed. "Alright, enough with that. You came to see me for some reason, and I don't think it was to inspire me."

"Ashton wants you to go over the landing procedure again after dinner."

Makara nodded. "Yeah, I knew that was coming." She gave me a sidelong glance. "Come on. Let's see what the old man wants."

We left the star-filled ports behind.

***

The plan was this: we were to land in a mountain valley, surrounded by dense forest, about one hundred miles northwest of Nova Roma. We needed to land far enough away so that our spaceship would remain hidden and unnoticed, but close enough that the journey to Nova Roma wouldn't take too long. From the landing site, we would travel south until we reached a settlement along the main Imperial road, which we had found from satellite imagery. This road, taken southeast, would eventually arrive at Nova Roma, the Empire's capital.

And that was just the easy part.

Once we reached Nova Roma, we needed to find the Imperial Palace and gain an audience with Emperor Augustus – which we could accomplish by name-dropping Cornelius Ashton. Once we had secured the audience, Samuel would explain the situation with the Blights and the xenovirus and give our solution – one that necessitated the Empire's help and the end of its war with Raider Bluff. And we had to hope Augustus agreed, and didn't decide to kill us instead.

It sounded impossible. It seemed that we could make it to Nova Roma alright. After all, what was one hundred miles when we had traveled a thousand miles to Bunker One in a mere three days? But trying to convince the most powerful man in the world to do something he probably didn't want to do seemed practically suicidal. However, if Ashton was right about a scientist or some high-ranking officer from Bunker One being in Augustus's court, we might be able to reach the Emperor through him.

There were *way* more ifs and buts than I was comfortable with, but I also knew we had pulled off much harder things – like surviving in the Great Blight and its constant onslaught of monsters. If Augustus could be convinced that those monsters would be his Empire's fate unless he acted, it might be possible to convince him.

Or at least, that's what we all hoped.

Ashton set a timetable for us to be done with everything in four weeks. That should be enough time to make it to the capital, secure the truce and troops from Augustus, and make it back to *Odin* in time to update Ashton, hear what he learned about the Voice during our absence, and head to Raider Bluff and let Char know the news. And after that, it was off to see the other leaders of the Wasteland, and find a way to coordinate everything to make the attack on the Great Blight work.

Yeah. This was going to be *real* easy.

Chapter 6

"Systems," Makara said.

"Check," Anna said.

"Engines."

"Check. Powering on engines."

Odin thrummed and vibrated. Makara and Anna sat side by side, pilot and co-pilot, Samuel and I strapped in behind them. Instruments on the dash glowed as the entire ship powered on. Makara clenched the control stick tightly. I couldn't tell of the vibration of her fist was from the ship, from nerves, or both.

"Go?" Makara asked.

Ashton's voice came from the dash. "Go."

Makara thumbed a switch on the control stick, causing *Odin's* deep, computerized male voice to speak.

Launch countdown: initiated.

A timer appeared in glowing green numerals on the LCD mounted on the dash between pilot and copilot seats. It read one minute, and began to tick down silently. We waited as the numbers decreased, as we felt the power of *Odin* surging throughout the ship's hull. I waited with bated breath, ready for the adventure to begin. When the countdown got to ten seconds, I couldn't help but smile. We were finally getting started.

"Here we go," I said.

With a thunderous roar, the fusion engine in *Odin's* stern powered up, causing a *thrum-thrum-thrum* to permeate the entire ship. That power crept into my muscles, tickling my nerves. The countdown timer reached zero. Slowly, *Odin* lifted from the launch bay. Makara watched the LCD as the ship autopiloted aft in the hangar. I saw the hangar wall recede. Soon, the blast doors behind us would open – but only after the air in the hangar had been pumped out of the hangar for use elsewhere in Skyhome. Air was too valuable a commodity to be wasted on the vacuum of space.

"Hangar depressurized," Anna said.

The LCD showed a shot of the hangar doors sliding open. As the doors opened, the oceanic surface of Earth glowed blue on the screen.

Next thing, we were out of Skyhome. The hangar doors shut ahead of us, and as our view panned outward, the outer cylinder of the Mid Ring came into view, continuing its steady rotation. I felt myself float upward, restrained only by my safety harness. We had attained zero-G.

"Bird's out of the nest," Makara said.

Everyone was quiet as we drifted further down toward the planet. As we fell backward at a controlled rate, the other Rings came into view – the Inner Ring first, followed by Alpha Tunnel connecting it to the Mid. After that, the rest of the tunnels came into view, connecting the Inner Ring with the Mid Ring with the Outer. All three rings rotated like wheels. The sky city circled away on its own orbit around the Earth, speeding away from us at an alarming rate. The solar arrays on the Outer Ring's side glowed like diamonds in the sunlight, among the myriad of stars that bore silent witness. Through the ports of the Outer Ring, green vegetation was visible. It was easy to just stare and be mesmerized by the station's beauty and ingenuity. I felt sad, realizing that it was a feat of engineering that would most likely never be achieved again.

"Bird falling," Makara said. "All systems are still go. Entering flight path in fifteen seconds."

Those fifteen seconds felt like the longest in my life. Skyhome raced farther away on its orbit as *Odin's* retrothrusters powered on, tilting the ship downward toward the planet.

"Go," Makara said.

Makara thumbed another button. In a surge of acceleration from the main thrusters aft, *Odin* powered forward. I was pushed backward in my seat from the force. Skyhome was distant, lost in a miasma of light cast from the wide rim of planet Earth. It had completely disappeared by the time *Odin's* nose finished angling downward for atmosphere reentry.

"Make sure you're strapped in good," Makara said. "Things might get a bit...bumpy."

As soon as she said that, *Odin* vibrated violently. I was afraid that the entire ship would disintegrate around me. The entire port glowed red from the friction of the passing atmosphere. I felt as if we were getting sucked into a fiery vortex.

A terrifying thirty seconds passed before Makara spoke again.

"Retrothrusters burning."

The ship lurched, sending the safety harness pulling against my chest. Again, I felt as if I were floating upward – not from a lack of gravity, but from the halting of our freefall. I felt the retrothrusters pushing us away from Earth, slowing our descent.

Finally, we reached equilibrium. Sweat trailed down my face as I fell back into my seat, breathing a sigh of relief that the most harrowing part of the descent was over. *Odin* flew horizontally, in much the same way as an airplane would. We had slowed from our speed of 17,500 miles per hour to one-twentieth of that in the space of minutes.

"Atmosphere reentry complete," Makara said. "Heading to target location."

Odin slid further down toward the planet. The ports revealed a dark and cloudy sky, within which light flashed periodically. It was storming on the surface. Other than that, I could not see anything. The LCD located us above the western Mexican coast, about halfway to our target location.

"Staying in the clouds a bit longer than planned," Makara said. "Altitude fifteen thousand feet. I'm not taking any chances with that storm."

"Roger that," Ashton said. "You're in Empire territory, two hundred miles northwest from Nova Roma."

"Copy that," Makara said. "Continuing course to target location."

Ten minutes later, Makara pressed a button on the control stick. "Disengaging autopilot, engaging in manual mode."

"Roger that," Ashton said. "You're ninety percent there. Knock 'em dead, kid."

Makara's face was covered in a thin sheen of sweat, I saw from my spot behind Anna. The copilot was calm, reserved, intently watching the many readouts on the dash.

"Nearing target," Anna said. "Might be a good time to descend."

"A little longer," Makara said.

Anna paused. "Makara, are you sure..."

"Last I checked, *I* was the pilot here." Makara said nothing for a long moment. "We can't be seen. Not yet."

The screen showed us nearing the end of our line. We were almost on top of our target.

Suddenly, Makara veered the ship to the left. I lurched to the right, the safety harness cutting into me. I barely held back a scream.

We were in freefall. We fell a couple thousand feet before Makara must have remembered we had thrusters. She engaged them, causing the ship, once more, to slow down. I felt as if I was being crushed into my seat from the g-forces.

We broke from the clouds. Night covered the land, and it was hard to see any discernable spot we could land on. How Makara and Anna could pilot this thing in the dark, I had no clue. Makara and Ashton must have practiced some nighttime landings.

"Pinging," Makara said.

Anna touched a few keys in quick succession on the dash, her fingers a blur. The screen view switched to one of a dot with by a long line below it.

Odin's computerized male voice responded to Anna's inputs. *Calibrating terrain.*

Finally, the line on the LCD changed. A few jagged, green spikes indicated nearby mountains. A small depression appeared on the other side of the screen.

Anna pointed her finger on the depression. "There it is."

"Heading down," Makara said.

We thundered forward, edging closer to the surface. We were a mere five hundred feet above it. Anyone watching from below would have been able to see us, not to mention hear us.

"Slowing," Makara said.

Makara guided *Odin* toward the depression on the screen, slowing it to a hover.

"Descending," Makara said.

I felt the ship going down, butterflies fluttering in my stomach.

From the windshield, I could finally see the land come into view. We were lowering into a clearing surrounded on all sides by tall, verdant trees, masked by darkness. It was more trees in one moment than I had seen in the rest of my life.

The ship paused a moment right above the ground, the fusion drive in the back going quiet. I heard the squeal of retracting struts. With a final lift, we alighted gently on the Earth. After two months, we were back, and it had only *felt* like we were going to get killed.

"Skyhome," Makara said, "we have landed."

***

Samuel and I began our return to Earth with a good old-fashioned recon. I was a little leery – after all, I felt I always had bad luck when it came to recons – but at the same time, it was fine by me because I was eager to get the lay of the land.

When *Odin's* blast door hissed open, we were met with a rush of warm, sticky air, pungent with the smell of vegetation. The wind blew softly, like a caress, folding the long grass on its side as it whispered through the blades. The warmth on my skin was foreign, yet definitely not unwelcome. The tall forms of trees bent slightly with the breeze, leaves rustling, as countless insects chirped in the night. The sky above was thick, pasty, misty, heavy yet unoppressive. To someone like me, who had grown up surrounded by machines, feeling nature felt strange and beautiful, like a primordial memory buried deep in my consciousness, a memory unremembered until I saw it before me. It was almost, dare I say, spiritual, or the closest thing to spiritual I had ever experienced.

Samuel was taking it in, too. He paused a moment, taking a deep breath of the humid air. In the distance, thunder crackled – not an angry, dry crackle like in the Wasteland. It was calm, sedate, almost...promising. It was very hard for me to describe something I'd only experienced once. The wind was coming from the north, the direction of the distant mountains lost in nighttime shadow. That wind was cool, smelling wet and fresh, carrying with it the smell of pine and other aromas I could not recognize. It was mid-December, though it didn't feel it. It must have been seventy degrees outside. I remembered Ashton's mentioning how Mexico's climate hadn't cooled as much as America's due to Ragnarok. Standing there, I could feel it.

"Let's get moving," Samuel said.

We hit the ground, walking quickly for the trees. I held my Beretta in my right hand. It was loaded and fully operational should the need arise. The grass and pliant turf under my boots was soft. Up until this point, I had always walked on hard surfaces – metals, linoleum, rocks. In places the ground was squishy from a previous rain. As it thundered again, I realized – it *rained* here. Rain was a miraculous thought, a thing of stories, a phenomenon I had only seen in movies, had read of in books, had heard told of by the old in Bunker 108. And now, I might finally get to see it. I might finally get to feel it.

As we walked toward the tree line, thunder boomed again. With it came a desperate rush of wind, and with that the first few, fat drops. The cold sensation as the drops splattered my face was pleasant, and made me smile.

We entered the thickness of the trees. It was dark, so we got out our flashlights.

"We won't go too far in," Samuel said. "I just want to make sure nothing's going to jump out at us."

Lightning cracked the sky, for a split second illuminating the forest in shadowy green.

"We need to be prepared for anything," Samuel said. He paused, listening for a moment. "This area's clear. Let's walk around the entire perimeter."

For the next ten minutes, we reconnoitered. We stuck to the outer fringes of the clearing as the storm advanced. The rain suddenly came down in a torrent, soaking and chilling me to the bone. It was as if some god had opened a heavenly window. The rain fell and fell, and lightning slashed the sky. It was apocalyptic and threatening and violent, in its own way. Gusts of wind bent the trees so far sideways that I could not see how they remained intact.

"Let's get back," Samuel shouted.

I didn't argue, and we headed back to *Odin*. Once we made it to the boarding ramp, soaking wet, I saw that both Anna and Makara were already standing there. They, too, must have never seen rain before. The ship itself provided an awning with its outstretched starboard wing. Waterfalls dripped from the wing's sides as the lightning continued to slash the clouds and to thunder in the forest.

We all said nothing as we watched. It was as if we were drinking in the raw nature we had been deprived of our whole lives.

As the storm gained in intensity, my feeling of calm wonder slowly became one of rising alarm. This came to a head when a jagged line of molten white speared itself from the sky, igniting a tall tree with a thunderous crack. I felt the heat of it, even from where I was, despite the coolness of the wind.

"Better get inside," Makara said.

I decided that was a good idea and followed her in. I paused at the open door, looking back at Samuel and Anna, who both stood as if transfixed. I thought about warning them. But Makara pulled my sleeve, and I stepped in after her. The door hissed shut behind me.

We said nothing in the metallic gray of the ship, merely turning left down the corridor to head to our bunks. On either side was an open archway – within each room were four bunks. Makara paused before the right-hand doorway, giving me a tired glance before ducking inside the dark room.

I went into my own cabin, and lay down on my back. Though we had left at morning according to Skyhome time, my sleep of the night before had been restless, and the dark night outside just made me want to sleep even more. Coaxed by the sound of falling rain and thunder, both dimmed from the ship's shell and walls, I closed my eyes, feeling sleep take hold almost instantly.

Chapter 7

The next day dawned hot and muggy. The water on the ground rose up in steam. It was hard to believe it was so warm, even though it was only early morning.

I started off by cramming myself into the ship's tiny shower. Once done, I stepped out and dried off, dressing in my green camo pants and a green shirt. The environment down here was a little different from the Wasteland, and for that reason I had decided to forgo my desert camo hoodie. That hoodie had been with me since my escape from Bunker 108, but I probably couldn't make it one mile wearing it now. It would be waiting for me here upon my return.

From the galley came the sounds of cooking – pots clanging, food simmering, a spatula scraping. I went to the doorway, finding Samuel cooking breakfast. It was a strange picture. The last person I expected to be the ship's cook was frying up four hearty omelets, filled with tomatoes, green peppers, mushrooms, and chopped onions. Four pieces of bread popped from the nearby toaster.

"Where'd you learn to cook like that?" I asked.

Samuel shrugged. "I cooked a lot when I lived in Bunker 114. I got pretty good at it." He gave each omelet a flip with his spatula. "I've only recently learned how to cook eggs. After all, I hadn't tasted a real one until Skyhome." He smiled. "Don't see how I got on without them."

"Either way," I said, "I'm starving."

Makara and Anna, still looking half-asleep, sat at opposite ends of the table in the wardroom adjoining the galley.

"*Hey,*" I said. "Breakfast."

They got up and walked to the galley just as Samuel finished putting an omelet and a piece of toast on each of four plates.

"This might be our last good meal for a while, so I don't want any leftovers." He eyed Anna and Makara severely. Both gave him a nonchalant grunt.

We took our food to the table and ate in silence. Even if no one was talking, it felt good to have the crew together again. I chowed down on the fresh food, washing it down with black coffee. I had taken to the stuff ever since coming to Skyhome, and hoped I wouldn't have to go too long without it.

While we ate, Samuel reviewed the day's agenda – head south, locate the settlement along the main Imperial road, and camp out until the next morning. Tomorrow, we would follow the road at a distance, scoping it out. If it was safe, we would follow it. If not, we would slog through the wilds all the way to Nova Roma. Hopefully, that wouldn't happen.

Once finished, Makara and I washed dishes while Anna and Samuel prepped everyone's gear. By the time Makara and I had put everything away, all our packs were lined neatly by the door.

I checked my Beretta one last time. It was locked and loaded, filled with seventeen rounds of ammunition. I carried two clips on my belt, opposite my combat knife, and had more ammo available in the pack. The pack was stuffed with food, water, and the camping gear we would need when we settled down for the night. My boots were laced, and I had managed to scrounge a headband to keep my lengthening hair out of my face while on the trail.

At last, we stepped outside into the hot morning. Makara pressed a few numbers into the airlock keypad. The door clicked itself shut.

"Don't forget that combo," I said.

"Oh no," she said, feigning distress. "I just did."

"Not funny," I said.

We got started, heading south through the balmy forest. Samuel took the lead, using nothing more than a compass to strike a course south. Hopefully, no one saw or heard our arrival last night. It was possible that the storm had completely masked our entry.

We entered the first line of trees. At points, the undergrowth grew so thick that Anna had to use her beloved katana to cut it down. She was strong and fit, but even she could not keep that up forever. After an hour, we had only gone about a mile.

At midday, we paused for a quick lunch of chicken sandwiches before moving on again. The day that had begun warm was now sweltering. It must have been in the nineties. It was hard to believe it was wintertime. In California, it was probably well below freezing. Even if Mexico was farther south, something just didn't feel right about this heat.

At last, the jungle broke, revealing a stream that ran quick and silvery over smooth stones. Green moss grew on its banks, soft under our feet. The stream veered south. Since that was the direction we were headed, we decided to splash through the water and follow its course. Our speed easily increased by a factor of two.

The thick canopy of green cast verdant shadows on the forest floor, lighting meadows and trees with an emerald hue. Bugs flew in giant clouds. Mosquitoes bit as we passed a bog. It was my first time being bitten by one, and it was a shame Ragnarok couldn't have taken care of them, too. My sweat clung to my shirt. Still, we pressed on. As the stream deepened, we were forced to the side. Thin rivulets fed the water's flow, broadening it. We had to head back into the thick forest again, and we were back to the same slow crawl we were at before.

Mercifully, around late afternoon, the trees broke, and we saw our first sign of civilization.

A huge tract of land, growing corn, filled my entire vision. The corn rose in green stalks, and here and there laborers worked the fields. No, not laborers. Slaves. Walking between the hunched bodies were their drivers, men in wide-brimmed hats with whips tethered to their belts. Across the fields was a low, circular wall, and within were buildings and lines of smoke rising into the blue sky. Several blood-red flags whipped in the breeze.

We ducked back into the forest, before anyone saw us.

"Welcome to the Empire," Makara said.

"What now?" I asked.

Samuel paused a moment. "We can't just come out of the woods like this. It'll look suspicious."

"Maybe just a couple of us could go in," Anna said. "Pose as traders from the Wasteland, or something. Could be a way to get some info."

"Sounds risky," Samuel said. "We are technically at war with the Empire. It might be best to try and make it all the way to Nova Roma without being seen at all. When we get to the capital there will be so many people that we'll escape notice."

"Do we have enough food for that?" I asked.

"We can travel at night," Samuel said. "Less people around. If we need food, we can steal it."

"Won't all that look suspicious, though?" Makara asked. "We'll be mistaken for escaped slaves."

"Our goal is to make it to Nova Roma," Samuel said. "We're not trying to make friends here. If we have to steal, or even kill, to get there, we all will do so...without hesitation."

None of us said anything as his words sunk in. Through the trees, I could still see the wooden wall of the settlement, distant.

"Now would be a good time to find a spot to camp," Samuel said. "We can catch some sleep and continue on through the night."

We trekked back upriver, toward a clearing we had passed on the journey down. There we set up camp, making some lean-tos out of some rope and tarps we had packed. We had a cold dinner – sandwiches again – before settling down to sleep with just an hour of sunlight left.

When night came, I was still wide awake. I wasn't sure how long Samuel planned on having us sleep, but I didn't feel tired at all. It was absolutely miserable with the humidity, the heat, and the bugs. I was already not liking this Empire place, and longed for my bed back at Skyhome.

As the sky darkened, stars began to appear. Ashton had been right; the meteor fallout from Ragnarok did not affect this area as much. It felt strange to sleep under a sky that was not much different from what my grandparents would have seen.

The clearness of the night caused it to cool off quickly. Soon, it was not so unbearable, and even the bugs mostly went away. The stars twinkled by the thousands.

Everyone else around me was sound asleep. Still, something just wouldn't let me relax. I didn't know what it was. As time passed, my feeling of unease grew worse, until I felt ready to wake everyone else up.

I touched Samuel's shoulder, next to me. His eyes opened in an instant.

"What is it?" he asked.

Everything was still. The insects had gone away – because the night was cooling off, or for some other reason?

The answer came soon enough when people ran out of the forest, right for us.

***

We didn't have time to react before I was trapped in a tangle of net. I tried clawing myself out, but to no avail. We were surrounded on all sides. Makara or Anna screamed, I wasn't sure which in the darkness.

I rolled on the ground, only ensnaring myself further in the net. Gunshots went off, lighting the forest like bursts of lightning.

I reached for my Beretta, but was so ensnared that I couldn't reach it. That was when I remembered my knife. Madly, I reached for it, and began slashing at the rope entangling me. I hacked, again and again, fighting my way out of the snare. Finally, I punched free, crawling forward into the darkness.

I was the only one free – the others around me were locked into place. The men did not have flashlights, and did not at first notice that I was free. I used this to my advantage, crouching low and heading for Samuel first, since he was closest. His eyes widened upon seeing me crawl next to him. I began cutting through his bonds.

A large hand grabbed me by the shoulder, pulling me back with a snarl. I tried to wrench myself free of the man's grip, but another pair of hands grabbed me and threw me on the ground.

But by this time Samuel had slunk out of the net. He fired two times, and the man gripping me screamed. I felt his hand loosen, and I ran forward, out of his grasp. I reached for my Beretta, still holstered on my belt.

I drew it, pointing it into the darkness. Samuel and I were alone. From the forest ahead, I heard both Makara and Anna screaming, and the shouts of our attackers. Accompanying the screams was a rustling, dragging sound, leading away from our position. They were fleeing.

That was when I noticed two large men barring our path. They had stayed behind to make sure we didn't follow. Each held a knife that glinted in the darkness.

Quickly, I brought up my gun, but not fast enough. One of the men charged forward, swiping it aside. It landed on the ground a few feet away and was obscured by darkness. As Samuel grappled with the other attacker, my own adversary advanced, stabbing toward me. I dodged. One of the girls screamed again, more distant. We had to take care of these guys, fast. And I had no way to reach my gun without leaving myself open.

The man took another jab at me. I jumped backward, my back slamming against a tree. Wincing, I dodged once more when the man came at me again. His knife plunged into the tree's bark. Cursing in Spanish, he struggled to wrest it free.

I didn't waste another moment. I took my own knife, slashing wildly toward him. My blade connected with his arm. He screamed, and I felt his warm blood splatter on my hand. He staggered away, meaning to run. With his back turned to me, the rest was easy. I jumped him, sending him crashing to the earth. With gritted teeth, I pinned him and gave him a deep gash in his throat. Blood spewed out, his scream silenced by my blade. His body grew still under me as what was left of his life ebbed away.

Right next to his body was my gun. I grabbed it, and turned to help Samuel, who was still going hand-to-hand with his adversary. I ended the fight quickly by placing my gun on the back of the man's head. He paused in shock right before I shot. His body fell forward, sprawling on the ground.

Samuel looked at me with wide eyes. He picked up his own handgun from the ground, and charged away in the direction the girls had been taken.

We ran for thirty seconds or so, pushing aside foliage and branches that slammed and scratched our faces and hands. Uncaring, we sprinted on. It was only a matter of time until we caught up to them, and we couldn't let any of them get away.

A scream came from our left.

We turned, and ran in the direction of the sound. A few seconds later, we came across one of the girls, netted in a clearing. She was alone, having clearly been abandoned.

"Anna, get Anna!" she yelled.

It was Makara. Not understanding, I ran forward to cut her bonds.

"They left me here, and took Anna with them."

"Where?" I asked.

"To my left," Makara said. "Opposite the direction you came from."

I bolted away. Samuel could take care of Makara while I went after Anna. I had to catch them before they really got moving. When I stole a look behind, Makara was out of the net, running with Samuel after me. Up ahead, I heard a whinny. They had horses. That meant there would be no catching them. I didn't yell Anna's name, though I wanted to. I needed all the surprise I could get.

I burst out of the trees, finding myself on a dirt road. Four horses stood there, two men already mounted while two others were securing Anna to the back of one of the horses. She was wrapped in her net, and unable to break free. The men looked my way. Two of them reached for guns.

Out in the open as I was, I had no chance against them. Cursing, I dove back for the trees, rolling behind a fallen, rotting log as the first bullets sprayed chips of bark in my face. From behind, Samuel and Makara slid next to me.

"They have horses," I said.

The gunfire ceased for a moment. The men were yelling again, the horses nickering and snorting. They were about to set off. We had to do something now or never. I wasn't about to let Anna become a slave.

Despite the danger to myself, I burst out of the trees, my Beretta aimed outward. The horses galloped down the road and into the night. They were heading in the direction of the settlement.

I fired a few bullets at the escaping forms, but nothing connected. Samuel, who had run up beside me, placed a hand on my arm, drawing it back.

I watched helplessly as the horsemen, with Anna, got farther and farther away. Despite the impossibility of catching up, I took after them.

"Alex!" Makara shouted, from behind.

This wasn't over until it was over.

Chapter 8

"Alex, wait!"

I didn't heed Makara's second shout. I sprinted down the road, the thunder of hooves dimming as the horses sped away. I didn't know how far it was to the settlement, but I didn't plan on stopping until I got there.

The road rounded a bend, and then it led straight toward the gates. The horses stood in front, their riders waiting to be admitted inside.

I increased my speed, my body protesting at the strain. I was fueled only by my desperation to reach Anna. If they got inside, there would be no getting her back. The walls would completely surround her and, obviously, the guards would kill us if we tried to get in.

The gates opened. The horses ran inside. I ran desperately, knowing, as the barriers began to close, that I would not make it in time.

"No..."

The gates shut, locking us out.

I stopped in the middle of the road. Makara and Samuel skidded to a stop beside me. I didn't say anything, watching the closed gates with a sense of defeat. Shapes of guards materialized on top of the walls. They pointed their rifles our way.

"Down!" Samuel shouted.

We fell together as the first bullets sprayed the dirt. I fought the tears that came to my eyes. We had been outdone. Anna was gone.

"No..." I said.

"We can't do anything about it," Makara said. "We've got to get out of here."

A few more bullets burrowed into the dirt road. For a moment, the fusillade ceased. That was when the gates began to reopen. I looked up, irrationally thinking that it could be Anna coming out. Of course, it wasn't. It was men on horses – maybe five or six of them. The horses broke into a run, heading right for us.

"We've got to *move!*"

We scrambled out of the dirt, and gunned it for the tree line. If we could make it there, the vegetation would seriously hamper the horses' speed. I looked back toward the city. It hurt, knowing Anna was in there, and knowing there was nothing we could do about it. We were leaving her behind.

"We can't fight them, Alex," Samuel said. "We'll all be killed, and the mission will be compromised."

"So, what, we're just going to *leave* her there?"

Samuel didn't answer as he and his sister pulling me toward the trees. Rather than fight them, I started running. As much as I hated it, they were right. I wasn't going to cause them to die, too.

Die. Is that what was going to happen to Anna? No. Her fate would be worse than death. She was going to be enslaved, worked to the bone with little food or rest. And if her master was cruel, or perverse, her fate would be much worse.

I turned back. I wasn't leaving her.

"No, you don't..." Makara said.

"She's alive. I know she is."

"We'll come back for her!" Samuel said. "We can't do that if we die here. Now come on, get your ass moving!"

Telling myself Samuel was right, I kept running. All the training in Skyhome had done me good. I had no problem keeping up with Samuel and Makara. Such wouldn't have been the case two months ago.

Behind, our pursuers chased us into the forest. We entered the first of the trees, pushing our way past brambles and underbrush, putting as much distance as possible between ourselves and our hunters. Fueled by shock, grief, and pain, I pushed myself on – for what, I didn't know. I wanted to run in the other direction and get to Anna.

Why hadn't I listened to Makara when we came upon her in the net? If we had done what she said and immediately gone after Anna, we could have saved her. If Samuel and I had kept running, we might have gotten to her in time.

I couldn't blame myself for long, however. A bullet whizzed past my ear, hitting a nearby tree.

"Keep moving," Samuel said, between breaths.

I could hear the men shouting from behind. They were on foot, having abandoned the horses.

The land began sloping upward. Mixed in with the dense vegetation were rocks and boulders. As we hoofed it up the incline, the trees began to thin. My lungs were bursting for air. Behind, men chased after us. We couldn't keep this up for long.

"They'll see us up here," Makara said, pausing a moment. "We need a place to hide."

Samuel pointed. "There."

Against the side of the slope was an opening, deep and dark, moonlight reflecting off the rock surrounding it. The last thing I wanted to do was go underground. Not only did I have a *lot* of bad memories of things that had happened underground, it would take us farther away from Anna. The more time that passed, the worse her chances got.

"We need to go in there, Alex," Samuel said. "It's the only way."

"Fine," I said. "But we're going back to the town tomorrow."

Samuel said nothing as we headed for the cave's opening. The men weren't far behind – they would come within view of us in seconds.

We climbed inside, sliding down a steep slope into the dark opening. The air was dank and moist. Where the slope evened out, I scuttled up, glancing up at the cave's opening. We had slid down probably fifty feet. In the darkness I heard an underground stream gurgling. I heard Samuel's pockets rustle as he searched for a flashlight.

Samuel's flashlight clicked on, its pillar of light scanning the cave. The cavern was huge, both tall and wide, and the stream ran before us, flowing down and away. The water had probably filtered through the ground from the recent rain. The air was cool, with an earthy smell. Nothing smelled rotted or Blighted, which probably meant there were no virus-infected monsters down here. Or at least, that's what I hoped.

"We'll follow the stream," Samuel decided. "Once it's safe, we'll follow it back out."

"What if they follow us in here?" Makara asked.

Samuel didn't answer for a moment. "I doubt they have flashlights. It seems they don't have as much technology as we do. But if they do, we'll hear them coming."

Samuel walked ahead, splashing into the water. We followed him. I glanced back toward the cave entrance. No one was there. Hopefully, they hadn't seen us come in.

As I waded into the stream, its coldness chilled my skin and made my muscles go numb. I stepped out onto the other side and rushed up the stream's bank to keep up with Samuel's pool of light. Above, stalactites glittered with both minerals and condensation. It was eerily beautiful, but it had no impact on me. My mind was somewhere else, thinking about the girl I couldn't save.

I felt numbness creep over me that had nothing to do with the cold water or cool air. I thought of Anna, bound in darkness and alone, all because I wasn't fast enough to save her. I hated myself, and knew I could never forgive myself as long as the thought that she was still alive haunted me. It was unbearable to think about my failure and what Anna would have to go through because of me.

I resolved at that moment, no matter what Samuel or Makara decided, that I was going after her.

***

An hour later, we were still walking. The cavern went on and on. Finally, Samuel came to a stop, clicking off the flashlight.

"We'll hold up here."

The darkness was absolute. Rather than being afraid of it, I felt safe in it. Nothing could attack me here. Only...

"We know the way back, right?" Makara asked.

"There's just two directions in this place: up, and down," Samuel said.

"What about Anna?"

No one said anything for a moment.

"We'll go back once we get some rest," Samuel said. "Scope out the town, see if there is a way in."

"And how are we supposed to do that?" Makara asked.

"We'll think of something," I said. "We can't abandon Anna like this."

"I agree," Samuel said. "But I will give it no more than a day. If there are too many guards, we will have to move on." Samuel paused a moment. "I'm sorry, Alex. The mission comes first."

"How can you say that? She's one of us. We leave *no one* behind."

"I understand that," Samuel said. "But you saw how many guards they have. I won't risk everyone on a suicide mission."

"There has to be another way in."

"We'll do what we can," Samuel said. "I can promise no more than that."

I wanted to yell at him, and just barely held myself back.

"I wonder how they found us to begin with," Makara said.

"I don't know," Samuel said. "But we're lucky to even be alive. It's a miracle all of us weren't captured."

No one said anything more. I heard someone sit on the ground beside me. The stream which we had followed trickled to our side.

We had nothing to our names. Our gear had all been left behind in our rush to escape, and had likely been looted. All I had were the clothes on my back and my Beretta. It was as if I had gone back to square one.

As I lay down on the cold, hard rock and closed my eyes, my only concern was how to rescue Anna.

I had to think of something by tomorrow, or she was going to be gone for good.

***

Later, we awoke. The only thing to do was get up and start heading back. Samuel clicked his flashlight back on, and we followed the stream back to the surface. Soon we were greeted with a bright spot of light in the distance – the entrance to the cave. The light illumined our surroundings, revealing stalactites and stalagmites once hidden in the darker regions. Parts of the stream veered off in separate directions, gathering in crystalline pools.

We crouched low as we climbed up the mouth of the cave. Peeking out, it was early dawn – far earlier than I'd expected. The morning air was crisp and cool. The dim light was blinding after the total darkness of the cavern.

Gathered below the cave's mouth was a circle of five men, four sleeping around a fire burned down to the coals. One of them was awake, warming his hands by the fire. He looked up. His eyes widened.

"Now," Samuel said.

We burst out of the cave, guns blazing. The man screamed as our bullets ripped into him, sending him sprawling to the earth. The other men jolted up, reaching for their guns – but two more were felled before they could even get shots off.

The other two ran for cover. Makara picked one off before he could find shelter, while the last man disappeared behind a boulder.

"Put the gun away, and we will spare your life," Samuel shouted.

The man threw the gun aside, coming out from around the boulder with hands raised and eyes wide. He fell on his knees, whimpering.

Makara walked ahead, holding out her handgun. "Shut up."

She shot him. The man fell backward to the earth.

Samuel shrugged. We looted their bodies, finding some ammo and a crumbly, yellow bread that tasted like corn. We also found some roasted white meat. Though both the meat and "cornbread" were dry, they tasted good. We drank from some canteens we found. Mine was filled with water that had a sweet, spicy flavor to it. The canteen had probably been filled with some sort of alcoholic drink – perhaps rum – before it was used for water. We found a nearby knapsack, and loaded it with ammo and leftover food. Samuel hoisted the pack onto his shoulders, and set off down the slope in the direction of the settlement.

"We are going back?" I said.

Samuel nodded. "It won't hurt to take a look. Don't get your hopes up. If I feel like it's impossible to get in, we're heading to Nova Roma – with or without Anna."

It was the best I could hope for. I just needed to think of something – anything – that could save her. The problem was, I had zero idea on how to do that.

Makara said nothing. She had been so against Anna when she had first joined us. I wondered if she felt the same way now. Anna was a part of our team, along for the ride when she had, at first, only been our guide to the Great Blight. She had saved the mission countless times, and it was wrong to leave her behind without any sort of plan to go after her. I didn't care what anyone said, or how rational they made it sound.

We followed Samuel down the slope. In the distance, smoke rose in lazy circles from within the trees. That was the location of the settlement. In the misty morning light, I could make out the wooden shapes of shops and houses surrounded by the circular palisade wall.

Somewhere in all that was Anna.

"Hang on, Anna," I said. "We're coming."

Chapter 9

Another hour passed, and we were in the outer stands of trees, scanning the wall of the town. It looked damn near impenetrable. The entire town was situated in a large meadow, and clearings filled with farms surrounded it. On the farms worked hundreds upon hundreds of slaves, growing crops. A road cut through the farms, entering the city by a gate, upon either side of which were two lofty guard towers. The road left the settlement's other side, veering off and curving into the forest.

That was the gate Anna had entered, and the one we had been chased out of. They were the only two entrances. In addition, several guards sat upon the three guard towers built into the walls that curved between each of the two gates, making a total of ten guard towers. Each tower had at least one guard in it.

Obviously, the Empire took security very seriously.

"Yeah," Makara said, "doesn't look like we're busting in that place."

"There *has* to be a way," I said. "We're just not thinking hard enough."

No one answered me, which was a bit discouraging.

"Would a disguise work?" I asked.

"Where would we get said disguise?" Makara asked.

I pointed toward one of the workers on the field. "Maybe he'll let us borrow his."

"Run out in the open and ambush a helpless slave?" Makara sniffed. "No thanks."

"We could start a fire," I said.

"Arson's always a win in my book," Makara said.

I couldn't tell if she was being sarcastic or not.

"A fire would force them out of the town, if it spreads enough," Samuel said. "That might mean Anna, too."

"She would still be under protection, though," Makara said. "Besides, we might end up hurting her."

"If we wait until nightfall, sneaking in might be easier," I said.

"Maybe," Samuel said. "But they probably have that place guarded 24/7." He paused. "I wonder what they're keeping in there that's so important."

We looked at the settlement longer, watching a caravan of camels leave by the north gate. When twelve camels had left, surrounded by guards and robed merchants, the gates closed once more.

"Not open to any sort of traffic, even in the daytime," Samuel said. "They *always* keep the gates closed. Either that's normal, or they are on lockdown for some reason."

I looked at Samuel. "Because of us?"

Samuel nodded. "Maybe. They probably thought we were escaped slaves. Or spies from Raider Bluff."

"That's right," Makara said. "We're technically at war with them."

"What would spies from Raider Bluff be doing in this Podunk town?" I asked. "Wouldn't we be in Nova Roma?"

"This place is on the way there," Samuel said. He pointed toward the road leading out from the left gate. "Follow that road far enough southeast, you'll end up in Nova Roma. Follow it the other way, it goes all the way up the Mexican coast, through a series of towns for over a thousand miles. Who knows? It might eventually arrive at Raider Bluff itself."

It seemed mind-boggling that a place like the Nova Roma Empire could exist, thirty years after the fall of Ragnarok. Augustus was obviously both a very well-organized and a powerful man. It was hard to see how Raider Bluff could stand a chance against him.

My thoughts turned back to rescuing Anna. Just staring at that town, I couldn't let her go – not without trying *something*.

"I don't think we can break in," Makara said. "We came here, we searched it out...there is literally nothing we can do."

My heart sunk. Makara was right. How would we break into that place?

I got an idea.

"The *Odin!*" I said.

Makara and Samuel looked at each other, confused.

"Alex, they'll see that thing from a mile away. There's no chance."

"Not if we fly it high enough."

"What are you saying?"

"We could parachute in. Do it at night, when no one can see us. Obviously, it would be just me and Sam. Makara would have to pilot the ship."

"That..." Makara began. I could tell she wanted to say my idea was stupid. I didn't care, interrupting her before she could speak again.

"We could learn to parachute," I said. "It probably isn't that hard. We have the ship – we can just take it somewhere safe, and practice until we're good enough to land where we want. After that we can get into the town."

"Yes," Makara said. "Even if we *did* do all that, how would we go about searching for Anna? How would we get *out* of the town?" She shook her head. "Those parts are pretty important, too."

Admittedly, they were. "We can figure that out later. Yes, it's risky, but isn't Anna worth the risk? How many times would this mission have failed without her?"

Makara and Samuel looked at each other. I could tell they were not saying anything, afraid to let me down. Cold logic said my idea was suicide – even if it was better than all the other ones I had thrown out.

"I know *Odin* has parachutes on board," Samuel said. "Unfortunately, none of us have ever used one before. And without anyone to teach us, I won't risk it."

"I'm sure there's instructions on the side."

Samuel sighed. "Alex, you're asking that we risk *both* of our lives for the minuscule chance that we save one. Our mission is to stop Xenofall – and yes, that might involve some losses. I would rescue Anna if there were any chance of success. But this is suicide."

"I don't care," I said, not concerned with how illogical I knew I was being. "I just *know* that if we don't try this, we'll regret it."

"We can't regret anything if we're dead," Makara said.

We said nothing, watching the town. I felt a mixture of anger and depression. I couldn't tear my gaze away from that town, even if I'd tried. It was my fault that Anna was gone, and there was no way I could live the rest of my life knowing I had done nothing to save her.

Finally, Makara spoke. "Fine. Let's practice it first."

I turned to Makara, disbelieving that she had changed her mind. "You mean it?"

Makara nodded. "It has to be daylight. And you, Alex...you're going to be the first one to throw your ass off the ship."

I wanted to hug her, but I knew there was small chance that she'd be receptive to that. "Done."

"Hopefully, parachutes can get reused," Samuel said. "We have a lot of practice to do." He shook his head. "The fact that I don't know if parachutes can be reused does not bode well at all."

I didn't care about that small detail. "So we're really doing it?"

Samuel sighed, and didn't say anything for a long moment.

"I don't like to leave anyone behind. We can go back to *Odin* and see if it's even a feasible option."

"What about Ashton?" Makara asked.

Samuel hesitated. "He won't like it. But spending a few days just to see if this could work isn't a small price to pay when it means getting Anna back."

"Exactly," I said.

"I can't believe we're actually doing this," Makara said.

"Believe it," I said.

"Let's not get ahead of ourselves," Samuel said. "Let's get back to *Odin,* and see what our options are."

Now that Makara and Samuel were on board for my crazy idea, I had no idea how we were going to pull it off. But if we could get into that town, find Anna, and escape, it would be the best thing we had done so far.

We weren't going to leave one of our own behind without a fight.

***

We spent the rest of the day double-timing it to *Odin*. We made it there by evening.

Unfortunately, by the time we made it, it was far too dark to practice. Instead, we got the parachutes out and tried to see if we could figure out how to use them.

Before we did any of that, however, we debated whether we should tell Ashton about Anna.

"He's going to find out as soon as the ship goes online, anyway," Samuel said.

We stood on the bridge, waiting to turn on the transceiver.

"I can deliver the news, if you don't want to," I said.

"I'm the leader of this crew," Samuel said. "In the end, this was *my* decision."

Samuel didn't take long to collect his thoughts. He turned on the transceiver and began to speak.

"Skyhome...this is *Odin*. Do you have a copy?"

Silence. It lasted a good long while. I began to get nervous. Ashton could probably hear us, but was in such disbelief that he couldn't bring himself to answer.

Finally, Ashton's voice crackled out of the speaker.

"*Odin,* what is your status? You should be in the city. What happened?"

Samuel paused before answering. "Anna's gone."

Ashton did not speak for a moment. "Are Makara and Alex with you?"

"Yes."

"We've been over this, Samuel. In the case of one of the crew members dying..."

"She's not dead, Ashton. There's a chance she may be rescued. I intend to take that chance."

"Christ, what happened?"

Samuel proceeded to tell the story. I internally winced when he got to the part about the town having a wall and many guards, and our plan to parachute ourselves in at night.

When Samuel was done, the other end was silent. It seemed that Ashton was having trouble processing all this information.

"Anna's a good fighter, there is no doubt of that," Ashton said. "But she isn't worth the risk. You know that, yet you came back to *Odin,* knowing what my answer would be."

"She's been with us from the beginning," Samuel said. "My crew would be crippled without her."

"You've never parachuted before!" Ashton said, voice rising with anger. "You intend to drop into a city under heavy guard, where you'll most likely be seen, even if it's done at night, and search every building until you find her? And if you do, how do you plan on getting out? All of you will be compromised! This is a *no-brainer!* What makes you think that you have even the remotest chance of success? Despite everything you guys have gone through, you are *not invincible!"*

No one answered Ashton for a long while. His cold logic was almost enough to cut through all my emotion. Almost.

"Ashton, we're doing this at great risk, because it is simply something we need to do," I said. "I can't explain it, but I know this mission will fail without Anna's help. She's our best fighter, and we can't go on without her. That's the truth, as truthful as anything you've just told us. Yes, it will be hard, but we will succeed. I have no doubt."

Ashton sighed from the other end of the line. He still didn't agree.

Samuel was about to say something, but in the end said nothing.

"Pack up, and get moving," Ashton said. "You're going to have to let Anna go. You have to meet with Augustus. That is your mission, Samuel. That is a direct order."

Samuel gritted his teeth, waiting a moment before answering. "You can say what you want, Ashton. We're going in."

"Like hell you are."

"Alex is right. Anna is family, and we don't leave family behind."

"Makara?" Ashton said. "Surely, you're not caught up in this madness?"

She shrugged. "My loyalty is with Samuel."

Ashton growled on the other end of the line. "If you all insist on being so bullheaded and stubborn, you leave me no choice."

We all looked at each other, eyes wide. What was he talking about?

"I didn't want it to come to this," Ashton said. "I'm far too old to be doing such insane things."

"What are you talking about, Ashton?" Samuel asked.

"If you are dead set on this fool plan, someone is going to have to teach you how to parachute without killing yourselves."

"You're coming down here?" Samuel asked.

"I'll be prepping *Gilgamesh* tonight," Ashton said. "I should be there by morning, your time. Try to get some rest. You're going to have a long day tomorrow."

With that, Ashton cut out.

Chapter 10

That next morning I awoke to the colossal sound of *Gilgamesh* landing right next to *Odin*. I rushed out of my bunk and ran outside.

The early morning sun tinted the large ship in a pale, orange glow. Three angular struts, two in back and one in front, unfolded from beneath the ship as it hovered above the ground. Slowly, it set down on the earth, its thrusters spewing blue flame. The ship's internal fusion hum dissipated as it powered down.

Like *Odin*, *Gilgamesh* looked like a giant, primordial insect. Ashton had told me the U.S. made its spaceships angular in order to be invisible to radar. *Gilgamesh* had a short wingspan for atmospheric flying, through the majority of its lift came from the four thrusters mounted aft. These thrusters could be turned to provide propulsion in whatever direction *Gilgamesh* wanted to go – up, and down, even left and right, or even directly backward. Two additional thrusters were located fore, which gave the ship the ability to hover. This also allowed the vessel additional mobility.

Gilgamesh's boarding ramp slid outward, and the blast door opened. A few seconds later, Ashton appeared, standing at the top of the ramp.

Samuel and Makara ran out to join me. We stood for a moment, watching Ashton.

Without a word, he motioned for us to come up the ramp and join him in the ship. When he turned to go back inside, we climbed the ramp and entered the ship. The blast door shut behind us.

The ship's interior was cool, lit by fluorescent lights. The interior design was not much different from *Odin,* but everything was slightly larger. Two tables were built into the wall of *Gilgamesh's* wardroom, whereas *Odin* only had one. *Gilgamesh* had been designed to carry a larger crew. The galley appeared to be in the same spot, connected to the wardroom, and to our left, a corridor led to the cabins and the clinic, and even further aft, the engine and fusion generator. On our right lay another corridor. On one side lay a conference room, toward which Ashton walked. We followed him down the corridor. Opposite the conference room was the armory – where not just weapons were stored, but other necessary supplies. The main difference between *Gilgamesh* and *Odin,* besides size, was that *Gilgamesh* was large enough to have a proper bridge rather than a cockpit. Before ducking into the conference room after the others, I paused to take a look.

Outside the angled windshields spread green, misty forest. Behind the pilot's and copilot's chairs was a large screen displaying a colored map of Mexico, along with *Gilgamesh's* location, a red dot on the map. A red line designated the flight path *Gilgamesh* had taken to arrive. A large deck allowed room for standing before the screen, and several jump seats had been built into the walls. In all, the bridge was probably twice as big as *Odin's* cockpit.

I entered the conference room. A long, stainless steel table sat in the middle, and eight chairs sat around it, bolted to the floor. A flat-screen, currently off, was mounted to one of the walls. Three packs were lined up on the table. Now that Ashton had arrived with *Gilgamesh,* Makara would also be making the jump.

Parachutes, I thought.

"Sit," Ashton said. "We have much to go over."

His tone was stern and businesslike. He was probably still upset about our decision, but what was done was done. The fact that he was here meant he wasn't *completely* against the idea.

Or at least, that was what I kept telling myself.

"I took the time to refresh myself on how to do this," Ashton said, indicating the parachutes. "Lucky for all of us, before Ragnarok fell, I was an experienced skydiver. My wife and I did it fairly often. There is not much to it, but it can be dangerous; especially for you all, who are lacking in experience. You will need to listen carefully, because there is not much time. The longer we wait to do this, the more danger Anna is in, and the more risky the operation becomes.

"Today, you will learn something that should take many weeks to accomplish. You will each learn to drop solo, and become proficient in all the steps, not only to ensure a safe landing, but also to land in a precise location of your choosing. Adding to this difficulty, you will be doing this at night, and will very likely be under enemy fire."

None of us said anything at Ashton's preamble. We were all listening, intent on what he was going to say next.

"The parachutes I have chosen are all dark. This will make them difficult to see at night although, of course, it's very probable that once you open the main canopy at an altitude of 2,500 feet you will be seen, shot, and killed. To avoid this as much as possible, we will practice as much as we can today – if all goes well, we will have as many as three trial runs. During these trials, you will learn how, and when, to deploy your parachute, how to steer yourself in the direction you want to go using the toggles, and, if all goes well, learn how to steer proficiently enough to hit a precise location. And hopefully, you will learn enough during daylight to do this under the cloak of darkness."

Makara leaned forward. "We will *really* be ready by tonight?"

Ashton looked at her blankly. "This is the group's decision. It is not my recommendation, but it is not too late for you all to back out. In fact, I encourage it."

"That's not going to happen," I said. "We're going to get Anna out of there, whatever it takes."

Samuel and Makara nodded in agreement.

"Humph. As I thought." Ashton reached for the packs, pushing one toward each of us. "I took the liberty of packing everything myself. Packing the chutes takes a while, so I have brought enough spares so that I don't have to repack them after each jump. That means we have twelve chutes to work from – three each for your training, and the three dark ones for when your drop comes tonight. Normally, the first step would be preparation, but since I have already done that, you won't have to worry about it. Everything has already been prepped for you.

"You will be dropped from an altitude of ten thousand feet. You will spend about forty-five seconds of that time in freefall. After forty-five seconds, you will deploy what is called a pilot chute, located in what's called the drogue, from an altitude of about 2,500 feet. The drogue is located at the bottom of the container, here." Ashton tapped a small pouch at the bottom of the backpack. "You pull the pilot chute out, like so..." Ashton pulled it out. It was surprisingly small. "It will catch the wind and inflate."

"How is that thing supposed to slow us down?" I asked. "It's so small."

"This is not the main canopy itself," Ashton answered. "The pilot chute will rise above, pulling on an attached piece called the bridle. The bridle is connected to the pin, which, once pulled, will let loose the main canopy itself from the deployment bag. When the pin is pulled, it lets out the risers, which connect the lines to the main canopy. The tension on the lines will cause the main canopy to inflate. There is also a piece of equipment attached to the canopy called a slider, which will automatically slide down the lines and prevent the canopy from inflating too quickly. At this point, the canopy should be out and working fine. You will look up to check that this is the case. If all is well, you can grab the toggles with your hands. Pulling the left toggle will veer you left – pulling the right toggle will veer you right. Pulling both will slow you down, and you want to do that before landing."

"What if the chute doesn't come out, or becomes tangled in the lines or something?" Makara asked.

"There are two main safeguards against that," Ashton said. "There is a reserve chute in case the first one doesn't deploy correctly. In order to deploy it, you must release your main canopy, which is done by pulling the release handle located on the right shoulder strap, here..." Ashton touched it. It was a series of three rings. "Pulling the release will cut away the lines on both risers simultaneously, sending you into freefall again. At that point, the reserve should deploy automatically."

"Should?" Makara asked.

"Yes," Ashton said. "Should. The chance is small that both chutes wouldn't deploy, but that is unlikely. By doing this, you are assuming the risks."

"You said there was another safeguard," Samuel said.

"Yes," Ashton said. "There is also a piece of equipment called the AAD – or automatic activation device. It is basically a computer that monitors air pressure and other factors. If your chute is not deployed by the time you reach 750 feet, the AAD will automatically deploy it for you."

"Why wouldn't any of us deploy the chute to begin with?" Makara asked.

"There could be many reasons – maybe you get hit by another skydiver and lose control. Maybe you lose consciousness for some reason. It's not likely, but there is a chance. Just another safeguard."

Either way, I was glad that there were checks in place. Hearing Ashton describe the entire process was a lot better than trying to figure it out for ourselves, and likely getting killed in the process. Rescuing Anna seemed more tangible than ever. We were *really* doing this. By tonight, we'd be flying over the settlement, dropping in, and finding Anna. We could all be together again as early as tonight.

"What about once we land?" Samuel said.

"We'll go over that after our last trial run," Ashton said. "We need to fit in as much practice as we can. Basically, you'll just be taking off your chute, finding some place to hide it, and figuring out how to find Anna and get out of there." He looked at all of us severely. "It is still your decision, Samuel. I recommend fully not going through with this."

"We need to find her," Samuel said. "We need to exhaust every option before moving on. Let's at least learn how to do this. If all three of us can land in the town, we can take care of the rest. We can fight any individual guard that crosses our path." Samuel smiled. "They'll never know what hit them."

"I hope so, Samuel. So, you do want to proceed with this?"

Samuel nodded. "Yes."

"Alright," Ashton said. "Makara, strap yourself in. Within thirty minutes, all of you will be back on the ground. I spotted a field nearby that is far enough away for our purposes."

***

Gilgamesh hovered over the green, forested Earth. A thin layer of cloud somewhat obscured the surface, but I still saw the field we were to land in, almost directly below us.

The ship was in hover mode, standing still above the clouds. Amazingly, *Gilgamesh* made little noise – had it been using conventional fuel, the sound of that energy expenditure would have been deafening. But the fusion reactor kept the energy flowing smoothly, steadily. The thrusters below the ship glowed a steady blue. When we did our drop tonight, the inhabitants would not hear the ship. Hopefully, the clouds could obscure the blue glow *Gilgamesh's* thrusters would produce.

Ashton stood behind us. "Wind speed is minimal. If it weren't for those clouds, conditions would be near perfect."

"Those clouds may be a blessing in disguise," Makara said. "No one has a chance of seeing us just hovering up here."

"That is true," Ashton said. "Remember – you will reach 2,500 feet after about forty-five seconds."

With the parachutes, Ashton had also brought us all digital watches. We each set the stopwatch for forty-five seconds.

"Try to space yourselves out, that way there's no chance of hitting one another."

"We know," Makara said. "We've already been over all this."

Makara's face was tense as she looked outside the open blast door. It was a long damn way to fall.

"You first, Sparky," she said, pushing me toward the door.

I yelped. I had nearly forgotten that.

"Sparky?"

"Yep. We had a deal."

Samuel gave a sly grin. "What are you waiting for?"

"Alright," Ashton said. "Whenever you're ready, Alex."

I was really doing this. I paused a moment, looking at the world below. In my head, I went over everything Ashton had said. Wait forty-five seconds. Pull the drogue at 2,500 feet. Try not to pass out. I took a deep breath. I fell forward, lying flat on my belly.

I was falling. The air pummeled my body and ripped cold past my face as I raced faster and faster toward the surface. I sailed through the cloud, fear and exhilaration coursing through my veins. This was *fun*.

Ten seconds.

I glanced above, unable to restrain a whoop. Both Makara and Samuel were small above me, falling at about the same speed. I had reached my max speed of 120 mph, maintaining equilibrium with the air resistance below me. I exited the cloud layer, and lost my breath seeing that green ground rushing up to meet me, closer than ever. There was nothing but green, and jagged peaks to my right, lost in cloud – no signs of civilization. It felt incredible, as if the whole world were mine.

I had twenty seconds until I had to open my chute. The ground rushed up toward me, faster and faster. Was I really supposed to wait *this long* before releasing the pilot chute?

I looked at my digital clock. It was time. I pulled out the pilot chute. It shot above me, pulling lines and popping the pin. The rest of the canopy filled up, cell by cell, and I felt myself shoot upward. I felt afraid that I might hit one of the others. But nothing happened. I felt myself lifted up, slowing from a hundred and twenty mph to a mere ten mph. I was floating down to Earth, not too far from the green field that was our target. My heart pounded like crazy.

On my either side, I grabbed the toggles with shaky hands. It was time to experiment with these controls. I pulled my left toggle slightly, feeling myself turn down and to the left. I tried the right. It had the opposite effect.

I pulled on both slightly, feeling myself lift up a bit. Butterflies flew in my stomach.

A gust of wind blew, veering me to my left. I pulled the right toggle to compensate. This was easy.

Except the clearing wasn't approaching fast enough. I would hit the trees below before I ever made it. Crashing into one of those things would be painful, not to mention tricky to get out of. If I were unlucky, the consequences might be even worse.

Afraid, I veered right, hoping to catch a draft of wind that would send me further ahead. The treetops were closer, reaching for me. I was going to crash into them before making the clearing. There was one tall tree in particular I was on a direct course to hit. I pulled up on the toggles, right before hitting the tree. I cried out, feeling myself lift above it, my feet scraping its top branches. I had made it. The clearing was ahead, and I allowed myself to sink toward the tall, waving grass. Right before I touched down, I pulled on both toggles, as Ashton had instructed me. I landed, rolling on the ground as my chute enveloped me.

I untangled myself, unstrapping my pack. As soon as I was free, I saw Makara land a few feet away, as nimbly as a cat. Samuel swung in from above, landing a good fifty feet away. It was a textbook landing, and this was only our first go. If we could have anywhere near this level of success tonight, I felt more confident about this rescue than ever.

"Close call, Alex," Samuel said.

"Yeah," I said, my voice shaky. "I'll have to release the drogue a bit sooner next time."

"Did you set your watch alright?" Makara asked, walking up. "Samuel and I released about the same time as you, and we spaced our jumps by about five seconds."

"I think I did," I said, looking at my watch. "Maybe it didn't start on time."

"Make sure it's working properly next time," Samuel said. "We were lucky."

Maybe things hadn't gone as swimmingly as I first supposed. "I will."

The shape of *Gilgamesh* descended from the clouds, still about 5,000 feet above.

It was time for takes two and three.

*** *** ***

That afternoon, we did our second jump. My watch worked fine; I must have hit the pause button in midair, and hit it again somehow. At least, that was what I decided. Who knew what really happened?

The nerves were still there for this jump, but they were easier to ignore. We landed in the clearing again, and this time there were no killer trees. Before evening, we did our final jump. This time, though, Ashton told us to pull the release on the main canopy, in order to get used to the reserve being shot out. This was a little scary, because releasing that canopy meant that the reserve was our only lifeline – and unlike the main chute, the reserve had no toggles – although, by the time we were to release our main canopy, we were supposed to be safely over the clearing.

We did get rid of our main chutes when the time came, and as we were told, the reserves deployed automatically. It wasn't easy pulling that release.

By the time we had gathered on *Gilgamesh* after the third jump, it was night. The only contingency we hadn't allowed for was the one where we *didn't* pull our chutes. Hopefully, that wouldn't happen.

After a quick dinner, we took a nap in order to prepare for our midnight jump. When we awoke, Ashton had black coffee ready to perk us up. After swallowing it down, we put on our jumpsuits over our clothing and readied our packs. I had my Beretta at the ready, along with my knife, both secured safely to my belt for use upon landing.

It was finally time. It had been a crazy day of shock and adrenaline, and we had yet to put ourselves through the craziest thing yet – the operation to save Anna.

Ashton piloted *Gilgamesh* toward the coordinates where the settlement was located. We were quiet on the journey there. We needed to get in and out of there, fast. Once done, we could make a new plan on how we were going to get to Nova Roma and reach Augustus.

I felt the ship slow. We had arrived. It was a matter of making the jump and praying that we didn't miss. Getting in was probably the easy part. We didn't know anything about the settlement's layout. We would be blindly searching for any clue to find Anna's location. But the fact remained – she was in there, and we were going to get her out, whatever it took.

The plan was to land as close to the center of town as we could, which was as far possible from the guard towers and walls. Preferably, we wanted to land on top of a building. The streets would be too risky. One person seeing us would be all it took for this operation to be compromised.

We just had to hope everyone was asleep – and that none of the guards looked up. It was a lot of ifs, but everything we had done so far was based on ifs. Maybe luck would carry us through one last time.

Despite the danger, I wasn't having second thoughts.

The three of us and Ashton stood next to the blast door. In his hands, he held three sets of what looked like goggles.

"These are night vision goggles," he said. "You won't be able to see without them."

I took a pair from him. They were very light, containing only a strap that held the goggles themselves. I strapped them to my head, finding the power button on the side. I flicked it on, and everything around me glowed bright green.

"Cool..."

"Bring them back," Ashton said. "These can't be replaced."

Ashton moved toward the control panel that opened the blast door.

"Stand clear," Ashton said. "The air's going to rush out."

We moved aside. I gripped a corner for extra support. Ashton pressed the exit button. When the door slid open, a gush of air rushed from the ship. My ears popped from the pressure change. The open door revealed the black night outside. The wind gusted as we hovered above swirling cloud made milky with moonlight. Conditions were perfect. We could not be seen from below. The moon hung crisp and clear in the sky, among thousands of stars, including the purplish band of the Milky Way. The air was cold and thin. In moments, we would be out there, on the wind. My heart raced.

"Remember the procedure," Ashton said. "Samuel first. Then Makara, and next, Alex. Follow Samuel's lead exactly, and remember to keep track of the time. Do everything to keep from getting noticed. If you are found, get out of there as quickly as possible. Don't take any unnecessary risks. You have thirty minutes."

This was crazy. Some would even say suicidal. Logically, it wasn't justified. But we were here, and Anna needed us.

"On my mark," Samuel said.

He stood a moment, taking a deep breath.

"One, two..."

He didn't wait for three. He jumped.

Makara stepped up to the opening.

"One, two..."

She, too, jumped, disappearing into the night.

I didn't even count. After a final glance at Ashton, I stepped out the door.

Chapter 11

I fell through the dark clouds, moisture cold and sticky on my skin, wind whipping my face. I did my best to control the tremors brought on by both cold and nerves. I had done this three times today; there was no reason why it should be so frightening. And yet, it *was*. Maybe because this time, it was night. But more likely it was because this was not a practice run. This was the real thing, and Anna's life hinged on whether or not we succeeded.

The clouds flew above me. I could discern Makara and Samuel's shapes against the landscape, lit green by my night vision. The green lights of the town were few and pale in the night. I had fifteen seconds until I was to deploy my chute.

Those fifteen seconds seemed to take forever as the lights below grew in intensity, glowing green through my goggles. Samuel's chute flared, his main canopy billowing upward. Makara's came next. They angled themselves toward the settlement, veering right.

I pulled my pilot chute free. It shot away, and I felt the strain of the harness as I slowed from my freefall. I felt myself lift from the drastic drop in speed. When everything settled, I grabbed the toggles, guiding myself after Samuel and Makara. I marveled at the fact that two days ago we had nearly all died outside the gates of this town. Now, we were coming back, tempting fate again.

The walls were still distant, perhaps one thousand feet ahead. I was still far above them. I saw that I was swinging in too fast. I would overshoot both Samuel and Makara, who were far lower than me. To compensate, I pulled on both toggles, slowing my speed. Samuel passed over the walls first, guiding himself toward the center of town. He was a mere shadow – I could only see him because of my night vision. It would be hard for anyone in the city to see him unless they were really looking. Makara followed, her path nearly identical to Samuel's.

I passed over the walls about two hundred feet beneath me. I spied two guards talking near one of the guard towers. They had no urge to glance up. I circled downward, toward the empty street Samuel had landed on. It wasn't a building, as we had planned, but it would have to do. Makara angled herself after Samuel, landing just a few feet away from him on the dirt street. Quickly, they grabbed their chutes, pulling them into a dark alley. Samuel and Makara were visible for all of three seconds.

It was my turn. I grimaced, doing my best to land where they had. But a sudden gust of wind lifted me above the street. Gritting my teeth, I tried to turn, but to no avail. The wind caught hold of my canopy, taking me above the flat roof of a four-story building. If I didn't do something, I would overshoot the building and draw dangerously close to the wall on the opposite end of the settlement.

It was now or never.

I pulled the release, and the main canopy shot away above me. Automatically, the reserve deployed. However, I had already landed on top of the building, tucking and rolling even as the reserve went limp from lack of air.

Panting, I cut the cords of the reserve with my knife, untangling myself from the lines. I gazed ahead, where the main canopy settled onto the corner of the roof, precariously close to falling off. I'd take care of that in a second. First, I threw off my pack, stripped out of my jumpsuit, and tossed them aside. I went to the roof's corner and picked up the main canopy, dragging it to the building's center, where there was a barrel. I stuffed the canopy inside the barrel, and stuffed my reserve and jumpsuit in as well. I didn't want the wind catching them and blowing them away. I crouched on the roof, holding my Beretta in my right hand. I crawled toward the edge of building in Samuel and Makara's direction. I took a peek over the edge.

The street was dark. Without my goggles, I probably wouldn't be able to see a thing. Only a few windows were lit in the early morning. Gazing upward, I saw clouds blanketing the whole sky, blocking out the stars. Somewhere high above, unknown to the town below, *Gilgamesh* hovered.

So far, so good. The town was fast asleep. We had not been spotted by any of the guards, and we had all landed relatively close to one another. It was just one of many things that needed to go right tonight.

Across the dirt road, Makara and Samuel kneeled between two buildings. Their faces stared at me from below, in the darkness. I had to find a way down and join them.

I kept low and searched the perimeter of the building for a way down. I was in luck; a metal ladder descended from the building's side, right into the alleyway below. All I had to do was go down it and dash across the street to where Makara and Samuel were, after which we could begin our search for Anna.

Before I stepped down, I surveyed my surroundings. The buildings were all old, mostly from Pre-Ragnarok times. Most of the paint had long since peeled off, and the buildings' sides were cracked, their original whitewash stained with dust and soot. The town wall had probably been built following Ragnarok, for additional security. In the distance rose one of the gatehouses. From its twin guard towers, flags flapped in the darkness. On the wooden ramparts stood two figures, guards facing outward.

I climbed down the ladder, taking the rungs carefully. It wouldn't do to slip and fall because I was in a hurry. When I reached solid ground, I allowed myself a small sigh of relief. I stepped lightly onto the dirt of the dark alley. A chill clung in the air, and a thin veil of mist covered the ground. In the distance, perhaps several buildings away, a couple of dogs howled, sending shivers down my spine.

I edged closer to the street. Everything was as empty as we could have wished it. I had expected there to be more people about, and for a minute, I was skeptical of the emptiness. Still, I crouched low, and ran across the street. When I reached the alley, I finally joined up with Samuel and Makara. They both looked relieved to see me.

"We're inside," I said. "Now what?"

Samuel motioned for me to keep my voice down. In the calm night, it had carried more than I'd intended. He took off his goggles, Makara and I following his example. I allowed mine to hang around my neck. It took my eyes a moment to adjust to the darkness.

"She will probably be under lock and key," Samuel said.

"Assuming she wasn't killed," Makara said.

Samuel nodded. "Yes, that is always a possibility."

"Maybe a guardhouse of some kind?" I suggested.

"Or a jailhouse," Makara said.

"Those would be good places to start."

I looked around, as if I might find those kinds of places in this cold, deserted alley. The settlement was a little bigger than I had thought. It was probably the same size as Oasis in the Wasteland, although the population density was much higher. The buildings were more packed together, most of them three or four stories. Obviously, this town had existed Pre-Ragnarok, and the Empire had appropriated it for its own use. Ashton had given us thirty minutes to complete the mission upon touchdown, and it would easily take hours to go through all the buildings. Even I wasn't feeling *that* lucky, especially when danger would be lurking inside.

I was about to ask where we should start, when a door slammed open in the building to our right. Yellow light spilled into the alley. A man was thrown out the door, crying out as he rolled through the dirt and into the brick wall of the adjacent building. He moaned in pain as three men exited the open door, brandishing clubs. They stalked toward their victim, surrounding him.

The downed man opened his eyes, looking right at us. His eyes widened, but he said nothing. He seemed to be pleading with us to help him.

The men had yet to notice us standing just a few feet off in the darkness. That wouldn't last long. Samuel urged us forward.

As the men closed in on their prey and began the beating anew, we sneaked up from behind. I silently retrieved my knife from its sheath, hoping for a quick and silent kill. We were close – just feet away, and they had yet to notice us. That was when the man closest to me turned around – fat, with a thick, unkempt black beard, and dark brown eyes. He cried out in alarm.

Samuel stepped forward, silently stabbing the man's neck before he could react. He screamed and fell to the dirt. Makara bounded forward, taking out the second man, tall and skinny, with a frenzy of knife swipes. She finished the job as Samuel had – stabbing the man through the throat once he was down.

I had the job of finishing the last one – a short, bald man who made up for his lack of height with plenty of muscle. He looked like a fighter to the core, covered with scars on his face and arms. He had drawn his own knife, backing away as he faced off against me. But his retreat was a feint. He lunged at me, eyes filled with lethal purpose.

Samuel and Makara pressed on him from either side. Knowing he was surrounded, he made one last-ditch effort to attack me, in order to cut his way free. I dodged his wild swipe. The attack had put him off-balance. I kicked him with my boot. He grunted, and was sent sprawling to the ground. He yelled in Spanish, probably calling for help, before Makara jumped on top and finished him, cutting him cleanly across the throat. Blood gurgled from his mouth. He quivered, and grew still.

The man we had saved still cowered against the wall, as if we might attack him next.

"It's alright," Makara said. "You can trust us."

The man looked up. "Thank you. I couldn't take all three."

The man was maybe in his mid to late twenties. He had coppery brown skin, and sported a full black beard. He wore a simple cotton shirt and rough pants fashioned from what seemed to be hemp or burlap. Whoever he was, he wasn't a wealthy man. He was covered in hard muscle, as if used to hard labor. He had striking green eyes, and several days' stubble covered his face. Several scars crisscrossed his forearms, and a small one underlined his right eye.

"Why were they attacking you?" I asked.

He shrugged, sitting up straighter against the wall. He closed his eyes, still obviously in pain.

"I'm a slave. This is nothing out of the ordinary." He looked at us, curiously. "Who are you? You are obviously Americans, but you have guns. Did you escape? Who was your master?"

"We're trying to find a friend," Samuel said. "She is short, with black hair. She was taken here two days ago, and we're trying to find her."

The man's face lit with recognition.

"Yeah, I know who you're talking about." He shook his head. "You just missed her."

"Missed her?" I asked. "What are you talking about?"

Makara glanced nervously toward the open door. From within came the sound of yelling.

"Guys," she said, "we better keep this short."

"They transported her, last night," the man said. "She fought against the slavers in the town square, even killing one of them."

"And she's still alive?" Samuel asked.

The man nodded. "They sent her to Nova Roma."

"Nova Roma?" I asked. "What for?"

"I don't know," the man said. "I saw her leave this morning, with the other slaves."

So she is *enslaved.*

"We have to go after her," I said.

The man stood up from where he had been sitting. "My name is Julian, by the way."

"Look," Samuel said. "Introductions can wait. If what you say is true, Julian, we need to get out of here."

Before Samuel could say anything more, two men ran out into the alleyway from the open door. They stood for a moment, shocked, upon seeing their fallen comrades soaking in their own pools of blood.

One of the men turned to Julian, his face a mask of fury. That was when he noticed us. Both men reached for their guns, but we already had ours out. In a moment, we were shooting them down. The shots reverberated through the quiet night, alerting everyone to our presence.

Julian looked at us in shock even as the bodies fell around him. Shouts filled the streets as doors slammed open.

"What now?" Makara asked.

"I know a way out," Julian said. "You have to trust me."

Julian bounded down the alley and was lost to darkness. Having no other choice, we ran after him.

Chapter 12

Julian took us over a mangled fence as more men ran into the alley, shouting in alarm upon finding the dead bodies.

"Where are we going?" I asked.

"There is a storm drain that leads outside the walls," Julian said. "I'm leading you there."

"Have you used it before?" Makara asked.

"Yes," Julian said. "Although that time it didn't work out."

"Didn't work out...?" Makara asked.

Julian ignored Makara's question, instead turning a corner and running straight down the street. Two men stood ahead of us, talking in front of an open door. Upon seeing us, they looked at each other and began to shout.

Before they could do us any harm, Makara aimed her gun and fired. The two men ducked into an alleyway. They stayed out of sight as we ran past the alley. They must not have had guns, but they would surely go find people who did.

"Here!" Julian said.

He threw open a door to one of the buildings as more men came from the alley behind us. We rushed inside and he slammed the door. Samuel locked it, placing a nearby chair under the handle. We all rushed up the wooden steps behind Julian.

"Where are we going?" I shouted.

"We have to take a bit of a detour. You have to trust me."

"This is the second time you've said that."

"Save your breath for the jump!" Julian said.

The jump?

Five landings later, Julian opened a final door. We were on the flat rooftop of the tallest building in town. Around us in the night were the shapes of other buildings, most slanted and decrepit from time and lack of maintenance. On the street below, several men were battering down the door of our building with a large piece of wood. The door fell.

"Why are they so set on coming after us?" I asked.

"Catching four escaped slaves is a huge payout," Julian said.

"But we're not slaves."

"Even if you're not, they don't know that, do they?"

I didn't have an answer as Julian bounded ahead. He was *fast*. Far faster than Makara, Samuel, or anyone I had ever seen for that matter. Not even looking down, he sailed through the air with a mighty leap. We all ran forward, watching him fall onto the next building across the alley, about a story down. He tucked and rolled upon landing, standing without injury to himself. He looked up, motioning us on.

"I hope this is the only time we have to do this," Makara said.

She backed up, sprinted, and jumped. Several men in the alley below spied her, shooting upward several times. I could hear shouts in the stairwell from the men running up behind us. There wasn't much time left.

Samuel and I jumped in tandem. I had done this enough times to be used to it. Upon landing on the next building, instead of letting my knees take the brunt of the impact, I rolled forward to distribute the force of the fall evenly. It still hurt, shocking my senses, but I stood on steady legs, shaking off the impact.

"Good," Julian said. "That was the hard part. The rest is fairly easy."

We ran, jumping from building to building. The buildings were of even height, so making the jumps wasn't too difficult. Behind us, our pursuers were beginning to make their first jump.

Julian was very quick. His lean, muscular body and long legs were built for speed. My lungs burned for air just trying to keep up with him. If I hadn't been working out, I'd have long since been left in the dust.

The palisade wall loomed in the distance. A couple guards stood on its ramparts, looking toward the city, drawn by the noise. Upon seeing us, they began to fire with their rifles. Julian ducked behind some crates, where we ran to join him. I slid on the flat rooftop, sliding right beside him. The men chasing us from behind were fewer, but they would be on us within a minute.

"Where is this storm drain?" Samuel asked.

"It's between this building and the wall." Julian paused. "It was how I almost escaped, two years ago."

"And you were caught," Makara said.

"Only because it decided to rain. *You* try escaping through a storm drain when it starts to pour and see how it works out. I'm lucky to even be alive. The drain leads to the river. Once we're there, we can escape into the forest."

We all looked at each other. It was a gamble, but we really had no other choice. We had to trust that Julian knew what he was doing. He had certainly kept us alive so far.

Stuck behind these crates, we were pinned between the guards on the wall and our pursuers behind us. The guards on the wall would shoot as soon as we left cover. But the men chasing us were only two buildings behind, and would surely kill us as soon as we were in range.

"There is a ladder on the side of the building," Julian said. "If we move these crates, we can have cover while we head over there. Once we're down the ladder, the building itself will be our cover."

We rushed to do what Julian said. We each scooted a crate. Bullets were fired, and those that would have hit us struck the crates harmlessly. The danger increased as the men from behind caught up and began to fire their own guns. A few bullets riddled the crates on our side. A bullet ricocheted off the rooftop just inches from my foot.

But by this time, we had made it to the ladder. Julian latched onto the metal, sliding down and gritting his teeth from the pain it caused his hands. Samuel went next, followed by Makara. As I slid down the side of the building, we were all out of our pursuers' lines of sight.

The metal and chipped paint burned and cut into my hands. I tried not to let the pain slow me down. The pursuing men were on top of the ladder, aiming their guns down. I hopped off just as they started shooting, rolling away into the dark alley. I ran after the others, who were already disappearing around the corner.

Upon circling the corner, I nearly ran into all three of them. They stood at the side of the street, staring at a metal grate covering the opening of the storm drain.

"It's gone," Julian said. "They've closed it off!"

The first of the men rounded the corner, while two other men from the ramparts above aimed their rifles down.

There was nothing more we could do. It was over. We had been captured.

***

The men surrounded us, pointing their guns. They did not say anything as one of them stepped forward.

That was when a repetitive thrum sounded in the sky. A blinding light shone down on all of us. The men cried out in alarm. Quickly, the light pointed away from us, and shined on the men. A second floodlight came on, shining on the men on the walls. They held hands up to their eyes.

"Ashton!" I said.

He couldn't lift us out of here – by the time he let the ladder down, the men would have long since recovered from their shock. We had to find another way.

Makara dashed for the gate, knifing a man in the throat as she passed. As the man fell, we followed. The men were yelling, and as we vacated the scene, *Gilgamesh* remained in hover mode. Its twin turrets opened up, raining lead on the street behind us. The men ran for cover.

Now *that* was the distraction we needed. The gate wasn't far, and we found ourselves in front of it in under a minute. It was shut.

"We have to go inside the gatehouse and open it," Julian said.

"How do we do that?" Samuel asked.

"I don't know, we'll figure it out."

Julian threw open the gatehouse door, which led to a narrow set of wooden steps. We spiraled around until we reached the top. To our left, an open archway led to the ramparts, where two guards stood transfixed, watching the *Gilgamesh*. Since they were not even looking our way, Samuel put his hand on a massive wheel, which connected to a giant link of chains. He gave the wheel a heave. Since he was not able to do it himself, we all joined him.

The loud cranking sound shook the guards out of their stupor. They aimed their rifles, but not before I shot one in the chest. He fell off the rampart toward the dirt street below. The other one, deciding not to take his chances against the four of us, jumped right off the rampart rather than get shot.

Below us, the large wooden gates groaned as they opened. We stopped turning the wheel, and ran back down the stairs. We burst on the street, turned the corner, and ran out of the barely opened gate and into the night.

Gilgamesh lifted off from where it had hovered above the settlement, angling our way. From the ramparts, the guards fired at us. We zigzagged our path in order to dodge the bullets.

Gilgamesh swooped overhead, knocking us all down with a colossal sound and gust of wind. It half-turned toward us, its landing lights still blinding. It settled maladroitly upon the ground, the boarding ramp extending. The blast door opened.

Men on horseback surged out from the gate behind us. We were about halfway to the ship.

"Run!" I yelled.

We sprinted for the boarding ramp, even as the horsemen gained on us. The ship loomed larger as we neared it, but the thunder of hooves behind let me know how close we were to being captured again.

Finally, we ran up the ramp, and the blast door closed behind us. Several bullets dinged off its metal outside.

No sooner were we in than the ship lifted off. I fell to the floor, and slid toward the wall as the ship leaned upward, surging toward the black sky.

Chapter 13

Once we were up and away, we all stood on *Gilgamesh's* bridge.

"Well, the operation wasn't a complete waste," Samuel said. "We found out Anna is in transit to Nova Roma with a group of other slaves. If we hurry, we might still catch her."

"And how did you find this out?" Ashton asked.

Samuel gestured to Julian, who stood next to him. "This is Julian. He saved our lives by showing us how to get out of the city. He also let us know what happened to Anna."

Ashton looked at Julian. "You are sure of this?"

He nodded. "They have auctions there, every Saturday, in Central Square. That is probably where they are taking her. She put up a big fight against all the slavers, even killing one of them. They probably see her as a potential fighter for *El Coleseo.*"

"*El Coleseo?*" I asked.

"It's the grand arena of the Empire, located in the heart of Nova Roma," Julian said. "They fight slaves there for entertainment."

"Great," Makara said. "How can people *watch* that?"

"They do not see slaves as people," Julian said. "Many came to seek refuge in the Empire, after the Rock fell – both native Mexicans and foreign Americans. Most were just enslaved as soon as they crossed the border. The lucky ones were sent to the farms. The unlucky ones, to the arenas. And the most unlucky...to *El Coleseo.*"

"You know this, how?" Ashton asked.

"I have been to Nova Roma many times as part of my duties for my old master. He attended these auctions at times. I have even fought in a few gladiatorial matches myself, though never in *El Coleseo,* thank God. They say that anyone who enters the Blood Gates is already doomed to die."

"Well, we'll just have to hurry," I said.

Ashton nodded. "You came along at just the right time to help us, Julian."

"How did you guys get into Itcala, anyway?" Julian asked.

I assumed Itcala was the name of the settlement. "We parachuted."

Julian's eyes widened. "That's crazy. You're lucky to still be alive."

"We know," Makara said.

"How did you come to be in the Empire, Julian?" I asked.

"I was hunting with my father outside my home, ten years ago. There were slavers there. They killed my father, and they took me. From that point on, I was sold from one master to another, until I found my way here. They fought me in arenas, from time to time, and I was lucky to survive. Because I can read, my last master found a use for me that didn't involve swinging a sword. He lived in Itcala, and sometimes traveled to Nova Roma, taking me with him to help him write contracts for his business. He mostly dealt with slaves."

"So you know the city well?" Ashton asked.

Julian nodded. "I've been there at least a dozen times. I know it well enough."

"Maybe you can help us find Anna," I said.

"I will," Julian said. "You guys got me out of there, so it's the least I can do." Julian looked around the bridge, as if he couldn't believe he was standing in such a place. "Although I have a lot of questions myself."

"That's understandable," Ashton said. "We have questions, too, but unfortunately, time is not on our side. We'll catch you up later."

"Can you use a gun?" Samuel asked.

Julian shook his head. "I've only used a sword and shield before. Gladiators are not allowed ranged weapons in the arena, unless they are javelins."

"Christ," Ashton said, looking away. "There will be time for that later, I guess. Makara can probably teach you."

"I can show him the basics," Makara said. "The finer points he'll have to learn on his own."

"Teach him what you can," Ashton said.

"Even if he can't use a gun, Julian can speak Spanish." I looked at him. "You *can* speak Spanish, right?"

He nodded. "Fluently. I knew it even before I came to the Empire because I am, well...Mexican."

Makara chuckled. "Well, that is something we didn't really consider before. How could we have missed that none of us spoke Spanish and we were hoping to find our way around Mexico?"

"It was a gross oversight," Ashton said. "Still, two months in Skyhome was hardly enough time to learn a new language."

"We're lucky to have Julian," I said. "He can translate everything for us so we aren't in the dark."

Julian nodded. "There is one thing...after we are done with all this, I'd like to be taken home."

"Where is home?" Ashton asked.

"A town called New America. It's in Texas, on the Gulf Coast. I don't know exactly *where,* but I know that much. That's where my community is, my family. They need to know I'm still alive. It has haunted me all these years."

"We'll do what we can," Ashton said. "We need you here. Are you willing to help us with this first?"

"Of course," Julian said. "You have already done more for me than I could have ever done for myself. Helping you find Anna will be the least I can do."

"Well..." Ashton said. "It's more than that. We have an important message to deliver to Augustus."

At the mention of Augustus's name, Julian's eyes widened. "How do you plan on doing that? And...*why?*"

Ashton looked at each of us. "We don't exactly know yet."

"It will be difficult," Julian said. "Very difficult."

"Maybe you can help us out there?" Makara asked.

Julian shook his head. "I don't know. It is all very overwhelming. Your goals seem impossible."

Julian didn't even know the half.

"Let's focus on one thing at a time," I said. "Do you have any idea where they might be taking Anna?"

"Auctions are held in Central Square every Saturday. Central Square is surrounded by all the major buildings of Nova Roma, including the Imperial Palace of Augustus, *El Coleseo,* the Senate House, the Grand Forum...if they are taking her anywhere, that's the most likely location."

"Can't we save her before they enter the city?" I asked.

"She will still be under heavy guard," Julian said. "The Slave Road is probably the most protected part of the Empire. A citizen can walk alone and unarmed from Jalisco Province to Oaxaca Province without fearing for his or her life. What's more, slaves travel with caravans, under heavy guard." Julian shook his head. "Attacking it head-on would be a bad idea."

"We can't just use the ship, either," Makara said. "We risk hurting Anna, not to mention the other slaves."

"So what can we do?" Ashton asked. "All I know is that we have to come up with something, quick. They'll be in the city by tomorrow."

"There's another problem," I said. "By the time we get inside the city, news of *Gilgamesh* might reach Augustus. Many might think it's just a story, but the Emperor will know better. Once he knows about it, he will know *somebody* from the United States in his

Empire." I looked at Ashton. "He might even guess that it's you."

"That sort of news could be in Nova Roma as early as tomorrow, if Itcala sends a messenger immediately," Ashton said. "Of course, that's something we have no control over. We can only hope for the best. In fact, that may even help us. It will add legitimacy to what we have to tell him. If he knows we're from the U.S., he will know we have access to resources that have given us knowledge about the xenovirus."

Julian looked at all of us, confused. "I have no idea what you guys are talking about."

"I know all this must be very strange for you," Ashton said. "Like I said, we'll catch you up when we can.

"How do you guys have a spaceship?" Julian asked. "Are you the United States government? What are you doing in the Empire? Everyone I know believes the United States is gone. *Is* there still a government, somewhere?"

"It's a long story, friend," Ashton said.

Julian sighed, obviously frustrated. "I'll wait for answers. But I want to know everything as soon as you get a chance."

Ashton nodded his assent.

"So, back to Anna," I said. "What do we do to find her?"

"Finding her will be the easy part," Ashton said. *"Gilgamesh* has high-resolution cameras. We can easily spot a slave train moving southeast toward Nova Roma, and get a head count of what we would will up against."

"Typically, the trains have anywhere from twenty-five to fifty slaves," Julian said. "Sometimes more. There is usually about one guard for every two slaves, along with the slaves' owners and anyone else who might be helping the owners. They take them to bidding blocks, set up in Central Square." Julian sighed. "To me, any sort of rescue sounds impossible, as she will be under constant guard at all times."

"And we still have our mission to accomplish," Samuel said. "If we make a huge ruckus, we'll get off on the wrong foot with Augustus."

"We can't just leave Anna to die," I said. "We've already gotten so far." I turned to Julian. "How many people live in Nova Roma?"

"Thousands upon thousands," he said. "It used to be an old city, but it grew from there. There are many foreigners living in Nova Roma, from the south, from the north...people will not notice you because of your foreign appearance. Although the Imperial Garrison might ask questions. Getting in is the tricky part. Anyone who looks like a foreigner has to present papers they received at the Empire's border."

"Dropping in like we did at Itcala might not work so well," Makara said. "Nova Roma has more people, and we are more likely to be spotted."

"No foreigner can be in the Empire without authorization from the Foreign Ministry," Julian said. "Anyone without transit papers is in defiance of Imperial Law."

"What happens then?" I asked.

Julian shrugged. "Whatever happens to anyone who is in the Empire without reason. You have no rights. You can be killed, enslaved...anything."

"With the war going on, papers might be hard to get for a Wastelander," Ashton said. "I'm sure by this point all trade has been cut off."

"War?" Julian asked.

"That, too, is something we have to catch you up on," Ashton said.

"We need more information," Samuel said. "I don't see how that's going to happen up here. We can find the slave train and see what we're up against. After, we have to find some way to infiltrate the city, never losing sight of Anna. If we watch closely, we might find an opportunity to rescue her."

It wasn't much of a plan, but at least it was something. Maybe an opportunity would present itself. But first, we had to find our way inside the city itself and get to Central Square before Anna did.

"It would be a good idea to get what rest you can," Ashton said. "It's near three in the morning, and you all will have to get an early start tomorrow."

Samuel turned to Julian. "I'll show you to your bunk. Tomorrow morning I will catch you up on everything."

***

We caught what little sleep we could. By the time we awoke, it was morning. After eating a small meal, we gathered once more on the bridge.

By midmorning, we were following the Slave Road at a slow hover above the clouds. We poked below now and again to get a glimpse of the road, trying to spy the caravan Anna was a part of.

The first few times we did this, we caught nothing. By the fourth time, however, the camera focused on exactly what we were looking for.

Julian was in awe of the equipment. Everything was different from what he was used to – the spaceship, the food, the way we treated him. He was remarkably resilient, and had taken to his new surroundings quickly. I wanted to learn more about him, but that would have to wait for another time.

"That is it," Julian said.

The LCD showed the curving line of road, along with the small shapes of pack animals and rectangular cages. On the sides of the caravan, guards walked slowly.

In the distance, below the clouds, I caught my first sight of Nova Roma on the horizon. It was situated in a large valley, and thousands of buildings rose from crisscrossing urban streets. A large stone wall surrounded its entire perimeter, and small wooden buildings spilled outside the walls themselves, as if they were leeching onto the city. Many large stone buildings stood within the city itself. In the middle was a tall, circular arena: the *Coleseo*.

Green mountains hugged the city's border to the north, and some low hills to the south and east. The main access point was from the west – the direction from which we were flying.

"We can't attack that caravan," Ashton said. "Not without killing Anna in the process."

It was hard to believe that Anna was *there,* heading straight for the city. What would she think if she knew we were watching her, that we were going to save her? Or did she feel we'd abandoned her? Just seeing the image on the screen gave me a reason to go on. It was *something*.

Ashton pointed to the north. "I can drop you off there, behind that mountain. The ship needs to remain hidden. If you hurry, you all can make it to Central Square before they do."

"Head that way," Samuel said.

Ashton changed the trajectory of the ship, carrying us above the clouds once more.

Chapter 14

We landed on an empty road behind the mountain. As soon as we exited the blast door, *Gilgamesh* lifted off. We took no radio, not wanting to risk our messages being intercepted. Instead, Ashton would keep an eye on this spot for when we were ready to be lifted out.

It wasn't perfect, but it was the best we could come up with.

The morning was gray and misty, the wind cool up in the green mountains. We followed the dirt road as it curved through a pass, leading to the valley below where the city was situated. We passed a farmer, his donkey, and cart on our way down. He eyed us strangely, but said nothing as we passed.

Samuel began to jog as the road sloped even more steeply downhill. As the sun rose higher, it burned through the mist. Before us was the city of Nova Roma, spreading throughout the entire valley. There were thousands of buildings, among which hundreds of stone streets crisscrossed. I could even see people walking in massive crowds in the distance, all of them tiny dots from here. The *Coleseo* stood out clearly in the center of the city. Its three tiers of stone arches rose above the other buildings, forming a perfect circle. Unlike the rest of the big buildings in the town, this had been built from scratch. It was amazing that Augustus could have achieved such a feat.

"Almost there," Samuel said. "Keep moving!"

We ran the rest of the way down the mountain. We came across more people walking both toward and away from the city – people dressed in robes, and the poorer ones dressed in rags. At one point, a set of guards came up the road. We ducked out of the way and hid behind a boulder until they passed, not wanting to risk questioning.

Back on the road again, we left the highlands and entered a thick forest. After running another couple of miles, we were there. Before us was an ivy-clad stone gatehouse that led into Nova Roma. The tall wooden doors were wide open, and crowds of people passed both in and out of the city. Some of the people had to pause before a set of guards to answer questions.

"How are we supposed to get in there with those guards?" I asked.

Julian stepped up beside me. "I don't see any way to avoid it. Your skin color and clothing alone will give you away. I'm the only one of us who could pass through."

"Is there a way you can talk to the guard?"

Julian shook his head. "The fact you only speak English will tell them you are slaves. English is the slaves' language."

"So we need to avoid confrontation," Samuel said.

Julian nodded. "Exactly."

We stood there for a moment, thinking of how we might get inside.

"Is there another gate we could go through?" I asked.

"There are five gates into the city," Julian said. "All of them are watched. All we can do is hope to sneak by and not get noticed."

"That doesn't seem like a good idea," I said.

"I don't know of any other way," Samuel said.

"Wait," Makara said.

She pointed to a large group of people, walking toward the gate from a dirt path leading into the forest. They seemed to be together in some sort of a religious procession. They were dressed in dark, fine robes. In the center, a silver tray was carried, spilling out smoke from an urn. The smell of incense tingled my nostrils. The urn was wreathed in colorful flowers of red and yellow. There were about twenty in the procession. Many held their heads low, as if in mourning.

"A rich man's funeral, most likely," Julian said. "There is a cemetery within the forest they are probably returning from. It's not likely that the guards will stop them. If we can somehow attach ourselves to them without anyone noticing..."

"That's our way in," Samuel said.

Samuel walked forward boldly, and we followed him. As we neared the gate, the crowds thickened. It was early enough in the morning that anyone living outside the city would still be making their way in – and that worked in our favor. It wasn't hard to attach ourselves to the tail of the funeral procession. By the time we were that close, there were enough people around us that we didn't stick out. We neared the gate, keeping our heads low like the mourners.

I tried not to think of how we would stick out, being dressed so differently from them. But a moment later, we were out of the sun and in the shade of the gatehouse. The chatter of the crowd echoed within the confines of the entrance, and I didn't dare glance to my left, where a group of people separated us from the guards. Finally, we were through the gates, walking into the sunlight of the city. Before stopping, we walked on with the procession for another moment.

I glanced back toward the gate. The guards there were questioning a new group of people.

"We made it," I said, hardly able to believe it.

But no one was listening. They were gazing in awe at the buildings surrounding us. The street was bursting with people, flowing down a long stone avenue like a river toward the city's center. Tall stone buildings lined each side of the street, and green trees occupied a median in the center of the avenue. Carts filled with sundries, anything from produce to glassware to clothing to household goods, lined the building fronts, behind each of which a merchant hawked his or her wares. Most people were dressed in robes of white and brown, the richer wearing more vibrant colors of yellow, red, and purple. Head scarves covered the faces of most of the women, obscuring almost all of their features except the eyes. The richer and more colorful the woman's clothing, the more her face was hidden. The poor wore simple tunics of burlap or cotton, all undyed and dirt brown.

The morning air smelled of unwashed flesh and animal dung. The thrum of human life was nearly deafening.

As we walked ahead, a contingent of guards marched down the street, resplendent in leather armor and carrying long pointed spears. Striding at the head of the contingent was a leader wearing a yellow and black-spotted jaguar headdress. The crowds parted before them, giving them plenty of space to continue walking. The guards marched past us without even a glance. As soon as they passed, people filled the void they left behind. It was a scene of chaos.

In the distance, the *Coleseo* towered above the other buildings. A large temple rose on our left, marble steps leading to an altar surrounded by both green trees and pillars. Smoky incense drifted from the temple's open doorway, trailing down the steps and into the street below. A vendor to our right shouted, hawking a sugary pastry which carried the scent of cinnamon. Despite my breakfast that morning, my stomach growled.

The entire city was overwhelming, and boasted the wealth and power of the Nova Roma Empire. The amount of things to see was a bit overwhelming, and it made Raider Bluff, the largest city I had seen to this point, look like a tiny dot.

"Come on, we're not here sightseeing," Samuel said, marching ahead. "We have to make it to Central Square."

I followed Samuel, along with the others, but I could not keep myself from looking around.

"Hide your weapons," Makara said. "They might not be as lenient here as in Raider Bluff."

Nodding, I slipped my gun underneath my shirt, where it would remain hidden.

We followed the curve of the street, surrounded by people on all sides. The main road split into smaller streets of stone, and the smaller streets split into alleyways. People came in and out of doors, groups hung out on corners, watching passersby. And always, the guards marched, stopping people on occasion to ask questions. Most people ignored the guards, giving them a wide berth. I saw two more men wearing jaguar headdresses, questioning a very nervous merchant.

"What are they?" I asked Julian.

"They are the jaguar warriors – the most elite force of the Emperor. They are brutal fighters with both gun and axe. They also serve as his police. During war, they lead the centuries."

"Centuries?"

Julian didn't answer for a moment as one of the warriors pushed the poor merchant. The man looked close to tears, but in the end, he reached into his satchel, producing a handful of small, silvery items. I realized they were batteries.

"In the Imperial Army, there are divisions," Julian said. "Largest is the legion, twenty thousand men. Next largest is the cohort – a thousand men each. The cohorts are split into ten groups of one hundred. These groups of one hundred are called centuries. The jaguar warriors, also known as the centurions, lead the centuries. They are known for their bravery, leadership, and martial prowess." Julian paused, watching the jaguar warriors turn away from the crestfallen merchant they had just shaken down. "They are also corrupt. You never want to have to fight one."

I had trouble imagining twenty thousand men in one place – much less an entire army.

"How many legions are in the Empire?" I asked.

Julian shrugged. "Four, I think."

Eighty thousand men. That could easily overwhelm the entire Wasteland, even if they didn't have many guns. If we could manage to gather all the people of the Wasteland, and that was a big if, we wouldn't even have a fourth of Augustus's army. It was all the more reason why he had to be convinced to join us.

We came to an intersection. Four roads entered a square plaza. In the center of the plaza, a step pyramid rose. There were six tiers total, and people could be seen walking up and down the steep steps.

"What the heck is that?" I asked.

"The Temple of Quetzalcoatl. An ancient god who has been appropriated into the Imperial pantheon. The Temple was here long before Nova Roma was. The city just sort of grew up around it."

My attention was distracted from the Temple when I heard the roar of engines coming from our left. A moment later, two all-terrain trucks surged into the plaza, coming right for us.

We rushed to the side of the street before we could be run over. Soldiers bearing guns and spears filled the trucks to the brim. Seeing the clash of technology with what could otherwise be an ancient city was shocking. The truck sped behind us, for the city gates.

"There seems to be something big going on," I said.

"Augustus is mustering his legions," Julian said. "They train every morning, and soon, they will depart for the north."

"The war is starting," Makara said.

"It is a long way to the Wasteland," Samuel said.

"It will take months for them to go that far," Julian said. "They don't have enough vehicles to carry all their soldiers. But Augustus means to conquer it."

Julian led us down a side street, where traffic wasn't as thick. We ducked through several alleyways, avoiding people where we could. Finally, the alley opened up into a large, paved area.

"Central Square," Julian said.

I knew from the moment I stepped into it that Central Square was the center of Nova Roma. On one side of the square were a series of tiled buildings fronted by pillars. Before the buildings stood a fountain and a large statue of a man on horseback. People milled across the square, mostly in fine robes. A steady stream of people walked toward the buildings. In that nexus of buildings, shirtless workers constructed a massive edifice at the top of a hill. Pillars lined the building's front.

"The new Senate House," Julian said. "The Empire has grown, and there are more representatives. The old one was getting overcrowded. Those buildings are all part of the Grand Forum – which is the main shopping district of Nova Roma."

"You know a lot about the Empire," Samuel said.

Julian shrugged. "I have lived in the Empire for much of my life. My old master had many dealings with important men in Nova Roma, and he would take me with him often." He pointed to our right. "The slave auctions are held in that corner, over there."

I followed Julian's gesture toward the far right-hand corner of the Grand Forum. Already, chairs were being set up, and a large stage was being mounted.

I turned my attention to the very center of Central Square, where a large square tower, about four stories tall, rose. On each of the two sides facing us were large television screens, and I could only assume there were two more on the sides facing away from us. On each of the screens was shown the sport of the Empire – the Gladiatorial Games. A bare-chested man appeared on the screen, beating his chest as his other arm held a gladius. Rocketing onto the screen was another man, wielding spear and shield. The shield slammed into the first man's chest, sending him sprawling backward into the dirt. People gathered below the screen cheered on, watching the fight unfold with revelry.

I was very surprised to see this place had the capability to televise anything.

Julian answered my unasked question for me. "There are cameras in the *Coleseo,* and cables run underground from there to here. Augustus wants everyone, especially the poor, to watch the Games."

"Why especially the poor?"

Julian gave a grim smile. "Because they are the most likely to rebel against him. Augustus is good at keeping them fed. Next on his list is to keep them entertained."

In the distance to my right, I heard the roar of a crowd. I turned to see it: the *Coleseo,* its three tiers of arches forming a perfect circle on one side of the Forum.

"Are the fights happening live?" I asked.

"Yes," Julian said. "There are fights all day most Saturdays, and sometimes during the week if there is a festival. Anyone who can't afford tickets can watch out here."

Even if it was grotesque, it was amazing what Augustus had been able to do with his Empire. If we could have something as powerful as the Empire on our side fighting the xenovirus, that would be a major win. But we had to talk to Augustus first. Before that, we had to rescue Anna.

"What now?" Samuel asked.

"We wait for the auctions to begin," Julian said.

We waited in Central Square for about an hour, watching the sun climb and burn away what was left of the misty air. With the loss of cloud came the heat. The televisions blared on, and the crowds grew, both to watch the fights and shop at the many stalls that were being set up. More crowds funneled in and out of the Forum buildings on the south side of the square.

I pointed to a walled enclosure that contained a massive, pillared building.

"What's that place?"

"The Imperial Palace of Augustus Imperator," Julian said. "Augustus lived here, first. Like the Temple of Quetzalcoatl, it is said that the city grew up around him."

"Amazing that it took only thirty years," Samuel said.

"Augustus is very powerful," Julian said. "Augustus used that power to put everyone to work, including architects and engineers."

As the day wore on, we noticed a crowd gathering before the base of the stage where the slave auctions were to be held. We made our way over there, keeping to the back of the crowd. No one noticed us as we stood, even though we were dressed differently from the other spectators. In fact, the proceedings had brought a lot of different kinds of people together. Most of the spectators, however, were the rich people of Nova Roma.

However, one man caught my eye in particular. He was short, fat, and wore rich purple vestments. A long scar cut across his left cheek. His keen brown eyes did not leave the stage. Rings bejeweled his fat fingers.

"That man's name is Ruben Barrios. He is a Lanisto," Julian said. When I looked at Julian questioningly, he answered. "A Lanisto is a master of gladiators. He is probably the richest one in the Nova Roma Empire. It's hard to tell from his looks, but he was once a gladiator himself, having earned his freedom from the Emperor Augustus during the Solstice Tournament."

"The Solstice Tournament?"

"It takes place every twenty-first of December," Julian said. "It is an epic tournament where the winner gains his freedom. The losers, if they do not die in the arena, are sacrificed at the Temple of Quetzalcoatl."

Makara sniffed. "And they think *we're* barbarians."

"Looks like they're starting," Samuel said.

Julian went quiet as slaves were forced on the stage by the guards. None of them even remotely resembled Anna. For one, all were men, and they wore nothing but crude loincloths. All were strong, fit, and chained hand and foot.

An auctioneer took the stage, conducting the proceedings in Spanish in a loud, booming voice. No more slaves lined the stage.

"She isn't here," I said.

"More might come," Julian said. "Just wait. Usually, they auction off the cheaper ones first."

We watched intently for the next hour, as the sun continued to climb to its peak. Once the last slave had been auctioned off, the auctioneer announced something in Spanish before walking off the stage. The crowd began to disperse.

"What's going on?" I asked.

"The auction is breaking up for the moment, and will restart in one hour," Julian said.

"Will Anna be there this time?"

"I think so."

"Instead of waiting, why don't we go take a look for ourselves?" Makara asked.

She pointed toward the right of the stage, where a line of carts was parked against a large stone building. The carts carried cages, and within them were people. Outside the carts stood guards.

"If she is there, we can at least see her," Samuel said. "When she is purchased, we can tail her to wherever she is taken. It will be too risky trying to break her out right now."

"We should get a closer look," I said.

We dispersed with the rest of the crowd, trying to edge closer to the slave carts. As we walked past the stage, down the crowded streets, we stood as close as we dared to the guarded carts. Crammed within were dozens of people. One of them had to be Anna.

It wrenched my heart to see it. Most were dressed in rags, and the citizens of the city passed the slaves and paid them no heed, as if they were nothing more than penned animals. Tools to be sold and used, and killed at will. I would have gotten closer, but guards flanked the entire convoy, directing anyone who got too close to go the other direction. Several men watched in the wings – prospective buyers that wanted an early look.

I saw her, holding the bars and staring outward at the city intensely. She was wearing the same clothing she had been captured in, and despite a bruise on her face, she appeared to be okay.

"Anna," I said.

She wasn't looking in our direction, and it wasn't as if any of us could call out to her. That would be a dead giveaway. Instead, I tried willing her to look our way. I just wanted her to know that we were here, and that we were going to take care of everything. In her face, I saw determination. I don't know where she got it from, but Anna was a fighter, even when the situation seemed hopeless.

"Do you see her?" I asked.

"Yeah," Samuel said. "She's right there."

"...And we can't do anything about it," Makara said. "There must be twelve guards around those carts. If we just went in there, we'd be captured or killed."

"Stick with the plan," Samuel said. "Whoever buys her, we'll follow him home. And there will be hell to pay."

I nodded. It was the best we could do. I just hoped it would be enough.

Reluctantly, I turned away and followed everyone back to the staging area for the second round of bidding.

Chapter 15

When the auction began again, Anna came on stage next to last. People were more excited about these prospects; the crowds were more numerous, and on the outskirts, even the commoners watched, percolating from the televisions in the center of the square to watch the bidding. The Lanistos stood in their own corner, laughing and joking. Anna was the only woman. The rest were bulky, muscular men that were probably destined for the *Coleseo*.

Anna kept her head straight, her eyes searching the crowd. When she didn't have her katana, something seemed off about her. I gritted my teeth. It angered me to see her up there. Most of all, I was angry at myself. If I had been more careful, we wouldn't be in this situation. I was willing to do anything to get her out of there. Anna had gotten this far. We would carry her the rest of the way.

The bidding began, and the first few men were auctioned off relatively quickly. As the auction progressed, the Lanistos ceased their joking and became more attentive, at time bidding aggressively on the prospects.

Finally, only two were left – Anna, and a bulky, muscular man who was shaved bald.

The auctioneer indicated for Anna to step forward.

She did, and the auctioneer began to speak in Spanish once more.

Julian translated. "He is saying that she is a beautiful warrior from the far north, an expert in the use of the katana. He also says that she has..."

The men in the audience laughed and smiled. I waited for Julian to continue.

"Has what?" I asked.

Julian a hesitated a moment. "...other talents."

My face burned with anger. There was nothing more I wanted to do than rush that stage and carry her away, danger be damned. My hand reached for my gun. Makara brushed it away.

"Don't do anything stupid, Alex. We'll have the last laugh in the end."

The bidding began. It seemed everyone was making an offer. Quickly, the poorer men were left in the dust and the richest men – the ones wearing the finest and brightest clothing – continued to bid in larger and larger amounts as if it were nothing.

"10,000," Julian said. "15,000."

"15,000 what?" Makara asked.

"Batteries," Julian answered.

That was probably more batteries than existed in all of Raider Bluff. And still the bidding continued. Fewer and fewer men continued to bid, bowing out as the numbers reached 20,000 and finally 30,000,

"How did they get so wealthy?" I asked.

"Many own plantations," Julian said. "Some earned their fame in more nefarious ways."

Only two men were actively bidding. One was the fat, bearded man with the many rings Julian had pointed out earlier – Ruben Barrios. The other was a tall, skinny man who reminded me of a serpent.

"Who's the skinny man?" I asked.

"He's Camilo Hidalgo. He owns much of the Subura – the poorest district of Nova Roma – and is also one of the few people licensed by Augustus to run gambling houses and brothels."

"Great," Makara said.

"Ruben is bidding 45,000 batts," Julian said.

There was a pause as Camilo considered. Finally he bid again.

"48,000," Julian whispered in disbelief. "I have never seen the bidding go this high."

Ruben's fat face reddened, and he turned and stalked away. Camilo gave a smile of victory.

Just as the auctioneer's gavel nearly fell, Ruben turned and shouted. "*Cincuenta miles!*"

50,000. A whisper overtook the crowd. Camilo Hidalgo paused, but said nothing. Everyone watched. Would the slumlord bid again? Finally Camilo waved his hand, ceding the floor to his rival. The auctioneer banged his gavel on the podium. Anna had been sold to the gladiator master. The crowd broke into an excited buzz.

That was it. A nearby guard ordered Anna to stand back as the last slave was presented. While the bidding for him began, some guards came on the stage, leading Anna away to meet the Lanisto, Ruben.

"It's go time," Samuel said.

We filtered out of the crowd, and edged closer to Anna. Already guards surrounded her, leading her toward the *Coleseo*. We pushed ourselves ahead, never for a minute losing sight of her.

That was when one of the men by the carts pointed our way, yelling something to his fellow guards in Spanish. He looked vaguely familiar.

"What is he saying?" I asked.

I recognized him as one of the slavers that had attacked us.

"They're coming for us!" Julian said.

The cart guards strode toward us. The commotion caused the guards escorting Anna ahead to turn around. Anna turned, too, just in time to see us sprinting after her. Her eyes widened in surprise.

I pulled out my Beretta and started taking my first shots. The bullets connected with one of the guards, felling him.

Taking our cue, Anna struggled against her captors, ripping free of two of them. Hands and feet bound, she hopped in our direction. Ruben the Lanisto went wide-eyed upon seeing Anna run away. He barked some orders to his guards, who came forward wielding not guns, but their clubs.

"He wants to capture us," Julian said.

I ceased my shooting. I risked hitting Anna. Instead, I ran forward, trying to reach her first. She was in my arms, and I was pulling her back. The guards raised their clubs upon reaching me.

Samuel and Makara joined me in the struggle, fighting off the guards. Julian dashed in from the side, trying, to no avail, to hold back the crowds that had encircled us.

Finally, we broke free, but the crowd was too close for us to break through. I roared in frustration. A pair of hands pushed my wrists together, roughly tying rope around them.

Makara grunted when a pair of guards forced her to the ground, binding her hand and foot. I felt a boot on my back, and I crashed to the street stones.

Next to me, the others were also on the ground. Surrounded by guards, we were all restrained and bound. Our worst fears were realized. Instead of rescuing Anna, we had gotten ourselves captured.

The guards forced us on our feet. Ruben, the Lanisto, cast an appraising eye on us all.

"This ended very well," he said, with an amused smile. "Instead of one gladiator, I have five."

It wasn't just Anna going to the *Coleseo*. It was all of us.

***

The crowds parted as Ruben and his guards escorted us to the *Coleseo*. I couldn't even look up as we passed under a large stone arch – the Blood Gates, Julian had called them. We approached a metal gate within the building, where two guards stood. Upon seeing Ruben, one reached for a key and unlocked the gate. He opened it, and behind the gate a set of stone steps led down.

We were forced down the stairs. The steps spiraled down into darkness. Soon, orange light appeared ahead. We were under the *Coleseo,* in a large antechamber. Several open archways led to adjacent rooms, and a stone corridor led out from each of the room's four corners. A wide set of stone steps led upward at the end of the anteroom – I assumed to the arena floor. This was a staging area for gladiators, before they were sent up to their deaths.

We were led down the corridor immediately to our left. Ruben threw open a door at the end of it. On the other side was darkness. We were pushed along in the dark, and we could see only from the few torches that Ruben's guards carried. From their light, I could discern that we were being led to jail cells. Metal bars rose from floor to ceiling from the cells on either side.

Ruben and his guards haphazardly threw Julian and me into one of the cells. We scuttled onto the floor, and the door was slammed behind us with a metallic clang. I heard Makara cry out as she was thrown into her own separate cell, while Anna and Samuel were thrown into the cell adjacent to mine. Two more metal-barred doors were slammed and locked behind us. Ruben, with his guards, stood for a moment surveying us. It was hard to tell if he was pleased, or angry.

Finally, without a word, he turned for the door from which we had come. Once all the guards were out, he slammed the door shut. I heard a key turn in the lock, leaving us in silence.

"Everyone alright?" Samuel called out.

Everyone answered that they were.

"You guys shouldn't have come."

Anna's voice was sullen.

I rushed to the side of my own cell, reaching my hand through the bars. "Anna, it's me."

I heard her get up, and I felt her warm hand on mine.

"I'm sorry," I said.

"You all should have left me here. I wasn't worth this."

"It's not over yet, Anna," I said. "Don't give up."

"By this time, you guys could have met with the Emperor and have gotten out of here. I definitely wasn't worth this mission getting compromised."

I didn't have an answer for that. Anna still held onto my hand. I put my other hand through the bars, grabbing her other hand. It felt good, just to touch her – even if it was a feeling that wouldn't last.

"We'll make it, somehow," I said. "I don't know how, but we've gotten through worse before."

I didn't know if that was true. It seemed as if we were all as good as dead, locked in these cells.

"How did you guys find me?" she asked.

I told her about how Ashton had piloted *Gilgamesh* above Itcala, and how we had all parachuted in.

"You...*what?*" Anna said.

"It was the only way in," I said. "It was my idea."

Anna sighed. "You're an idiot."

"Yeah. I know."

"Julian?" Samuel called out.

"I'm here," Julian said.

"Who's Julian?" Anna asked.

"I'm Julian. I met your friends in the town. Anna, right?"

Anna didn't answer. Samuel spoke again.

"What can we expect now that we're here?"

Julian didn't answer for a moment. "Nothing good. For what we did back there, our penalty will be death by combat. Whether they will have us fight each other, or simply be executed, I don't know."

"What about Anna?" I asked. "Surely, Ruben wouldn't have spent all that money just to kill her."

"Imperial Law warranties a slave for up to three months," Julian said. "Rebellion is included in that."

A hand banging on metal sounded throughout the narrow confines of the cells. Someone was trying to force the door open.

"Makara, that isn't going to do anything," Samuel said in his deep baritone.

"At least I'm trying *something*," she said. "I'm not going to be forced to fight."

"I've never seen a Lanisto pay as much for a slave as he paid for you," Julian said to Anna.

"I don't blame him," Anna said. "I took down one of the slavers with my bare hands as soon as they untied me. When they finally got me under control again, I thought they were going to kill me. Instead, they *still* wanted to sell me. Word got out about what I did, and that's when they shipped me here. I looked for chances to escape, but I was tied up and in a cage the entire time. There was nothing I could do. I couldn't even take a piss without some bastard watching me."

"If I know the *Coleseo* at all," Julian said, "we won't be here long. A day, at most. After that, we'll be the entertainment of the crowds."

"What's going to happen?" Makara asked. "Do we stand a chance of surviving at all?"

"Likely, we all die," Julian said. "I was an escaped slave and you attacked Ruben's guards. The fact that we're here in this arena tells the entire story."

Makara harrumphed, just as the door to the corridor slammed open. The torchlight at first blinded me. I shaded my eyes, watching the forms of the four guards and Ruben striding forward. He paused in between our cells. We watched him warily from within our prisons.

"As criminals and slaves who have broken the law of Nova Roma, you are all my slaves," Ruben said. "You will fight tomorrow in the *Coleseo* in an execution match."

"What about Anna?" I asked.

Ruben sniffed. "Who, the slave girl? She fights, too. I have no tolerance for insurrection."

With that, Ruben exited with his guards. The door was locked, and we were all left in darkness once more.

"Well," Anna said, "that's it, then."

"No, this is *not* it," Samuel said. "This isn't over until it's over."

A long quiet followed Samuel's statement. I wished I felt as sure as he did, but at least for now, that wasn't to be.

***

I awoke sometime later to the sound of dripping water. I had no idea what time it was. It was quiet, and I heard deep breaths coming from the adjacent cell. The others were sleeping.

"Still awake?"

I jumped at the sound of Julian's voice.

"Julian, you scared the bejeezus out of me."

"Sorry about that. I can't sleep in these kinds of places."

"It's alright. You find yourself in these kinds of places often?"

"Not really. At least, not anymore."

We said nothing for a moment. Finally, I had a question for him.

"You said it's been ten years since you were enslaved?"

"My father and I were hunting south of New America. Slavers found us there. My dad died protecting me, and I ran back for home. Still, I was caught because they had horses. My mother and sister probably think me dead. Naturally, they would have found my father's body. But me...they will not know the rest of the story."

"Were slavers common in your area?"

"They were always a threat. Even at sixteen, when I was captured, I wasn't strong enough to fend them off."

"I don't see how anyone could have. Hell, even *we* couldn't fight them off, and we've done some pretty incredible things."

"Samuel told me what you guys have done, and what you are doing." Julian paused. "I think it's great. I haven't heard anything of this xenovirus, but if anything Samuel says is true, I wish you all the luck in the world."

"Well..." I said. "We definitely need it, now."

"Yeah, I guess that's true. Only – I had hoped to go back to New America, someday. I guess there's little chance of that happening."

It seemed so stupid, that one mistake – choosing the wrong place to set up camp – had led us all here, to this dark moment, which none of us would survive. The fate of the entire world depended on our success. But that same world was going to kill us before we even had a chance to save it.

"What about you, Alex?" Julian asked. "What's your story?"

I gave a bitter laugh. "It's long, and sad. I lost my home two months ago, to the xenovirus."

"I'm sorry to hear that."

"My entire life, gone in a single night."

For the next hour, I told Julian my own story. Once I'd finished, he was interested in everyone else's. I gave him the basics – Makara's life as a Lost Angel and ex-Raider, Samuel's life as a scientist, and Anna's life of surviving with her mother after losing her home to Raiders, and how she became Char's bodyguard following her mom's death. He listened in the darkness, not saying much.

After I finished, he was quiet for a long while.

"That is a spectacular story," Julian said. "Although I think your message to the Emperor will fall upon deaf ears."

"Why?"

"He thinks he is God. He thinks he was born to rule all men, and he will not stop until he accomplishes that goal. Everything fits into that. Even if he agrees with your message – and he likely will, if what you told me is true – he will somehow use that to give himself more power. You wait and see."

"We have to deliver the message, all the same."

Julian sighed. "I hope that can come to pass. Tomorrow morning, we shall see."

I frowned, and lay back onto the cold stone. I closed my eyes, and tried to get what sleep I could. Perhaps the last sleep I would ever get.

Chapter 16

The next morning, the guards arrived to escort us out of our cells. Ruben wasn't among them, to my surprise, but if we were being led to our match, I supposed that he was already waiting in the stands.

The guards pushed us along the dark, narrow passageway and into the anteroom we had first entered. We were led up the wide stone steps. As we walked up the hot breeze blew from the outside. At the top, at the end of a broad stone passageway, stood a large gate, through which bright sunlight filtered. When my eyes adjusted to the light, I saw the gigantic circle that was the arena floor, the dirt raked cleanly for our ensuing match. The crowd's drone sounded through the gate. Our execution match would be starting any moment.

I felt as if I were in a daze. We were each hastily handed a weapon by a grim guard. Anna received a long, two-handed sword, not her katana. I could tell from her frown that she wasn't pleased. Makara received a spear and buckler, while I received a gladius and shield. Julian also got a gladius and shield, while Samuel took a two-handed mace laced with cruel spikes.

I wondered if they were really going to let us hold these weapons with all of them standing so close to us. It was at that moment that a gate fell from the ceiling, crashing onto the floor and separating us from the guards. A cloud of dust rose from the ground, sending Makara and me into fits of coughing.

A gate behind us, blocking our escape. A gate ahead, that led into the *Coleseo*. We were trapped, and the only way out was forward, into the arena.

"Well played," I said.

"Focus," Samuel said.

The gate to the arena floor began to rise. The *Coleseo* erupted into thunderous screams as we strode forward into the sunlight. As we walked toward the center of the field, I spun around, trying not be stunned by the enormity of it all. Thousands of people stood, booing and hissing at us. We were the only ones out there, and it seemed the Novans did not like us. I dodged a rock thrown by someone from the stands.

At long last, the crowd subsided, and soon a loud voice shouted from our right. The voice sounded from an exclusive section of the stands. Here, the seats were bigger, and the people more colorfully dressed. This was the rich people's area. Over these stands fluttered colorful sheets of linen that served to block the sun and provide shade for the seats below. One man in these stands was resplendent in full purple, sitting upon a seat more akin to a throne, looking bored as he munched on some food.

"That's him," Samuel said.

Emperor Augustus was not an imposing man. Even from my distance, I could tell he was a bit small. He had coppery skin and short-trimmed black hair, and sat next to a beautiful woman whom I assumed to be his wife. Two children sat in front of him, one a teenage girl, and another a boy maybe eight years of age. They were among the thousands that watched us, that wanted to see us die simply for trying to save our friend. I wondered if their bloodlust would be satisfied if only they knew our story and what we were trying to do.

To the right of the Imperial family, a fat man was standing on a stage. He was the source of the yelling. Every face turned to him, and in order to hear, the crowd noise diminished to an astonishingly low volume.

The man began to orate in Spanish. Julian translated.

"Friends, citizens, noblemen of Nova Roma!" the man's voice boomed.

Cheers. Quickly, they died down as the man continued his introduction.

"We have for you today a rare spectacle – an execution of the spies sent by our mortal enemy, the barbarians of the ignoble Wasteland!"

The sound of boos and jeers thundered all around us. After a while, the crowd's noised lowered, and the fat man proceeded with his speech.

"This week, the armies of the Empire march north, to deal a mortal blow to our enemies! In expectation of the Empire's victory in the north, Emperor Augustus himself is pleased to present..."

The fat man paused. Everyone in the crowd leaned forward, hanging onto his every word.

"The Battle...for the Wasteland!"

The man bowed away from the dais, and as he did so, the gate on the opposite side of the *Coleseo* began to rise.

"Ready yourselves!" Samuel shouted.

The gate opened and released those it had confined. Six men filed out, each wearing a headdress of jaguar fur. They were the jaguar warriors, the Empire's most elite fighting force – the ones Julian had told me I would never want to face off against. Each of them wore leather armor and was armed with two axes.

Upon seeing the jaguar warriors, the crowd cheered, as if at an unexpected surprise. The jaguar warriors began to fan out. They were six against our five. Following Samuel's lead, we backed away, so as not to get cornered. The crowd booed at our maneuver. But we weren't trying to win the crowd. We were trying to win our lives.

After that, things got going immediately. Anna stepped forward, hoping to incite one of the warriors to attack. Taking the bait, one of them fell on her from the side with a dual flash of axes. But she had expected that. She sidestepped him, cutting him in the back, with great economy of motion. With wide eyes, the warrior fell. Nimbly, Anna stepped away, rejoining our ranks.

The crowd roared in fury that the first blood was drawn by us. Only five of the warriors were left, and they leapt into action upon seeing their comrade fall. They completely encircled us, causing Makara and me to go back to back, Makara pointing her spear outward. Anna's training came back to me – even if she had taught me with her katana, her lessons of keeping calm amidst danger steadied my resolve.

Three of the jaguar warriors surrounded Makara and me, each wielding his dual axes that shimmered in the sun. The other two faced down Samuel, Anna, and Julian. Since we were outnumbered, Makara and I had to do our best to hold our own until the others could take care of their own adversaries.

Samuel wielded his mace as his group's two jaguar warriors sprung forward in tandem. Samuel sidestepped and spun, clobbering one of them with his mace in the back. The crowd hissed again as the warrior fell to the dirt. Samuel, with a baleful roar, bashed the warrior's skull in with a squishy crunch. Anna, meanwhile, had no trouble dispatching the other before he could reach Samuel. The warrior sprang forward, and Anna did the same to him, taking him off guard. As the jaguar warrior's axe fell toward Anna's midriff, Anna did a barrel roll, the axe blade missing her body by inches. At the same time her sword, held outward, cut the man deep into the gut as she landed acrobatically on her feet. The blade remained embedded. With the full strength of her torso and legs, Anna ripped straight through the man's abdomen, severing his spine. The top half of the jaguar warrior's body toppled and crashed into the dirt while the legs buckled from underneath. The crowd screamed in both horror and revelry as blood splattered the ground in a torrent.

The three remaining jaguar warriors retreated as the five of us lined up and advanced slowly. Judging by the rising drone of the crowd, this was not the way it was supposed to go.

Finally, the men turned tail and fled for the gate from which they had come. Makara launched her spear. It sailed through the air, arcing downward toward the last warrior. It nailed him in the back, sinking below his right shoulder blade. Soundlessly, he fell to the dirt, quivered, and grew still.

The last two warriors were completely routed. They banged on the gate, desperate to escape the arena. We stood in front of them in a semi-circle. Makara, next to the body of the man she had speared, pulled out her weapon, pointing it at the two remaining warriors.

At last, the gate was raised, and the men fled inside the staging area. It was shut again.

The echo of the closing gate reverberated throughout the *Coleseo,* leaving in its wake dumfounded silence.

***

The silence lasted a few seconds before the arena was filled with jeers, boos, hisses, and the maddened faces of the crowd. Several men tried to jump from the stands onto the dirt ground, restrained only by loved ones and friends who understood the foolishness of such an action.

We had won the fight. That was what mattered. But something was wrong. We were still alive, and they weren't letting us out. Were they going to send more warriors after us this time?

"We stay here until we die," Julian said. "It is that simple."

My hopes sank. "They're just going to send more in until we are all dead?"

Eventually, they would overwhelm us. We could fight all we wanted, but it was not going to do any good. My only hope was that Ashton would drop out of the sky and save us all. Of course, he had no way of knowing that we were here, so that would never happen. We couldn't get lucky every time.

Finally, every head in the *Coleseo* turned to the Emperor's box. Here, long-bearded men in rich, multicolored clothing sat, looking on in silence. The Emperor himself was speaking to the fat man who had announced the beginning of the match. At this very moment, they were discussing our fate.

At long last, the fat man returned to the dais. The entire *Coleseo* fell into silence. He kept his hand raised, outward, commanding the attention of all present. The five of us stared upward at him.

"The Emperor commands," the fat man's voice boomed, "for your entertainment, Wastelander blood, this very day!"

A roar of approval met this pronouncement.

I was nearly jolted out of my skin when I heard the rattle of chains come from all around us. Four square-shaped holes appeared on the arena floor, descending into darkness. I wondered if we were meant to go down them. The clinking of the chains ceased.

"Trap doors," Julian said.

"For what?" I asked.

Samuel knelt down, ready to fight. "Whatever they plan on using to kill us."

The chains clinked again. The trap doors rose back up, and as they did so, the crowd waited with anticipation.

Finally, the doors' payloads were revealed. There were four of them, yellow with black spots, thin, as if starved, but all the more deadly for it. They were jaguars – real ones this time.

The crowd cheered as the four beasts prowled toward us at a low crouch. I gripped my gladius, ready to jab the first one that got too close. Makara stood next to me, doing the same with her spear, while Samuel and Anna stood nearby.

"Bring it on," Makara said.

The first jaguar sailed through the air right for Anna. But that was a mistake. She held her sword aloft, and with a cracked yowl, the jaguar impaled itself through the gut. The crowd oohed, unable to help being impressed by Anna's skill.

However, holding her sword that way left Anna's side exposed. A jaguar dashed from the side, going for her exposed abdomen. I rushed forward, scaring it off with a swing of my blade. The other two jaguars, with lightning speed, circled around me, going for my back. Samuel and Makara stepped in from behind, keeping my back protected. The three jaguars encircled us.

The five of us formed a circle as the three deadly cats stalked around us.

"Stay in formation," Samuel said. "Don't break for anything."

It continued this way for five minutes, and another five. The heat of the sun baked my skin, turning it red. My throat was parched, and every part of me ached. But I did not lower my shield. Not for anything. This was a waiting game, and we would not be the first to break ranks.

The patience of the cats was unsettling. I tried hard not to stare into their black, hypnotic eyes and become transfixed. Their mouths salivated in anticipation of their meal, sticky saliva dripping from their jaws and onto the dirt. The crowd had deadened, talking amongst themselves. I told myself to be ready for anything.

Still they circled, and none of us spoke. We had been standing here at least fifteen minutes, maybe longer.

The crowd started to get bored and restless. I glanced up at the Emperor's box, noticing that the rich men were talking to each other. I saw one man nod, and disappear into the arena. What was going on?

One of the cats yawned, settling itself into the dirt.

Five minutes later, the crowd started booing. But I couldn't let that break my concentration.

Something happened that we could *not* ignore. It came as a steady clinking of chains from our right.

"The gate is rising," Anna said.

The gate was halfway up, and from the darkness behind it I heard a high shriek. It was a familiar, horrible sound – cold and unyielding, making you want to run, scream, and cower.

"Oh no..." Makara said.

They came out of the gates, at a low, dead run. It was a part of my home that I didn't want to be reminded of.

"Crawlers," I said.

***

The first to fall were the jaguars, not us. If there was anything that could knock the boredom out of them, it was crawlers. These were big ones, too, not like the ones in the Wasteland. They were long, serpentine, and scuttled about on multiple legs. Their three eyes were haunting white orbs without pupils, so that you could not see which way they were looking. Their long tails swung back and forth like scorpions'. How the Empire had managed to capture them and transport them here, I couldn't guess.

There were three of them, and that was more than we could handle on foot. The first crawler surged out of the tunnel, leaping right for one of the jaguars. The cat gave a pained yowl as the crawler swiped it with its tail, red blood spewing into the air. The crowd gasped in shock as the torrent of blood fell, splattering onto the dirt. The cat fell lifeless.

The other two cats, hair on end, tried to slink away out of sight. It was pitiful to watch them as they were put against the walls, the three crawlers surrounding them on all sides. The crowds in the stands pulled back as the hideous monsters approached, flexing their tails to strike. In tandem, they stabbed the jaguars, over and over. A fine mist of blood collected in the air from the momentum of the stabs. The cats, after giving a few pitiful wails, fell silent, and the crawlers began to feast on their flesh.

The five of us stood in the center, weapons ready. It was only a matter of time before they lost interest in their fresh kills and came after us. Samuel motioned with his hand, taking a step forward. He meant us to follow him. I saw that he meant to take them by surprise. We had no other shot, anyway.

We snuck forward, and with our movement, the crowd began to get excited. Still, the crawlers dug into the fallen jaguars, the sounds of their chewing and gnashing sickening. Flesh ripped and bones crunched, and nasty slurps sounded in the air. As we neared, the monsters' stench made me want to retch. I had almost forgotten how *horrible* everything infected with xenovirus smelled. It was like corpses dead for weeks, like garbage, like untreated sewage.

The crawlers didn't seem to have much intelligence, even if they were powerful. We were ten feet away. Up close, they were even more giant-sized, still munching away at their prey even as Samuel gave the signal to attack the one on the far left.

Letting out primal yells, we charged forward, hacking at various parts of the crawler's body. Anna slashed at the tail, giving a good chop that only went halfway through, causing the tail to hang askew. The creature shrieked, turning on us and glaring at us with those white orbs. As it reared up, Makara stepped forward, stabbing it in its soft, white underbelly, where its dark crimson scales were not so impenetrable. Purple blood gushed from the wounds. It thrashed about, catching Julian with an insect leg, sending him sprawling to the dirt.

Alerted to our presence, the other crawlers encircled us, blood dripping from their fangs. Their mouths opened, revealing forked tongues and rows of sharp, yellow teeth. They gave unearthly bellows, their breath smelling of rot and decay.

Samuel dealt a killing blow to the first crawler. He swung his mace down, pummeling its head into the dirt. Dazed, the creature remained still as Samuel hit it again and again. The creature twitched and grew still.

There were two crawlers left. One broke from the other, going right for Samuel, mouth agape. Anna jumped forward, but the crawler tackled her, sending her to the dirt.

The crowd was on its feet, cheering. As Makara rushed to help Samuel, and as Julian was getting back onto his feet, I ran to Anna. Anna tried to force herself up, but the crawler snapped its face downward, its mouth opening...

"No!"

I was too far to save her. I hurled my gladius toward the face of the creature. I had a lucky throw; my gladius spiraled, connecting with one of the crawler's three eyes. The creature roared in pain, turning to face me. It stamped the ground with its front four legs, and scuttled toward me at an alarming rate.

I dove to the side, but it wasn't enough. Its teeth snapped at me, grabbing me by the shirt. It picked me up with its mouth, swinging me left and right. The bottom half of my shirt ripped, and I flew through the air, landing right on top of the body of the downed crawler Samuel had killed just a minute before.

I crashed into the armored creature, wincing in pain. I had barely missed landing on the row of spikes jutting from its back. I thought the crawler was going to leave me alone at this point. I was wrong. It was dead set on killing me.

Just as it was nearing, I heard Makara scream. She stood right in front of it.

"Makara, no!"

The creature tore into her. She screamed in pain and toppled to the ground, her shirt wet with blood.

"Makara!" Samuel shouted.

The evil creature flashed its teeth, as if in a triumphant grin. But that wasn't to last. It didn't even scream in pain as Anna stabbed downward, right into the back of its head. Closing its eyes, the crawler slumped to the ground.

All three crawlers were dead – somehow, the other had been felled while I was occupied with this one. I didn't care about that. All that mattered was Makara.

I ran to her. She held her side and shook. Blood gushed from a deep wound – the kind of wound a person did not survive. Her face was pale under the bright sun.

I pulled off my shirt, pressing it against her side. But even that couldn't stop the flow of blood.

"Makara..." Samuel said.

He touched her face. Makara's eyes focused, if only for a moment.

She looked at Samuel. She said nothing, her eyes fluttering. She turned to look at me. She smiled slightly, I didn't know what for. The ground around her form was stained with her blood.

"Why?" I asked, tears coming to my eyes.

She looked at me a moment, her green eyes growing hazier every second.

She didn't answer. She faded, and closed her eyes.

Chapter 17

I couldn't be shocked. I couldn't be anything. I was dead to everything. I couldn't believe what had just occurred. Makara had saved me, countless times, and she had saved me one last time.

And I didn't deserve it. I didn't.

I stared at the ground, tears welling in my eyes, refusing to believe. But there she lay, on the ground, her brother's hands still unable to stem the tide of red leaking out. My mentor, the one who taught me how to survive. My friend was dead.

Samuel was on his knees, tears in his eyes. He still held her wound, blood soaking through his hands. But no matter how tightly he held the wound, the blood wouldn't stop. The pain wouldn't stop.

I fell to the ground, and didn't want to remember anything anymore. Anna was by my side. Tears were in her eyes, too. Julian watched, eyes glistening with tears, as if he too couldn't believe what he was seeing.

It seemed impossible. We had all gone through so much together. And now this.

Something had finally gotten to us.

The ground shook, I didn't know from what. I thought it was the crowd at first, somehow making a constant thumping noise. I realized it was more like a set of legs.

"Look out!" Julian shouted.

I turned to see what would be our final doom. A Behemoth, and there was no Recon to outrun it this time, no spaceship to drop from the sky and give us a ladder. Only four of us, once five, with our paltry weapons and a whole Empire against us.

The Giant wasn't like the Behemoths we had seen in the Waste. This one was less humanoid, and more reptilian. It was at least ten feet tall, had stout, thick legs, and hard green scales that none of our weapons could pierce.

It would be our final battle.

I cried out. Fueled by grief and anger, I readied my gladius for a jab. The Behemoth lowered itself, opening its wide mouth to reveal its needle teeth. It gave a scream, its warm breath toxic and putrid. Still, I ran forward. The others joined me in my berserk attack. As the creature arched its neck to take me out, Anna swung in from my left.

Not you, too...

Thankfully, the creature ignored her, coming straight for me. That was fine. I didn't want anyone else to die because of me.

The teeth snapped closed, right on my gladius and inches from my hand, rending the hilt in two. I had nothing left but my bare hands. Unthinking, I leaped on top of the monster's head, straddling it with my legs. Annoyed, it shook itself, but it wasn't going to be rid of me so easily. I took my right hand, and, making a fist, jabbed it in one of its two completely white eyes.

It roared in pain, and this time the Behemoth successfully threw me off. I fell ten feet to the ground, rolling and landing sprawled on my stomach. I scrambled to get up, but every part of me hurt. Every damn part. I stood on unsteady legs, but fell again.

I rolled over to see the Behemoth coming for me again. One of its eyes dripped purple blood. The purple stuff was all over my hands, stinging them. I wiped them in the dirt, grabbing a handful of the arena dust. The creature shot its face down again, mouth widening. I dodged to the side, throwing the dirt directly into its other eye at the same time.

It hissed. That gave me the moment I needed to kick it, right in that eye.

It pulled up again, screaming in agony, shaking its colossal head. It stepped forward uncertainly. I had completely blinded it.

Anna took up Makara's spear, and with a primal yell, stabbed downward into the creature's clawed foot.

The creature screamed again and again as we slashed and stabbed and pummeled its legs, forcing it to the ground. The crowd was on its feet, watching and screaming like crazy. Crying out, I slashed at the back of the Behemoth's knees, until it was completely grounded.

As she had done with the crawler earlier, Anna hopped onto the Behemoth's back, finding the sweet spot at the base of its skull. There she stabbed her sword. The creature let out a horrible wail as she twisted the blade, grimacing with the effort. She rotated the blade one time completely before leaving it in. After giving its left leg a final twitch, the monster grew still. It was dead.

The crowd was up on its feet, cheering madly, but I was deaf to it all. I ran and went to kneel beside Makara, who was still on the ground.

Almost afraid of the confirmation, of what I would feel if I did it, I placed my hand on her neck. I waited one. Two. Three seconds.

I thought I felt a thump.

I could scarcely believe it, so I kept my hand there.

Another pulse. It was unmistakable.

"She's alive!" I said.

Everyone rushed up around me. Samuel placed my shirt, which was on the ground, back on the wound to stop what blood was left in her from flowing out.

"She won't last long," Samuel said. "Not without help."

He waved to the stands. Instantly, an outcry went up. They wanted Makara to be saved, too.

Trumpets blared, and from one of the gates, out of nowhere, ran two men with a stretcher.

"About goddamn time!" I said. "Where were they before?"

"This was supposed to be an execution," Julian said. "Only we killed our executioners."

"What does that mean?" I asked. "Will they save Makara?"

Julian didn't say anything. He didn't believe she could be saved.

God, if you are really there, please save Makara...

I was willing to cling to anything at that moment, willing to reach out to anyone who might listen to me, God included. I watched as the men loaded Makara onto the stretcher and carried her away. We started to follow, but at that moment, guards filed out of the gates, rushing to keep us back.

"Hey!" I said. "You can't just take her and not expect us to follow."

Anna placed a hand on my arm. "We don't have much choice. We can only hope they're taking her to get treated somewhere."

By the tunnel, they lowered the stretcher. One of the men carrying it retrieved a syringe from one of his pockets. He injected Makara with it, right in the chest.

"Oh my God..." I said.

I saw Makara's eyes open, and saw her legs sprawl out. She really *was* alive.

Makara was carried up the tunnel, out of sight.

We waited there a good two minutes before two columns of guards streamed out of the gate, wearing steel-plated armor and purple capes. They wore leopard mantles as well, but these were different. They were completely white. From their steel helmets rose tall purple plumes, and their spears gleamed silvery in the afternoon light. Their bodies were etched from stony muscle, their dark and tanned skin lined with jagged scars from the Empire's numerous wars.

The soldiers continued to file out. We remained still.

"The Praetorians," Julian said.

"Who are they?" I asked.

"When I said the jaguar warriors were the best, I was wrong. The Praetorians are. They are the Emperor's personal bodyguards."

The Praetorians fanned out to encircle us, their steps resolute and unyielding. There were twenty-four of them.

"They have come to finish the job," Julian said.

This was it. This was our last moment on Earth. But if they were here to kill us, why bother to save Makara?

The Praetorians stopped in their tracks, facing in once their circle was completed. The leader shouted out, his voice booming off the awed crowd. As one, they lowered their spears, the collective sound sending a shock throughout me.

No. There would be no surviving this.

I grabbed Anna's hand. "We're not going to make it."

In the corner of my vision I saw her shake her head. "No."

"Anna, I just wanted to let you know that..."

The trumpets blared again, their sonorous tones echoing off the stands. The crowd buzzed with excitement. Something had changed.

"I don't believe it," Julian said.

"What?" I asked.

Julian shook his head. "The Emperor is coming."

"The Emperor?" Anna asked. "He's coming *here?*"

"We will meet, at last," Samuel said.

That's when *he* came out, flanked by yet more Praetorians. Short and small of frame, Emperor Augustus still walked as if he were the biggest and most powerful man on Earth. Indeed, he probably was. There was nothing spectacular about him, other than his pure white toga with purple trim, with two eagles emblazoned in gold on his chest. His face carried a neutral expression, and had no distinguishing features. He was neither handsome nor ugly. It was the eyes, however, that carried his entire personality – forceful, bold, and confident. There were wrinkles on his brow and on the edge of his eyes, the only sign of his age other than the few gray hairs intermixed with the dark brown of his head. He was probably in his late fifties. His skin was dark from exposure to the sun. This wasn't a man who lay around doing nothing. He was outside, commanding armies, constructing public works, touring his domain. Augustus was a man of action.

He raised a hand and flashed a toothy smile, and the crowd cheered. He strode toward us, his smile fading somewhat, but still lingering. There was a genuine sparkle in his eyes, and though it had no effect on me, I saw how it would endear him to many people. I had to remind myself that he had killed thousands of people in his quest for power.

He stepped into the circle of Praetorians, pausing in front of us all. He carried no weapon. He had no need to. We just stared at him.

Go, Samuel.

"Congratulations on your well-earned victory," Augustus said.

Samuel hesitated before answering. Was he going to go straight into what we came here for, or was he going to play along? Any sudden move, any disrespect, might get us killed. But was Samuel thinking along the same lines?

"What is going to happen to my sister?"

"She is on her way to the best hospital in the city. She will have my own doctor care for her."

There was a questioning look in Samuel's eyes, but he said nothing more.

"Perhaps you are wondering why I have extended such a kindness to you," Augustus said.

Yes, I thought. *We were wondering* just *that.*

"You came here criminals, and became slaves. How would you feel to be elevated to the rank of Praetorian within my guard?"

The Praetorians around us gave no sign of surprise, other than a slight widening of the eyes. I was shocked, but did my best to hide my astonishment.

"Why are you offering us this?" Samuel asked.

"In all my days, I have not seen anyone fight the way you have," Augustus said. "I would be a fool to pass up this opportunity." He held out a hand. "So, what say you?"

We had to play it cool. If Samuel said no...

Samuel reached out, grabbing the Emperor's hand. "We would like nothing more than that, *Princeps.*"

Augustus smiled widely, letting go of Samuel's hand. *"Princeps.* You address me by the moniker of the Emperors of old."

Samuel bowed his head. "You are saving my sister, and you have given us our lives when we deserved nothing more than to die. It would be my honor to serve you, and I am sure I speak for the rest."

What was Samuel doing? Surely he couldn't be serious about this. Even Augustus couldn't be serious about this. When was Samuel going to get to the reason for our coming here?

"That was the finest fight I have seen in all my days," Augustus said. "Do all Wastelanders fight with such ferocity? Perhaps I should think twice before sending my army there."

"The Wasteland is a harsh land," Samuel said. "And it produces an even harsher people."

Augustus nodded. "Maybe so." He thrust his hand to the side, toward one of his guards. "Sword."

Immediately, a sword flashed out of the Praetorian's scabbard. Augustus grabbed it.

"Kneel, all of you," he said.

We looked at each other. Kneeling would leave us exposed. But considering how many guards there were around us, it was the only thing left to do.

One by one, we knelt in the dirt. As we did so, the crowd's cheers escalated. What was going on? Was the Emperor going to execute us himself?

First, he tapped Samuel on either shoulder. "I pronounce you...free."

He did the same for each of us.

"Rise. I hand you over to Maxillo, Chief Centurion of the Praetorians. He will see to your training."

Augustus handed the sword back to Maxillo, and began to turn away.

"Emperor," Samuel said.

Augustus halted, a bit annoyed. It was a breach of protocol. A recently freed slave did not stop the Emperor in his tracks.

Augustus turned, facing Samuel. "Speak, quickly."

Samuel stared Augustus directly in the eye. "Cornelius Ashton sends his regards."

Augustus's face paled as he looked Samuel up and down. Clearly, he had not heard that name in a long, long time. And clearly, he didn't *want* to hear that name.

He turned fully around. "Where did you learn that name?"

"My crew and I were sent here by Ashton himself." Samuel paused. "We found your own crew in Bunker One. Their names were Harland, Drake, and Kris. They attacked us, but we escaped with our lives. They are all dead. We found the Black Files."

Augustus eyes widened. "Who are you? Are you from Raider Bluff? Where is Ashton?"

"I will tell you all of that, and more. But I need guarantees."

"You have no guarantees," Augustus said. "You are surrounded by my Praetorians, and you will tell me what I wish to know."

"I hope the knowledge I give you is enough to persuade to put down your weapons and point them where it matters – at the monsters in the Great Blight. What we found in the Black Files suggests that there is not much time left, for any of us. We must all come together to fight it, or none of us will be left. That is why we are here. We are messengers."

"You are saying *it* can be stopped?"

Samuel nodded. "Dr. Ashton and I are both researchers. We have come up with a plan that we believe will stop the xenovirus. But we can't do it alone. We will need your help."

Augustus turned away, nodding slowly. "I sense no lie in your words, Wastelander." Augustus gestured to Maxillo. "Lead the Wastelanders to my audience chambers. The fights here will continue, but my family and I will retire to the palace." He looked us up and down. "And clean them up as well."

Maxillo nodded. Augustus turned back to Samuel. "We will be speaking soon..." His words trailed off on an interrogative note.

"Samuel."

Augustus nodded, turning away from us. He strode out of the arena with a rapid gait, his guards closing in around him.

Maxillo stepped forward. "Set down your weapons, and follow me."

We did as commanded, and Maxillo turned away, also toward the exit of the stadium. The crowd murmured with confusion. Despite everything bad that had happened, despite what had happened to Makara...

Makara. All we could do was hope that she could be saved. We had thought her dead, at first. Perhaps she would *still* die. There was nothing we could do, except trust that she was being taken care of. That trust was very hard for me to place.

I shook my head, the tears forcing their way to my eyes again.

"Come on," Anna said, pushing me lightly on the small of my back. "We're moving."

The guards flanked us, making a square box. Inside that box, we were marched out of the *Coleseo*, where I had been so sure we were going to die.

The hardest part had been accomplished. Augustus was on our side, and we would be able to tell him more inside his palace.

Chapter 18

The Praetorians marched us out of the *Coleseo* and into the white-tiled Central Square tinted golden from the setting sun. We were in rags, bloodied and bruised, but we were still standing – at least, all of us except Makara. We went right across Central Square in the middle of the Praetorians' box formation, the crowd parting and the *Coleseo* fading with distance. We approached the outer gates of the Imperial Palace.

When the contingent of Praetorians stopped before the gate, it opened slowly, revealing a circular, gravel drive, in the middle of which were colorful gardens and trees. The green grass had been mowed in neat, diagonal rows. The palace itself was something from Pre-Ragnarok times – made of pink granite with fluted Corinthian columns. It was a vestige of Spanish colonialism.

Guards stood in front of the massive, intricate wooden doors. But we weren't led to these doors. The Praetorians passed them, instead circling to around the back of the palace.

"Where are you taking us?" Samuel asked.

Maxillo turned his head, but continued walking. "You cannot set foot in the palace in your current state. You will be washed and given new clothes first."

None of us argued as we marched along. I couldn't stop thinking about Makara. I didn't want to be here. I was sure Samuel felt the same, but now that we were on the grounds of the Imperial Palace, we had to make the most of it. This is what we came here for. Makara wouldn't want it any other way.

The grounds were a stark contrast to the rest of the city. Here it was spacious, green, and beautiful. The air smelled sweet with flowers and freshly cut grass. It was hard to believe that one man and his family would ever need all this space.

We passed the side of the palace, and I looked back to see rows of gardens, trails, and trees growing and blossoming behind the Emperor's home. The outer stone porch was tiered, and columns rose to support the overhanging red-tiled awning. Curving steps led downward from the wide-open back doors to the end of a long, clear swimming pool, surrounded by gardens and rock formations. From the rocks, waterfalls tumbled into the water made violet from the fading light, sending a fine mist into the evening air. It made me angry to see such luxury when so many suffered just a minute's walk outside the walls.

Finally, a smaller building behind the palace came into view. It was two stories, built in the same colonial style as the main house. It was probably a guest house.

The Praetorians paused before the door. Maxillo turned, and with a soldier's posture, came to stand before us.

"Stewards will see to your needs inside," Maxillo said.

"What about our weapons?" Samuel asked.

"I had a katana," Anna said. "It is very personal to me."

"I will ask about your weapons," Maxillo said. "I'll start with the Lanisto, Ruben. They are probably still in the *Coleseo,* but keep in mind I can't give them to you unless the Emperor permits it."

Maxillo turned to go, leaving us in the hands of one of the house stewards. I hated the idea of wearing clothes that were not my own. If they were anything like what these Imperials considered fashionable, it was going to be even worse. I was not too keen on wearing robes that seemed like nothing more than a bed sheet wrapped around me.

Several stewards rushed out of the door, both male and female, obviously told beforehand of our arrival. They led us inside the house.

One of the male stewards pointed me toward a shower on the bottom floor. I stripped down and stepped inside, and the water came out hot and steamy. The runoff that went into the drain seemed more like mud than water. There was soap, not to mention shampoo from Pre-Ragnarok days – and *that* I had never even used before. Clearly, Augustus was trying to impress us with his wealth. The smell of the soap tingled my nose.

I didn't take long. I toweled off, wondering where my new set of clothes was. A knock came at the door. I opened it slightly, and the steward, with bowed head, presented me my vestments.

Well, not really vestments. The clothes, miraculously, were much in the same style as I was used to: camo pants, a clean cotton tee (albeit of finer quality than I was used to), complete with boxers and athletic socks.

"Forgive me, but I could not find a pair of boots similar to the ones you came in," the steward said. "Although we took the liberty of cleaning them as best we could. They were rather...dirty."

"That's fine," I said. "Thank you."

I dressed, and returned to the atrium of the guest house. Ten minutes later, everyone had cleaned up and redressed. Samuel was wearing dark pants and a black muscle shirt, revealing his heavily muscled arms and broad chest. Julian wore long black pants and a white tee. Anna wore lightweight, wear-resistant dark gray pants with a tight green shirt with thin shoulder straps.

"Couldn't they have given me something a *bit* more conservative?" she asked.

The stewards either pretended not to notice, or just didn't care, because they ushered us toward the doorway.

"I think you look fine," I said.

"Yeah, I'm sure."

We exited the guest house. Maxillo and his waiting Praetorians escorted us to the marble steps leading to the front doors. The two guards posted there swung the doors open, revealing the entry hall within. We walked inside.

It was hard not to be wowed by the grandeur of Augustus's home. A massive chandelier overhung the room, sparkling like crystal. Light reflected off the white marble floor overlaid with oriental rugs. Two sets of staircases curved toward the center of the room and the second floor, where a balcony overhung the entry hall. Fine paintings were mounted on the walls – probably stolen from museums to grace Augustus's own halls.

"This way," the head steward said, taking us away from the door and farther back into the palace.

We passed under the balcony and through a set of open French doors. We had entered a plush living area, with cozy leather couches and more priceless paintings on the walls, along with a white jaguar fur hanging above a marble fireplace. A chandelier, smaller than the one in the entry hall but no less opulent, hung over the area. A set of doors led out into a garden – open to let in a cool evening breeze laden with the scent of jasmine. A tuxedoed butler stood by the door, holding a silver tray with a bottle of champagne that sat chilled in a bucket of ice.

"Please, be seated," the steward said. "The Emperor commands it. He will be with you shortly."

There was nothing left but to sit. We crowded onto the long, leather couch, sinking into its well-worn comfort. I had never sat on anything so relaxing in my life. It felt as if all the stress of the day melted from me – at least physically. However, Samuel, Anna, and Julian gave no sign of relaxation. They sat up straight, and looked ready to bolt at a moment's notice. I did my best to follow their example.

We were sitting in the living room of a man who had killed thousands to forge his empire. A man who would kill thousands more, if need be.

I straightened myself in my seat just as Augustus entered from his gardens. He regarded us for a moment before speaking.

"Your friend has stabilized," he said.

Relief came over me to know that Makara was safe.

"How bad is it?" Samuel asked.

"My chief doctor, who is personally overseeing the case, told me no major organs had been hit. The creature gave her a horrible wound, and she nearly died of blood loss. They have sanitized it and stitched it, but she will not regain full health for at least a few weeks."

Samuel nodded. "It is the best we could have hoped for."

"You can visit her following this audience," Augustus said. "Although she will not likely be conscious."

I frowned. If Makara's condition was this bad, it meant we could be stuck here for a while. It also meant Augustus had yet another bargaining chip – he held the health of Samuel's sister in the palm of his hand.

"I hope you don't mind meeting in this informal setting," Augustus said, sitting down in a well-worn leather chair. "I felt you would appreciate a comfortable place, where I could speak to you as an equal rather than as an Emperor. After all, you have a connection to Cornelius Ashton. My relationship with him precedes the founding of Nova Roma, and as such, I thought it would be appropriate." Augustus paused. "By what names am I to call the rest of you?"

Anna, Julian, and I told him our names. When Augustus's gaze fell on me, it was intent, though friendly. I had imagined the leader of the Nova Roma Empire to be more domineering, more ruthless, more...mean.

Then again, meeting Augustus here meant that if anything went wrong, guards could rush in at a moment's notice. This was the best we could have hoped for. At least we had his attention.

"Tell me," Augustus said, leaning forward and crossing his left leg over his right, "what did you learn from the Black Files?"

Samuel hesitated slightly before giving him the information that we had all learned. Samuel started with the Guardian Missions, and how each had failed. None of them had been able to successfully divert the course of Ragnarok. He talked about how the United States government had covered up the reason for the failure of the third and final Guardian Mission – that its crew members had been attacked by an alien force, known as the Xenos.

Samuel got to the part that was most important – that the xenovirus had been implanted in Ragnarok by the Xenos. The virus would infiltrate all life – and anything infected with the virus was under the control of an entity called the "Voice." The Voice was a consciousness, based in Ragnarok Crater, that controlled xenolife. If the Voice could not be stopped, the xenovirus would be able to spread indefinitely.

Samuel laid out his and Ashton's plan to stop the Voice – by entering Ragnarok Crater, seeking the Voice's source, and destroying it.

When Samuel finished, it was hard to judge Augustus's reaction. The Emperor's face was taciturn, almost bored.

"And you need my help to do all of this?" Augustus asked.

"Your armies are the most numerous," Samuel said. "That is why we came to you first. In addition, we know you have an interest in the xenovirus. After all, you sent a team to Bunker One to learn more about it."

"And you came here to stop me from marching on Raider Bluff."

Samuel nodded. "Yes, that is part of it."

"Do you have a copy of the Black Files for me to read?"

"Not with me, no," Samuel said. "However, if we can get access to your networks, we can send it wirelessly."

Augustus smiled. "The Empire's networks are not your concern, Samuel. What you have told me confirms my fears about the pestilence to the north."

"You were looking for the Bunkers, weren't you?"

Augustus nodded. "I admit, there are many resources within the Bunkers that I envy. We have stripped twenty of them bare, mostly in the southern United States."

"Twenty?" I asked. "That's so many."

"We are efficient," Augustus said. "And we are determined."

The way he said that made me wonder – had the Empire been responsible for some of the Bunkers falling to begin with?

"We noticed the alien growth many years ago," Augustus said. "Although we did not think it was a concern until we began to lose our far patrols. With the fall of Bunker One, some refugees came into our borders, with tales of horror from the north. We saved all that we could, including a scientist."

"Ashton mentioned there might be a scientist from Bunker One in your circle," Samuel said. "He said that was how you might have found out about the Black Files in the first place. Is that the case?"

Augustus shook his head. "Ashton is correct in saying that I learned about the Black Files from one of his scientists – a man by the name of Roger Carrolton. However, he died several years ago. He told me about the Black Files, but he himself was not privy to the information within. So I hired Wastelander mercenaries, though I sent them to investigate far later than I should have. I thought they would do a better job fighting those monsters than native Novans." Augustus sighed. "I see that I thought wrong."

"At least you know what the Black Files contain," I said.

Augustus nodded. "Yes, that is true. So your plan is to attack into the Great Blight?"

"The attack will be a feint," Samuel said. "In reality, we will fly into the Crater to deal the death blow."

"Fly in?" Augustus said. "You have access to an airplane?"

Samuel wasn't going to lay that card on the table. "We do."

"At Bunker 40?" Augustus leaned forward. "That area is covered with the Great Blight."

"There is still a plane outside of Los Angeles that we can use," Samuel said. "The Raiders control it."

Augustus frowned. Something wasn't adding up to him.

Samuel changed the subject. "Regardless, that is the plan. Following this meeting, I hope to have your support."

Augustus eyed Samuel for a moment, before breaking into a smile.

"You have my full support, Samuel," Augustus said. "I will help you with this."

I looked at him in disbelief. Was it really going to be this easy?

Chapter 19

"My armies will be marching north within a week's time," Augustus said. "I hope you can let the other cities in the Wastes know of our arrangement. Of course, you and your crew are welcome to travel with us."

"Wait," Samuel said, "what do you mean by 'arrangement'?"

"The Wasteland is fractious, disjointed. It will be difficult to convince them to join you in this endeavor – even if it's their very lives at stake." Augustus made a fist. "I can guarantee that they will fall in line."

"You want the Wasteland for yourself."

"It is the price for my help."

Samuel frowned, and turned away. He knew he couldn't just give up the entire Wasteland to Augustus. None of them would agree to that, least of all Char and Ashton. But Augustus likely wouldn't see things that way.

"You don't leave me much choice," Samuel said.

"That is part of my charm." Augustus gave a rueful smile.

"Raider Bluff, the L.A. gangs, Oasis, and the others...they won't much like this."

"I'm not asking what they will like," Augustus said. "I'm telling you how it must be. Two weeks ago, I received word that my emissary, Rex, was brutally murdered by Alpha Char in Raider Bluff."

"He was going to make us slaves," Anna said, face red.

"He was under orders to offer fair terms," Augustus said. "However, your people are faced with a choice. Safety and joining with me. Or...freedom and death."

None of us said anything. Augustus held all the cards. He had the soldiers, he had the power. It would take a while for his army to reach the Wasteland. But once it did, who could resist him?

"Why do you want to own the Wasteland, anyway?" I asked. "The cost of gaining it might outweigh the benefits of owning it. It is desolate and poor."

"I will tell you this much, Alex," Augustus said. "I believe I was preserved for a reason, even when I believed myself dead following the fall of Ragnarok. Your Dr. Ashton barred my entry into Bunker One, but I made the best of it. I funded the Bunker Program greatly, but I *still* was not allowed in. My blood wasn't good enough. My money wasn't good enough."

"You were a drug lord," Anna said. "You really think they would have let you in?"

Augustus's face reddened. "This is not about revenge. This is about destiny. *My* destiny. The world is a harsh place – but the Nova Roma Empire offers the best chance for everyone's survival. By the time I'm dead, I hope to unite all of the former Americas into one whole – to rebuild a society greater than anything that ever existed before Ragnarok. Obviously, this will take decades – perhaps centuries. The xenovirus stands in the way. And we will deal with that when the time comes. But I want you to think about this." Augustus leaned forward. "The Xenos are coming, Samuel. You know this. In defeating the Voice, you are only thinking short-term. When the Xenos come, humanity must be united under one banner. The banner of the Empire. As you have already told me, Xenofall could be decades from now. Centuries. Or it could be tomorrow. But once we defeat this Voice – with my help, under my orders – we must continue our work building the Nova Roma Empire. It offers the best chance of fighting back against the

Xenos. If the Xenos come and find nothing but squabbling leaders – the way the world is now, as it stands – we will crumble like a clump of dried earth in a fist."

Samuel frowned, thinking. I didn't blame him. Augustus had given him a lot to think about, and a lot of what he said actually made sense.

"I don't know what Ashton told you about me, but it wasn't the entire picture," Augustus said. "Always remember, there are at least two sides to every story, and most times more. Always be skeptical of what people tell you, especially your friends. You are more liable to believe them."

"Our loyalty is to Ashton," Samuel said. "First and foremost. I do not have the authority to give you what you ask. Only Ashton does."

Augustus smiled again. There was something...insistent about it. "Believe me, Samuel. At the head of my army, we can be very persuasive. And Ashton...if he cared so much about the fate of the world, why was he too cowardly to come and meet me himself? I would have let him right in."

"Because *you* still have a score to settle," Anna said.

"That is all in the past," Augustus said. "I am looking to the future. If I hadn't been looking to the future, could I have built all *this?*"

He gestured around the room, and in so doing, we knew he was talking about Nova Roma.

The light of the day had almost been extinguished, and the sitting room was darkening. Despite the warmth of the breeze, I felt a chill pass over me.

"Your Wasteland is nothing more than a series of fractured city-states, gangs, and competing agendas. You will accomplish nothing there without my help, Samuel. Surely, you know of the man Carin Black?"

Carin Black. He was the leader of the Black Reapers, the gang that had supplanted the Lost Angels in L.A. Had Augustus been corresponding with him?

"Of course we know of him," Samuel said. "He is our enemy. He destroyed the Lost Angels several years ago."

Augustus nodded. "It would be wise not to consider him an enemy, Samuel. He is a powerful man – the most powerful man in the Wasteland at present. And he will not give up his power easily. Trying to convince him otherwise, as you plan to do, might be even more suicidal than walking into my Empire." Augustus smiled in the darkness. "We all know how that almost turned out."

"Nonetheless," Samuel said, "He is an evil man. He has committed unspeakable crimes, against the Lost Angels, against my sister, and against me. Carin forced my sister into a life that I will never forgive him for. And the way he treats his slaves makes your Empire look like paradise in comparison."

"My Empire *is* paradise."

"A paradise for the few."

"Don't be naive, Samuel. It has always been that way, even before Ragnarok. The world is a harsh place. All I can hope to do is dim that harshness. It will take time, yes. But as they say, time heals all wounds."

Samuel said nothing in response.

"If you agree," Augustus continued, "you will find a ready ally in Carin Black and the Reapers. Give me the locations of the other Bunkers, and we will have all of the weaponry we will ever need to take on the Blights. It is the simplest solution, and you know it."

"The freedom of the Wasteland is not something to be bandied about," Samuel said.

"If we give you the locations to the Bunkers," I said, "those weapons will make it easier for you to conquer the Wasteland. Why would we do that for you?"

Augustus smiled. "Because you have no other choice. I will not hide my intents. I am laying it all out on the table, as any man should. You, however, Samuel...I can tell you are made uncomfortable by this. I tell you now, in my time as Emperor, I have learned that safety *always* comes with a price. You must decide for yourself if you are willing to pay it."

Samuel sighed. "And should I disagree?"

Augustus shrugged. "You have no reason to. But if you disagree, nothing changes. I march on the Wasteland. I meet with Black. And there will be war. I will have more trouble finding the Bunkers without the coordinates, but they *will* be found. I will overwhelm the other Wasteland leaders with sheer numbers, leaders who will undoubtedly cobble together a poor, fractured defense. I will march on the Great Blight, and using the knowledge you have given me, attack the Voice and destroy it. You will have no choice but to help me at that point, because I will be the only one with the power to stop the Voice."

Samuel glared at Augustus. "I will not sell you the Wasteland. This mission will be under the direct control of both Dr. Ashton and myself. We are the only ones who know what must be done in order for it to succeed."

"I grant you that," Augustus said. "But without me, you cannot succeed."

"I can say the same for you. So the best we can do is compromise – so that you can get what you want, and I can get what I want."

"Clearly," Augustus said, smiling. "I am glad we have come to this consensus. But I will have you remember – the Empire was the only nation that survived the horrors of Ragnarok. I saved thousands of *your* Americans when your own country could not even do that. True, most of them are slaves. But they are not dead, and they are treated well in accordance with Imperial law."

"What about the arenas?" I asked, angrily. "What about the *Coleseo?*"

"You know nothing. The *Coleseo* is for the transgressors – the prisoners and malcontents who cannot follow Imperial law. I do not allow innocents to fight there."

"What about us?" Anna asked. "What about Makara? We came to your Empire to speak with you, and instead I was enslaved the very day I came here. Something is *broken* about this place that you say is the best hope for humanity. Forgive us for being a little skeptical."

"It isn't perfect, I admit," Augustus said. "But don't forget that it was *my* hand that saved you, and I had every right not to." Augustus turned back to Samuel. "We can either do this the easy way, or the hard way. You can join with me, and by force of arms have all your Wastelander leaders fall into line. Or you can go your own way. You will never be able to muster all the armies of the Wasteland quickly enough to resist me – and I would overwhelm them with great force. They are too disjointed, and I will be there in two months, ready, organized, capable."

Samuel said nothing, merely brooded over what must happen next. Augustus didn't know we had *Gilgamesh* and *Odin*. If he did, that would change the balance of power. It meant that, if we could somehow get out of Nova Roma, we could reach the Wasteland and have the time to mount a defense. But even two months would be cutting it very close.

"I would need to let Ashton know about this arrangement," Samuel said.

Samuel couldn't be serious. If he was playing along with the Emperor, he was playing a dangerous game. I was all too aware of the guards surrounding us, and the fact that we had no weapons.

I could tell from Augustus's eyes that he was very interested in meeting Ashton. Perhaps that was what he was *most* interested in. He had to have had great self-control to play it cool for so long. "Yes. Go and speak with Ashton, and bring him here to finalize this arrangement. Until this occurs...Makara stays here. Until I am *completely* satisfied she has recovered from her injury."

Anna opened her mouth to protest, but Samuel placed a hand on her shoulder, silencing her. "You have a deal."

A shadow passed over the garden in a rush of wind, darkening the room. At first I thought it was *Gilgamesh*, come to our rescue once again. But the shadow passed, and there was no sound of an engine. It must have just been a cloud.

"You will remain free, obviously," Augustus said. "I consider you dignitaries representing the entire Wasteland. But I hope you will consider joining my Praetorian guards. Perhaps, when all of this over, I can arrange a joint governorship for you all over the entire Wasteland."

"You would let us rule the Wasteland?" I asked.

Augustus shrugged. "Why not? Nothing is impossible. But this is merely speculative. I just want you to be aware of the benefits of working with me – benefits many cities in Mexico have already accepted."

Augustus rose from his chair, and we stood with him. "My Praetorians will accompany you to Ashton. I hope we can have an arrangement before the day is over."

Augustus was not taking any chances, and I didn't blame him. I wondered what Ashton's reaction would be when he saw us coming down the road surrounded by Augustus's most elite guards. Seeing us hostage, would he have no choice but to land *Gilgamesh* and be escorted back to the palace, where anything could happen?

"I think you will find that the past can be forgiven if we can all agree to work together," Augustus said. "However, I am a terrible enemy." He smiled bitterly. "Perhaps it was fate that I was left on the surface when Ragnarok fell. Fate often has a funny sense of justice."

"We will not bring Ashton here if you are only going to hurt him," Samuel said.

"No," Augustus said. "I would never do that. I need him to stop the xenovirus, and besides, I am not wantonly cruel – even if Ashton was to me, thirty years ago."

Augustus gestured toward Maxillo, who had entered the room while we were speaking with Augustus. "Have you found the Wastelanders' weapons?"

"My men are waiting outside the gates with the weapons," Maxillo said. "Shall I return them?"

Augustus nodded. "Hand them over there." He looked at us. "As a sign of my trust, I will let you walk with weapons within Nova Roma, a privilege that is only granted to my legionaries. I hope you will not squander this trust, and that it may be a good sign of our future partnership."

Trust. Augustus was only giving us those weapons because he knew we couldn't do anything...not with Makara still in the hospital, and not surrounded by twenty-five of his best guards.

"May I see my sister before we leave?" Samuel asked.

Augustus shook his head. "I would like to conclude this arrangement as soon as possible. I am hoping that Ashton can be here within the hour. Granted that everything proceeds smoothly, then yes, you may visit your sister."

"Very well." Samuel looked toward us. "Let's go."

The grim-faced guards led us out of the reception room, and back into the glittering entry hall. The bright chandeliers illuminated the pastel colors of the walls, giving sparkling life to the paintings, giving the rich oriental rugs beneath our feet a vibrant hue. I couldn't help but feel that we were on a death march, and that Augustus had us where he wanted us. How could this have ended any other way? We were stupid for coming here. With Makara hostage, and our lives at stake, we couldn't just leave. We had to play this out until the end.

But there still might be a chance to get the better of Augustus. There had to be, or this mission could fail.

The same two attendants from earlier swung the front doors open, letting us out into the cool night. Our footsteps clicked on the marble steps, crunching on the gravel drive. Anna impulsively reached for her back, where her katana would usually be sheathed. Of course, there was nothing there.

As Augustus had assured us, a group of Praetorians waited on the other side of the gates. I saw that one carried Anna's katana. Its black sheath glimmered under the light of faded lamps.

The guard by the gate opened it, and we strode outside. I received my Beretta. Feeling it in my hand was good, and made me feel immediately safer. I checked the clip, finding it loaded with nine bullets. It would have to do. I stashed it on my belt. Anna took her katana, strapping it to her back, along with her handgun sidearm. She didn't look right without that katana, and now that it was back, there was more confidence in her step. Samuel received his handgun, and strapped it to his belt without a word. Julian holstered a handgun too, for the first time in a decade.

"I don't know how," I said to him. "But we'll get you home."

Julian nodded. "I appreciate it. But right now, I'm worried about bigger things."

Maxillo turned to Samuel. "Lead, and we will follow. But first, tell us where we are going."

Samuel turned to look at us, his eyes surprisingly calm. It was as if he were saying, "play along."

"It is a long walk," Samuel said.

"Where?" Maxillo asked, impatient.

"Outside the north gate. Up a mountain road."

Maxillo frowned. He was suspicious. "That doesn't lead anywhere. There aren't even any farms up there."

"It might be a trap," another Praetorian said.

"If it is a trap," Samuel said, "it wouldn't be a very good one. There are only the four of us, and there are twenty-five of you. That is simply where Ashton is staying. We thought it was safer if he remained outside the city."

Maxillo nodded. From his expression, he still didn't like it. But there wasn't much he could do about that.

"Onward, then."

Samuel started walking, and the rest of us followed.

Chapter 20

We walked across Central Square as night finally settled over the land. With the night came a thin mist that overhung the entire city in a wispy blanket. The *Coleseo* appeared haunting in the nighttime fog – maybe it was just the wind, but I thought I heard screams echoing in that direction, like ghosts in the air.

The city was a different place at night. Central Square was mostly empty and ill-lit. Most windows were dark – lighting must have been an expensive commodity – though behind us, the Imperial Palace's many windows glowed in the night. As we exited Central Square, the tall, shadowy buildings and twisting streets imbued a sense of claustrophobia. Raucous laughter emanated from taverns.

At long last, we reached the northern gate. We passed through them, the nighttime guards giving us questioning stares. The mist thickened as we walked up the wide dirt road. One by one, the Praetorians clicked on flashlights, but they did little to illuminate our surroundings. The mist was cool, creeping onto my skin, chilling me. On either side of the road was thick forest, from which the sounds of insects came. A high screech emanated from the woods – the yowling of a jaguar, perhaps?

The Praetorians did not seem afraid, however. They marched on, their demeanor stony and determined. We kept up with their pace.

"About how far is it?" Maxillo asked.

"A few miles," Samuel said. "He is staying where the road goes through a pass. It's just a little bit beyond that."

"Sepulcher's Pass," Maxillo said. "It is a haunted place. Many dead kings are buried there from an age long past."

"Kings?" I asked. "What kings?"

"The land is forbidden to normal citizens," Maxillo said. "There, many of the Aztec kings buried their dead. There are pyramids covered in forest and jungle. They were discovered by the Empire's armies years ago during the First War."

"The First War?" Anna asked.

"The war the Empire fought with Old Mexico."

"I thought Mexico fell after Ragnarok," I said.

"It did," Maxillo said, growing tired of our questions. "Because of us."

Nothing more was said as the road began its steep incline. We went back and forth as the road snaked up the mountainside. The mist thickened, making it very difficult to see. Behind, the lights of Nova Roma glimmered dimly in the darkness. Even the thick fog could not mask a city of that size.

Again the screech sounded from the forest, closer.

"What is that?" Julian asked.

Maxillo shrugged. "Probably a jaguar. They are active in the forest, at nights."

I knew that was *not* a jaguar. I had fought those things inside the *Coleseo,* just hours before. This was something different. Something...worse. It was all too reminiscent of...

"Crawlers," Anna said.

An unmistakable scuttling of dozens of legs sounded from ahead.

"Box formation!" Maxillo shouted.

The Praetorians hurried to make a square around us, each facing outward, pausing in the center of the road. We remained in the middle.

"Whatever comes out of the forest, shoot first," Maxillo said to us.

Another screech sounded, deadly close to us. A shadowy crawler pounced from the night and onto the misty road. It landed on top of a Praetorian, who screamed as the creature tore into his flesh. With a flash of spears, two more Praetorians charged the creature, skewering it through the belly. It went limp, even as more shadowy shapes came from the woods.

"There's too many!" Anna asked. "We have to break through and make it to the ship!"

"The ship?" Maxillo asked. "What ship?"

A pair of crawlers attacked the group's left flank. Three Praetorians lined up, pointing their spears into the darkness. The battle-hardened warriors did everything their training had taught them, but they had never fought anything like this. More crawlers appeared, swarming over the warriors, whose spears did little against the creatures' thick exoskeletons. The crawlers screeched in victory as they ripped gobbets of flesh from the Praetorians' corpses, sprays of blood adding a reddish hue to the mist.

"Do as she says!" Maxillo roared. "Clear a path ahead!"

The Praetorians responded, cutting their way through a pack of crawlers that *still* grew in number. Where had they all come from? There were no Blights around here, were there?

That was when a crawler appeared in front of me, a scythe-like fang flashing by my side. I tucked and rolled onto the ground. As I lay on my back, the crawler appeared above me, exposing its soft underbelly. I aimed and fired my Beretta. The creature squealed in pain as each bullet connected, purple blood oozing from the large holes I had created at point-blank range. I rolled to the side as the creature crashed down.

The others were ahead of me, but Anna had stayed behind.

"Alex, get your ass moving!"

Another crawler appeared at Anna's side. She turned, dodging its lightning strike, all the while swinging around to catch it with her katana. The creature turned its stomach away, and instead the katana glanced off the creature's side in a shower of sparks.

The crawler had cut us off from the rest of the group, and more were coming from behind.

I ran forward, pointing my gun toward the hideous monster.

Bam. Bam. Bam.

The bullets ricocheted off its tough skin. I had succeeded in nothing more than pissing it off. The crawler charged for me, and in so doing exposed itself to Anna. She surged forward, swiping her blade underneath it.

The crawler gave a horrible screech that pierced my ears. The fetid stench of its guts filled the air as they spilled out onto the dirt path. The creature's body slumped, twitched, and grew still.

"Come on," I said.

I grabbed Anna's hand and ran up the mountain path. We passed the bodies of both man and monster as we ran ahead. Thankfully, none of them were our own.

A baleful roar sounded from above. The mist darkened as something...*flew*...over us. It wasn't *Gilgamesh*. This was something alive.

We both paused on the road. I hoped the mist was thick enough that *whatever* was up there couldn't see us.

The thing passed overhead, giving an unholy bellow as it plied the skies above. The mist was too thick to get a view of it.

"What *is* that thing?" Anna asked.

"I don't know. We need to find the others."

We continued our sprint, wheezing for air. The sounds of the screeches and gunshots were getting closer. Men's screams sounded in the night. I could only hope that they weren't either Samuel or Julian.

Finally, the ground leveled, and the road turned. We were getting close to the rendezvous point.

We passed the corpse of one of the crawlers. Huddled against its frame were two forms. It was Samuel and Julian.

"Samuel!" I said, running closer.

He held a finger to his lips.

"We thought you were dead," Julian said.

"It'll take more than a few crawlers to kill me," I said. "Did you guys see that flying thing?"

Samuel nodded his assent, his eyes wide. "It swooped down and took Maxillo with its claws..."

"What was it?" Anna asked.

Samuel waved us over. We got on the ground, scooting against the corpse's back.

"I have no idea. But Ashton is up there. If we don't let him know..."

"How is he going to find us in this mist?"

"We need to find a spot to hide, until things clear up a bit," Samuel said.

"Where can we go?" I asked. "The forest is down the mountain, and it seems like there might be a Blight nearby..."

"A big Blight, if one of *those* things lives in it," Anna said.

Samuel shook his head. "No. I don't think there is a Blight. If there were, Augustus would surely know about it. I think there is some other explanation."

"The Praetorians?" I asked.

"All dead and scattered," Julian said. "We only survived by hiding against this."

The flying monster gave another roar that echoed from the mountains. In response, the crawlers screeched in the distance. They had gone away. For now.

"They might come back," I said.

"We need to get back to the city," Samuel said. "The plan has changed. With the Praetorians gone, we need to get Makara and get the hell out of here."

"I can lead us to the hospital," Julian said. "It isn't far inside."

A colossal rush of wind pummeled us from above. The ground shook as *it* landed, sending the mist scattering. At first I saw giant, claw-like feet, covered in crimson scales. The talons were as long as swords, and they curled as they buried themselves in the dirt. A massive body flared upward, crimson and snakelike, along with a massive spread of wings – wings impossibly large. They must have been at least a hundred feet wide. The creature was enormous – it was like a gigantic crawler, only with wings. From its back hopped two creatures to the ground – additional crawlers, who seemingly had been piloting the monster. The monster's long serpent neck lowered. It had two white, blazing eyes. Two massive nostrils opened at the end of its short, scaly snout, quivering as they sniffed the air. The head was round, bald, black as night, the darkness of the head fading to the deep ruby red scales that covered the rest of its body.

It opened its mouth to reveal rows of thin needle teeth, already stained with red blood. It opened its mouth and screamed, two forked tongues quivering as the roar emanated, shaking me to the bones.

And all I could think was: *is that a dragon?*

"Run!" Samuel shouted.

We scrambled up, just as the crawlers that had been riding the dragon flanked us on either side. The dragon stepped forward, neck and head extended. We ran, but it was too fast. Its mouth opened and closed, snapping as it neared us.

That was when the roar of an engine from above deafened us, sending us all to the ground. It was *Gilgamesh*. A blinding light flashed on, causing the crawlers to screech in pain. The dragon still kept coming forward, terribly close.

Gilgamesh's twin machine guns opened up, deafening and thunderous. Lines of bullets entered the dragon's body, causing it to scream in pain. The creature loomed above. Its body shook and convulsed as the bullets entered its chest, its neck, its hideous face. It opened its mouth to scream, but nothing came out. It started to fall forward.

"*Out of the way!*" Samuel yelled.

We crawled forward as fast as we could, the creature falling into the spot we had just vacated.

The crawlers, on their multiple legs and with white orb eyes, looked upward at *Gilgamesh,* hissing angrily. They turned on us.

As *Gilgamesh* lowered itself to land, the crawlers charged for us in unison. I could do nothing but dodge the first one as it tore past me, right for Anna. Anna fell to the ground, the creature looming over her. She skewered it with her katana, quickly pulling the blade out of its stomach and rolling aside before it could fall on her.

Samuel and Julian attacked the other crawler. Samuel kept his gun pointed at its front, distracting it while Julian swung around. Julian leapt onto the body. The creature turned, as if to swat off a fly. Julian tumbled to the ground, but it gave Samuel the opening he needed to fire on the creature's gut. Samuel emptied his entire clip as the creature screamed, again and again. Anna rushed forward, dealing the final death blow by slashing a deep X on the monster's abdomen. The crawler screeched again as its entrails burst from the wound, spilling onto the ground.

Behind us, *Gilgamesh* alighted on the ground, boarding ramp extending.

We rushed up the ramp and into the open door. As the door shut behind us, we lifted off from the mists and into the night sky.

It was time to go after Makara.

Chapter 21

We ran to *Gilgamesh's* bridge, finding Ashton intent on the controls and white hair wild.

"You got here just in time, old man," I said.

Ashton turned his head, blue eyes wide. "You kids have got my blood pumping! I had to dodge *three* of those things just to get here..."

He saw Anna, for the first time. He smiled. "Good to see you with us, Miss Bliss. Now, if we can just get out of here..." He frowned. "Where's Makara?"

"Down there," I said.

"What? You left *her* behind now?"

"We had no choice," Samuel said. "She was injured in the *Coleseo,* and she is in the hospital. Augustus is holding her hostage until we bring you to him."

"Like hell you're bringing me to that bastard! We need to get to Makara!"

Ashton turned the ship toward the city. "If we can find a spot to land, you guys can get there on foot."

"With those...*things*...flying around?" Julian asked.

"They're dragons," I said.

"No," Anna said. "They're not."

"Well, whatever they are, I think I lost them back in the clouds..."

"Maybe not," Samuel said, pointing.

Shadowy shapes of wings descended, not for us, but for the city of Nova Roma.

"The invasion picked a hell of a time to spread to the Empire," Ashton said. He looked at Julian. "Where's the hospital?"

"Well, from the sky it will be difficult to find, but if you could land in Central Square..."

"Central Square," Ashton said. "Find something to hold onto, kids. Things are going to get dicey."

We rocketed forward, having to hold onto the sides of the ship as we descended toward the city. There were at least two of those things flying around, causing chaos.

"Maybe those dragons will change Augustus's opinion about things," I said.

"Stop calling them dragons!" Anna said.

"Why? That's what they are."

"It's so unoriginal. Surely you can think of a better name."

"This isn't relevant," Ashton said. "I guess the meeting went poorly?"

"Yeah," Samuel said. "But he wants to use the Xenos as an excuse to conquer the rest of the Wasteland."

Ashton sniffed. "It doesn't surprise me. I was right to keep him out of Bunker One." Ashton focused more intently on the controls. "We're getting close."

"Just land us in Central Square, and fly off again," Julian said. "That would probably be the easiest."

"And how will I find you again?" Ashton asked.

"We have flares, right?" Samuel asked.

"Yes, there should be some in the ship's armory."

"I'll get one," Anna said, rushing off the bridge.

"When you have Makara, get to the hospital roof and shoot the flare," Ashton said. "Night like this, I'll be able to see it easily."

As we passed over the city walls and descended, some of the dragons veered in their courses to come our way. At least three of them were flying toward us at full speed.

Anna rushed back onto the bridge. "You better hurry up!"

"Hold on to your britches, girlie," Ashton said. "We're in for a rough landing. You find the flare?"

Anna nodded, holding up a flare gun. My stomach did a flip when the ship suddenly descended. *Gilgamesh* plopped on the square awkwardly, scuttling a few times before coming to a stop.

"I can lose them in the clouds," Ashton said. "Get your butts out of here!"

"Follow me," Julian said.

We ran off the bridge, down the corridor, and out of the ship. As soon as we cleared the boarding ramp, *Gilgamesh* thundered toward the sky. A roar sounded from above. One of the dragons was diving for *Gilgamesh*. Ashton, with a slick sideways maneuver, dodged the blow as he blasted for the skies.

But we had our own troubles to deal with. Several guards rushed from the palace gates, staring upward in disbelief as *Gilgamesh* shot away with several xenodragons in tow.

"Does xenodragon work?" I asked.

"That's even worse."

"Come on!" Julian said. "It's this way!"

Julian's voice snapped the guards to attention. The lead guard yelled in Spanish, sending his cronies after us. Thankfully, none of them had guns. The Empire was so big that likely not everyone in its army had the privilege of owning a firearm.

We saved our ammo, instead rushing ahead across the square. It had completely emptied. The city was a ghost town with all its inhabitants hiding indoors.

Anna took her handgun, aiming it behind her to fire a few times. The guards took the warning, stopping their tracks.

"Nos dejen en paz!" Julian shouted. *"Guarden sus familias!"*

The guards looked at each other, considered, and scattered.

"What did you say, Julian?" I asked.

"I told them to leave us alone and save their families."

"Good advice," Anna said.

We exited Central Square, turning down a side street. People watched from the windows as we blazed by. My lungs burned for air, but Makara was in danger. If any of the crawlers had followed their dragon mounts...

As if thinking of them were a summons, two crawlers appeared at the intersection ahead. They saw us, and scuttled down the street toward our position.

"This way!" Julian said.

He jumped through an open window, and we followed him in. We found ourselves in a living room, a large family looking at us with wide, surprised eyes. The mother and father looked at our weapons.

Julian didn't stay long. We ran out the apartment's front door, finding ourselves on a staircase. We ran up the steps, even as the monsters began to batter themselves against the door leading into the building.

We reached the top of the stairs, Julian bursting onto the apartment's rooftop.

"The hospital is just two blocks away," Julian said.

We were going to have to building-hop again. The dragons were nowhere near us, instead circling the city near Central Square, about a half mile away. In the distance came the screams of another victim. More crawlers screeched from the street below. The dragons appeared to be ferrying them inside the city, right over the walls.

I ran after Julian and the others, making the jump to the next building with ease. The buildings were so close together that it would have been hard to fall. We hopped from one to the other, silently through the night. Finally, reaching the end of the apartment row, we took a ladder down to the bottom. For now, the street was clear.

Once we hit the ground, we ran to the left. Julian was very fast, and hard to keep up with.

He took a right turn. After passing shops, cafés, and more apartments, we came to a large open area filled with grass. A driveway circled around in front of a large four-story building.

"We're here," Julian said.

We ran up the drive and through the hospital's front doors. The building was one of the few in the city powered with electricity. The glass doors slid open, leading into a lobby. Blood and dead bodies covered the floor. From within the building, I could hear screams of victims and the horrible wails of predators.

"We can only follow the noise," Samuel said. "Get your weapons ready."

We ran down the hall and up a flight of stairs. When we arrived at the door that led to the second floor, a low hiss sounded from the other side, followed by a woman's scream.

With a shout, Samuel kicked open the door, pointing his gun down the hallway. A crawler leaned over a small woman's frame, ready to tear her to shreds.

Samuel fired, hitting the creature's face. As the creature cried out and faced us with its angular head, its former prey forgotten, I realized that these crawlers were different from the ones in the Great Blight. Their armor was thicker, covering nearly every spot on the body. Their bodies were lower to the ground, affording them better speed and balance. Their legs were thicker, and the blades at the end of their tails were longer. The cruel spikes growing from their backs were curved and sharper than I'd ever seen.

During our two months in Skyhome, we were not the only ones getting stronger. The virus was evolving its alien army to become more powerful than ever before.

Instead of attacking outright, the creature curled into a ball, its spikes jutting out on all sides. It rolled forward, right toward us.

Our bullets glanced off its armor, doing nothing. We shut the door to the stairwell, backing up the steps. The door burst open, and the monster's head slithered in. It opened its mouth to give a bloodcurdling shriek. It scuttled up the stairs after us. We could do nothing but back away, run faster...

We exited onto the third floor, and ran down the hallway, passing rows of open doors. Most of the rooms were empty. When we passed the final door, we found a familiar form lying in the bed, her eyes shut.

"Makara!" Samuel said.

The crawler burst into the hallway, slinking low to the ground, its white eyes afire with bloodlust. We faced the crawler. We couldn't give another inch, or Makara would die. This was where we stood our ground.

The narrow confines meant we couldn't defeat the creature in our usual way – flanking it and getting a good attack on its soft underbelly. It completely blocked off the hallway, making it impossible to get around it from the front.

"Samuel, you and Julian keep it occupied," I said. "Back up if you need to."

I grabbed Anna by the arm, pulling her back.

"What are we doing?" Anna hissed.

"This hallway probably circles all the way around," I said. "If we can get behind it..."

"Hurry!" Samuel said.

The creature charged forward. Samuel and Julian backed up to the corner as Anna and I broke out into a dead run. We had to make it all the way around before the creature could hit Samuel and Julian. Hopefully, the creature would be so distracted as to avoid Makara altogether.

We rounded the corner, finding a short hallway that led to the right again. We took the corner. We were on the side opposite where we had been.

"Faster," Anna said.

The monster screeched from behind. I heard Samuel roar out, either from pain or exertion.

We turned another corner, finding ourselves in a short hallway. Just one more turn, and we would be behind the crawler.

But when we made that last turn, we found the hallway completely empty.

"They must have backed up further," I said. "Keep going!"

We kept running, circling a corner yet again. The hallway was still empty. There were no sounds of struggle, no signs of a fight. I was beginning to wonder if we might have taken a wrong turn somewhere.

Until the crawler surged out of a door right behind us.

"Run!" Anna said.

We did run, but the creature snatched onto my leg. That's when I heard gunshots. Somehow, Samuel and Julian had gotten behind the crawler. The crawler screamed horribly as it turned to deal with the new threat. Its grip loosened on my leg, and Anna ran forward, wedging her blade between the wall and the creature, angling it toward the monster. With a thrust, she managed to stab the crawler in the gut.

The creature collapsed to the floor and thrashed about, its tail swinging back and forth madly. Anna's katana remained embedded in the creature as purple blood spilled from its gut, both from bullets and blade. We backed away, allowing the creature its dying spasms. A minute later, its movements had diminished into feeble twitches. It settled into death.

Anna ran forward, retrieving her katana. It was coated in slimy, purple blood. She ran into a nearby room and wiped the blade on some bed sheets before sheathing it.

Samuel and Julian ran to Makara's room, Anna and I following behind. Inside, Makara sat up in the bed, her eyes half opened. She was still dressed as she had been in the *Coleseo*. The skin surrounding her wound was angry and red, and white gauze wrapped her entire abdomen. Her face was pale and strained.

"I tried to get up," she rasped, "but…"

"Come on," Samuel said. "Ashton's waiting up above. We're getting out of here."

He picked her up as if her weight were nothing, placing her gently over his right shoulder. She winced in pain, but said nothing.

"Glad you're alright," I said.

Makara forced a smile. She wasn't looking at me, though. She looked at Julian.

"Thanks for guarding the door," she said.

Julian's face reddened as he gave a shy smile. "It was nothing."

They shared a look, but it didn't last long. Samuel strode out the door, walking quickly to the steps. The rest of us guarded him, making sure nothing else jumped out at us.

As we entered the stairwell, the power in the building shut off, leaving us in blinding darkness. It was dead quiet, but from below we could hear crawlers, their scuttling legs heading for the stairwell. I heard one of them hiss from below in the darkness.

"Go, go, *go!*" Samuel yelled.

We ran up the stairs. The creatures below were out of sight, but they made their presence known by their screaming. The metal of the stairs rattled as the crawlers ran up at lightning speed.

After two flights, Samuel bust the door open, revealing the hospital's flat rooftop. As the last one up, I shut the door, barring it with my back. Julian joined me in holding the door closed.

"The flare, Anna!" Samuel yelled.

Hastily, Anna reached for her side, withdrawing the flare gun from its holster. She pointed upward and fired. A long streak of red surged into the dark sky, arcing high above and falling again toward the ground. It left a trail of smoke that lingered and glowed in the night.

The door shook as a crawler battered it. The shock nearly made me fall over. From the clouds, a light descended. Instantly, several winged creatures screamed in the distance, making their way toward the speeding spaceship. *Gilgamesh* raced downward to our position.

We had to hold on a little while longer.

The creature rammed the door again, throwing it off its hinges and sending Julian and me sprawling to the ground. I crawled ahead, scrambling up before the creature could set itself on me.

Ahead, the shape of *Gilgamesh* came level with the building rooftop, hovering at a standstill. The dragons in the distance were closing. The ship's blast door slid open, revealing the lit interior.

We were going to have to jump.

Samuel ran with Makara on his back. With a roar and the force of his powerful legs, he jumped through the air, landing in the spaceship. Anna followed close behind, making the jump with ease.

Julian and I ran forward, abandoning our positions by the door. A xenodragon dropped from the sky, heading directly for *Gilgamesh's* nose. As its claws extended, the ship's twin turrets fired, nailing the monster with a shower of lead. The dragon roared in pain, arcing to the side and out of the way.

Julian jumped, rolling neatly into the spacecraft. With three crawlers behind me, I gave a mighty leap, pushing off with my right leg. I sailed through the air, arms outstretched. As I landed, the ship turned away. The turn caused me to teeter on the edge. I was about to fall through the open doorway. But as I fell backward, the door shut, and my back was stopped by the cold metal.

A bump came from the side of the ship, where one of the dragons had pummeled it. After rocking slightly, *Gilgamesh* arced at an even steeper angle, going straight for the clouds.

We lay on the deck, holding on for dear life as Ashton gave the ship all it had. We flew higher and higher, until finally there were no more roars of flying monsters. The ship evened out, and we all lay, bloody and beaten, but still alive.

After the horror show we had just gone through, I almost couldn't believe it.

Chapter 22

Almost an hour later aboard the bridge of the *Gilgamesh*, Samuel and I stood next to Ashton. Anna and Julian were asleep aft. As much as I wanted to be back there with them, Samuel wanted me here to update Ashton on the situation. Makara was resting in the clinic. Ashton had seen to her care, making sure there had been no damage during the escape from the hospital.

"What's the report?" Ashton asked.

"Augustus is on the move," Samuel said. "His army is marching north and will be in the Wasteland in two months." Samuel paused. "His first target will probably be Raider Bluff."

"That doesn't give us much time to muster a resistance," Ashton said. "I take it he was counting on that."

Neither of us answered Ashton. He sat, his blue eyes concentrated, his fingers steepled. It was a stark contrast to his dishevelment before.

"Any damage to *Gilgamesh?*" I asked.

"None to speak of," Ashton said. "Let's hope it stays that way." He gave a long and tired sigh. "It's a miracle everyone got out of there alive."

Ashton's mention of miracles reminded me of my moment of weakness in the *Coleseo*. I had prayed that Makara would live. For some reason, that didn't bother me now. We were all grappling with forces, seen and unseen – forces far beyond our control. There were mysteries that no science would ever be able to explain.

Thinking of that prayer reminded me of Julian for some reason.

"When can Julian go home?" I asked.

Ashton's tired eyes looked up at me. He looked every bit his age and more, but some light came to those eyes at the mention of home. He was quiet, thoughtful.

"We can take care of that when the time comes. We have bigger fish to fry for the moment."

"Understood," I said.

"He was a huge help," Samuel said. "He saved Makara when I wasn't able to. He blocked off that doorway and kept the crawler off her."

"Heroic," Ashton said.

"I would like him to become part of our crew."

I looked at Samuel. We could use someone like Julian. But would he agree when home was so close?

"Talk to him," Ashton said. "See if you can get him on board. I'm inclined to agree with you."

"He hasn't been home in ten years," I said. "Shouldn't we let him go?"

Ashton and Samuel looked at each other. Finally, Ashton spoke. "We need every able man we can get. But if he would rather stay in New America, I won't stop him."

"What's our next course of action?" Samuel asked.

"We need to refuel," Ashton said. "We're running on vapor, but luckily the Pacific isn't too far. Once there, we can refuel and head to Bluff. We need to update Char on the situation. And from there, we must find the other Wasteland leaders. Carin Black must be either dealt with or brought to our side."

"I think Augustus might be in league with him," I said.

Ashton frowned. "That's disturbing news. What makes you say that?"

"Augustus told us not to even try to persuade him," Samuel said. "Like he knew something we didn't."

"He also said that we would be smart to bring Black to our side," I said. "That's if we joined up with the Empire."

"Makara won't hear of it," Samuel said. "Black is the reason the Angels fell four years ago. And the Raiders don't really like the Reapers, either." He sighed. "We will need to choose one side or the other."

"How is that even a choice?" I asked.

Samuel didn't say anything as both Ashton and I waited for his response.

"A lot of what Augustus said made sense," Samuel said. "I hate to say it, but if we give Augustus what he wants, his army and Black's can control the entire Wasteland. They can force everyone else there to help us...Char included. The alternative is to organize the Raiders and any other group who will listen to us. We have two months to do that if we go down that road. The Reapers and the Empire together will be hard to stop."

"I don't trust Augustus," Ashton said. "There's a reason I didn't give him that berth in Bunker One. He tried wheedling it away from Dr. Keener, Alex's grandfather. He might have been able to charm President Garland and the others, but I saw right through that bullshit." Ashton sighed. "I know you're tempted to believe him. Hell, I am too. He makes it sound so easy. But this is anything but easy. We won't sell our souls unless that's what it comes down to."

"We need every major player in the Wasteland to stand with us," I said. "When they are warned about the Empire, they will have a reason to stop bickering. If we can take out the Reapers first, before the Empire arrives..."

"We have two months to do it," Samuel said.

"We *have* to do it," I said. "Augustus knows we have *Gilgamesh*. How could he have not seen it flying into his city? He had counted on us taking a while to get back to the Wasteland. If Augustus is smart, he'll do his best to get his army to the Wasteland as soon as possible. The Wasteland is a long way from the Empire. And if the Reapers join him, we'll be fighting two forces, one on either side." I shook my head. "Raider Bluff, not to mention the other settlements, won't stand a chance. But if we can take out the Reapers first..."

"The Empire will be easier to deal with," Samuel said.

We said nothing for a while, letting our thoughts collect.

"All this talk has reminded me of what the Wanderer told me," Samuel said.

The Wanderer. That strange and mysterious man had told each of us something we must do, in order for us to be successful in our mission. I remembered what he had told me, seemingly ages ago – that the success or failure of this entire mission hinged on me, somehow. It was an awesome responsibility, and those words were no clearer today than they had been. I wondered what he had told everyone else. I was about to find out what he'd said to Samuel.

"What did he tell you?" I asked.

"He said that I would be tempted," Samuel said. "But in that moment, I would need to trust my ideals. Part of me feels agreeing with Augustus would be easier and safer. But a future where he is in charge is no future at all. I have to trust in my ideals – the people of the Wasteland must remain free."

At first, I agreed with him. I thought about whom we were siding with. Sure, Char was on our side. But was he really better than the Empire? After all, the Raiders stole, they raped, they enslaved, albeit on a smaller scale. What difference would a Raider Empire be from the Novans?

"You're right," I said. "But we need a new agenda. A new vision."

Both looked at me, curious. I had it.

"It's time to reform the Lost Angels."

Both stared at me for a moment before Samuel broke into a rare smile.

"That is quite the idea. But how do we do that? Who will lead them?"

"She's in the back of the ship."

"You mean Makara."

I nodded. I don't know why I chose her over Samuel. It just felt right, for some reason.

"She was closest to Raine," I said. "Though Raine is dead, his legacy can live on through her. From what she told me about him when we first met, Raine had been the best thing to ever happen to the Wasteland. He kept no slaves. Los Angeles was prosperous while his gang ruled. He helped people rebuild communities. People were kept safe from violence. If we could create something like that, a society that people could believe in..."

"You're talking about a resurrection." Ashton said. "It could be powerful. People know of Makara's connection to Raine. She was like a daughter to him. If she were to rise to the mantle, gather any Angels who escaped as well as anyone else who was willing to follow her..."

"This could work," Samuel said. "This is what we need. If Makara could get the other Wasteland leaders to band with her, we just might be numerous enough to stop the Empire, as long as we took out the Reapers first."

"We may not even need to go that far," I said. "We need to avoid as much bloodshed as possible. The more of each other we kill, the stronger Augustus's army is by comparison. We need to be more cunning."

"What do you mean?" Samuel said.

I took my index finger, dragging it along my throat.

"You mean...assassinate Black?"

"You know how any gang of violent men is," I said. "As soon as the head is chopped off, the rest of the body dies. Once Black is dead, the reformed Angels can acquire the Reapers. Once we are in that position, we can ally with Raider Bluff and anyone else...all before Augustus arrives. He will find us united, rather than separate."

"What about the xenovirus?" Ashton asked. "What about these dragons?"

"That might actually work for us," I said. "Augustus might be afraid to move out if the xenodragons are threatening his Empire. They can keep him pinned until he has his house in order. And, he might be more reluctant to send as many troops as he planned on to begin with. But at the same time, he is desperate. He needs to take us out before we have a chance to prepare. He will be wrestling with that in the coming days."

"I need to speak to Makara about this," Samuel said.

"Let her rest," Ashton said. "Actually, it would be a good idea for all of us to rest. We have been through a lot on very little sleep."

"So rest, refuel, get Julian home..." I said. "Am I missing anything?"

"We need to go back to Raider Bluff and let Char in on our plan," Ashton said. "He is close to Makara, and may have some information and advice on how to proceed."

"We also need to get *Odin* back," Samuel said. "It's still parked in the forest."

"Yes, there is that. It should be fine where it is, but I can drop you all off there before returning to Skyhome. There are some matters I must attend to there."

"Like what?" I asked.

"Well, I was in a middle of a research project before I was called down here. I was setting up some wavelength monitors to plant around Ragnarok Crater."

"I'm glad you didn't end up doing that," I said. "Ragnarok Crater is probably a bad place to be."

"With these xenodragons, I guess so," Ashton said.

I smiled. Despite Anna's illogical hatred of the word "dragon," I was happy to see my name sticking.

"That is something I still need to do," Ashton said. "Preparing the monitors will take some time, but I can drop them around the Crater from a height. They only need to be there for a few minutes to triangulate the point of origin of the Voice."

"We'll be on our own for the next leg?" Samuel asked.

"It's looking that way. But we will still be in contact through radio."

As Samuel and Ashton continued to discuss plans, I began to feel a bit overwhelmed with everything that needed to be done, and the short amount of time it needed to be done in. I was grateful for both Samuel and Ashton, because doing things and making decisions quickly seemed to be their element. Ashton was brilliant, and Samuel was decisive. Together, they made a good team, and it made me wonder what they even saw in me.

"This Lost Angels thing..." Samuel said. "It's brilliant. In Skyhome, Makara was always so down. This will give her something to work on."

"Well, it's not anything, yet," I said.

"It will be, though," Ashton said. "Everything great begins as an idea. A good idea inspires. The fact that this idea has unlocked everything else, unbarring our progress into the future..." Ashton paused. "It will do the same for others. I know it will."

Well, maybe that was my answer. Maybe *this* was why they had me here.

Chapter 23

We landed on a pristine white beach in what used to be Baja California. After setting up the thick blue water intake lines and anchoring them in the sea, we took the rest of the day to relax. It was going to cost some time for the ship to refuel. After catching up on some much-needed sleep, Anna and I came outside to enjoy the warm sun. We found a place to lie down and be alone. Together, we watched the waves in silence, enjoying each other's company.

It was the best day of my life. We ran into the cold water together. The shock was refreshing on my skin. I dove under, and came back up to see Anna's face, her black hair framed around her pale face, her hazel eyes looking into mine. It was good to just be with her, with no pressure or pain.

The air was warm, yet not too warm, and the late afternoon sun was a couple of handbreadths above the blue line of the sea. Everything was calming and beautiful.

We returned to the beach, and lay down to dry off. About half a mile away, Samuel was walking with Makara, trying to get her some light exercise. She had said she needed it or she would go crazy in the clinic bed. Julian spoke with Ashton atop a twisted rock formation jutting out into the sea, against which wave after wave crashed.

Everything about the day was perfect. I wish life were always like this – more about peace than fighting.

"Do you think this is what people did before?" Anna asked.

I smiled. "They would have been crazy if they didn't."

A large, cold wave came. Anna laughed as the water lapped at our feet.

For some reason, my thoughts turned to love and friendship. To people who had never experienced love, it was scary. That was how I had felt, once – closed off, reserved, rarely talking to anyone except for maybe Khloe or my dad. But once you had loved, you couldn't live without it. I knew, because I had lived both sides.

It was sad that my entire life had to be burned away for me to learn lesson. I wished I could have learned without the pain, but that was the way life was: you can cannot learn and grow in the absence of pain. I could only be grateful that I had found these people: Samuel, Makara, and Anna; even Ashton and Julian. It was a good warm feeling that was all too rare in this world.

Perhaps it had been rare in the Old World, too.

"Even if we've done some crazy and suicidal things that I would never, ever want to do again," I said, "I'm glad we've met, Anna. I wouldn't have had it any other way."

"Even with the Bunker?"

Anna had hit on something. It was hard to let go of that. The ghosts of my father and Khloe would always haunt me. But after almost three months, I knew I would never be the same person. I remembered what Samuel had told me in Skyhome: that I was going to change and become who I was always meant to be. I didn't know when that was going to happen. I didn't know if that was already happening. All I knew was that I had changed a lot. I had seen too much. I had loved too much.

"No, I don't regret anything. Because without that, I would have never met you."

Anna smiled, but said nothing as we continued watching the ocean. *Gilgamesh* hulked above on our right, the ship's thick blue water lines issuing out of its sides and into the sea. The water would be desalinated and filtered, once inside the ship, before being converted into the deuterium and tritium needed to fuel the fusion reactor. The process took a while, and ironically, it took almost as much energy to create those two isotopes of hydrogen as we got out of fusing them. Which meant that we were stuck here for the next two days until both canisters of isotopes were completely filled.

Which was completely fine with me. It gave us a much-needed break, and a chance for Makara to heal. Maybe it gave *everyone* a chance to heal.

"So," Anna said, "why did you come back for me?"

I turned to look at her. Her long, black hair was still wet from our swim in the ocean earlier. The salt and sand clung to her hair. She looked at me with her warm hazel eyes. She was so beautiful that it was hard to find words.

"We all came back for you."

"But it was *your* idea."

I smiled. "How do you know that?"

She turned away, whipping her hair around flirtatiously. "You just told me."

I turned on my side. "Told you? How?"

"I can just tell."

"That doesn't explain anything."

Anna shook her head. "Apparently, you've never heard of this thing called women's intuition."

I laughed. "Alright. You got me there."

It was quiet for a moment before she spoke again.

"You haven't answered my question yet."

Well, there was no getting out of this one.

"I came back for you because..."

She turned to me, her eyes telling me she didn't want a joke, which was what I was tempted to do. Being serious was always hard for me. If you really wanted to be serious, you had to mean it or you risked hurting the girl. And hurting Anna was the last thing I wanted to do.

"I came back because...of a personal reason. And that's all I'm going to say for now."

She smiled, but said nothing more. I couldn't tell if she was disappointed or not. Still, I felt my answer was lame. The three words I wanted to say were somehow the hardest to say of all. It was a guy thing, I guess.

"That's cool, I guess," she said.

I turned to face her. She was looking at the sea.

"You were going to say something to me, in the arena," she said. "When we thought those guards were going to kill us. I haven't stopped thinking about it."

"I was going to say..."

Anna leaned forward. Those eyes again. I knew, looking at them, that she had never looked at anyone else like that before. It both exhilarated and terrified me.

"How about I just *show* you what I wanted to say?"

I leaned forward to kiss her. Her face was so close to mine. We paused, right before our lips touched. When they did, I felt a surge of energy run throughout me. I moved my lips against hers gently, and she kissed me back. I reached my hand to touch her face. We stayed like that for a while, and it was the most wonderful thing I had felt in a long time. It was something I had wanted to do for a while, something I had even dreamed about.

After another moment, I pulled away, my eyes still closed.

When I opened them, she was looking at me. And smiling.

"So that's how you feel?"

I nodded. "Damn straight I do."

Anna laughed, and nestled against me. Together, we watched the waves and the sun fall, tinting the sky and sea in light pink and orange. It was too perfect, and even if I knew such perfection wasn't meant to be in a world so fallen as ours, that didn't take away from its beauty. It only made it more beautiful.

***

It took two days, but we found New America. It was on the Texas coast, as Julian had said, about fifty miles south of Houston – a small, non-walled village in the center of a thick stand of trees not too far from a brown, winding river. On its western side were farms, growing rows of green crops. To the east were the apocalyptic ruins of a massive industrial complex, once silvery towers and tanks, now shattered and ruined. It could not have been a safe spot to pick for the founding of a new city, but I guess home remained home to people, no matter how bad it got.

If anything, it was hundreds of miles from any Blights, which probably went a long way toward explaining how the town still existed after so many years. But for a town called New America, it was humble. There couldn't have been more than two hundred people living there, judging from the couple dozen or so buildings it consisted of.

We landed in a field to the south of the town, not even trying to hide the spaceship. Julian walked outside into the warm, muggy air, and we followed him from behind. The sky was mostly clear, though tinted with red. The meteor fallout was not as thick as in the Wasteland, but this land still carried wispy traces of it. The people came out of the wooden buildings, one by one – ragged, dirty, thin, their eyes wide. It was such a stark contrast to the Empire, and it was a sign of how far we had fallen, how low America had been made by Ragnarok. Isolated as it was, it came as a surprise that this community had survived for so long. And yet, they *had* survived.

As we walked forward, Julian in the lead, several goats crossed our path. Weeds and tall grass grew thick, and from the low-hanging trees, insects chirped.

Julian stepped into the center of the gathering.

"I am Julian," he said, tears coming to his eyes. "After ten years, I have finally come home."

At first, there was silence. From the crowd there came a wail. A woman, maybe in her late forties, had fallen on her knees, hands outstretched.

A collective gasp went through the crowd. The people stared in disbelief, turning their attention from the spaceship and to Julian, who ran into the embrace of his mother. She held him tightly. The tiny woman gripped him with such ferocity that it seemed as if she would never let him go. Julian was crying like a baby, doing nothing to restrain his emotion. The mother stroked his back, her eyes closed in contentment, tears streaming down her face.

"All these years, *Mijo,*" she said. "I knew that you were alive. I knew it."

Another, younger woman came from the crowd, with tears on her face. It was the little sister Julian had spoken of, now grown up. She threw herself on her mother and her brother.

As the crowd marveled and we watched, the women led him toward the town. A tall, lean man with bright blue eyes approached Julian. He was beaming, and he gave Julian a strong embrace. The man wore blue-jean overalls and a large straw hat. All of his clothing looked as if it had seen better times.

As Julian walked away with his family, the man approached us, extending a hand to Samuel.

"I am Herbert Shaw, mayor of New America," he said. He looked up at the *Gilgamesh,* from which Dr. Ashton emerged. "Is there an America anymore? That's who you are, isn't it?"

Samuel shook his head. "It's a long story, Mr. Shaw. A very long story."

"Well, it's a Sabbath day, and we have all the time in the world. Why don't you come inside the Gathering Hall and sit a spell? We have food and water."

Julian stopped, turning our way. "These people saved my life," he called out. "I was a slave for ten years in lands far to the south. It was unspeakable hell and misery. But they kindly took me here and gave me my freedom."

"Thank you," Julian's mother said. "You have no idea what this means to us. My heart was broken that day, but now it is healed. My son is home!"

All around her, the people of New America cheered and clapped. Judging from their faces, it was the first good thing that had happened to them in a long time.

"We will join you for dinner," Samuel said, "though we cannot stay long. There is so much that you and your town must know, and it will take hours just to tell you everything. Julian will fill you in later."

"I can see you are being very serious," Mayor Shaw said. "I won't press you. I'm glad you want to stay and get to know us, humble as we are." He looked at all of us. "What are your names?"

We told him, and Mayor Shaw led us into the town, where everyone was still gathered, crying and celebrating at the reunion. The town was nothing more than a series of cabins, built in several circles. It had probably existed before Ragnarok, but for what purpose, I couldn't guess. Some other buildings had been constructed – one of which was the Gathering Hall the mayor had spoken of. It was little more than a thatched roof supported by thick, wooden poles driven into the ground. Though humble, it was wide, and beneath its awning were a couple of dozen tables, at the center of which was a large fire pit.

That night, we dined with Julian, his family, and the rest of New America. His mother, Gloria, was a small, yet pretty Mexican woman, who could not stop smiling. His younger sister, Yasmin, was also very pretty, and was probably in her twenties. She had two children who scampered about, and her husband, a man named Craig, sat with us. The new faces and environment were a bit overwhelming, but there was a sense of warm community among everyone here. It was clear that everyone loved each other, even if they didn't always get along.

Over the course of the day, goat meat had been roasting over the fire. I had never eaten goat before, or much meat in fact, but the smell was tantalizing. When it was finally served, we also had fresh vegetables and bread with our meat, along with coffee and cool water. The water, Mayor Shaw had said, was filtered. He seemed very proud of that fact.

These people didn't have much, but the extent to which they were willing to share it was humbling. It was clear why Julian had wanted to return to this place. And it was another reason to fight. We couldn't let this community, and any others like it, fall to the xenovirus. I was glad to see the Great Blight hadn't extended this far. But how long until it set its sights on this community?

I turned from these dark thoughts when Anna grabbed my hand, offering me a smile. I pulled her close, resting my cheek against the top of her head. She was another reason I was fighting.

After everyone had finished eating, Mayor Shaw stood. He whistled loudly to get everyone's attention.

"I just wanted to say that one of our own has returned here today," Mayor Shaw said. "It's God's grace that it has happened, and we would all do well to remember that."

Everyone murmured their agreement.

"I know times are hard. They're always hard. But we have each other. We thought the Lord had taken Julian from us, but he has been returned. He left us a boy, and has come home a man. God works miracles, every single day. With Julian sitting here, with us, how can anyone deny it?"

Several people cheered. Gloria touched her son's arm, and her sister gave him a radiant smile.

"Life will keep on being hard. I can guarantee that. But God will see us through to the end. We are lights for each other in the darkness. Today, a miracle occurred, and we would do well to remember that."

Next, the mayor led everyone in a prayer, thanking God for Julian's safe return. I had never seen anyone pray as he did, never seen religion practiced the way it was being practiced here. It was startling, yet not unwelcome. There was so much love in the gathering, it almost overcame me and shattered my beliefs. Almost.

Anna reached for my hand, and held it.

"You don't have to believe," she said. "I don't."

I looked at her. I placed my head against hers.

"I know," I whispered. "It's amazing, isn't it?"

"What?"

"That they can believe, after everything. I don't understand how."

Mayor Shaw continued his prayer. Around me, I could hear whispers, people ushering their own wishes to the heavens. Whether the heavens were silent, or whether they answered, I couldn't tell you at that moment. But in the light of that fire, in the collective light of those people, it felt as if they did.

"I don't understand, either," Anna said. "Maybe someday we'll figure it out."

Shaw concluded his prayer, and a collective amen passed over the crowd.

Soon after that, the people went their separate ways, turning in for the night in their cabins. The dream was over, and tomorrow there was work – working for survival and bringing forth fruit from the land, so that they could work again, and dream again.

Shaw approached us, along with Julian, with whom he had been speaking.

"Thank you for bringing him back," Mayor Shaw said. "You have given these people hope beyond what you can even imagine. I have no idea what happened down there, but Julian will tell me everything in the days to come."

"You have decided to stay?" Samuel asked.

Julian nodded. "I must spend time with my family. This is my home, and I won't be parted from it. But when you need me again, I want to be there for the final battle. I will speak to everyone here, and let them know what is going on with the world. If you return, I will be willing to fight for you again, and hopefully, others will as well."

Samuel nodded. "We will come back. We will need the help, when the time comes."

"So you're just going to leave us like that?" Makara asked.

Instead of getting angry, Julian looked at Makara tenderly.

"We will see each other again, Makara," he said. "This isn't over yet. There is much I have to do, to help my community."

She nodded, accepting his answer. "You better remember those words."

Julian nodded gravely, as Makara turned toward Samuel. "We should go."

"We appreciate your hospitality," Samuel said to Mayor Shaw. "I have not eaten like that in...well, ever. But time is short, and we have a mission to carry out. In the coming days, Julian will tell you some very incredible things. Believe every word, Mayor. There is not much time left. Not even for New America."

The mayor frowned, disturbed by what Samuel said. He looked at Julian, but Julian was holding out a hand to Samuel.

"Goodbye, Samuel. We will speak again soon."

Samuel took the hand and shook it. Julian next took mine. He said goodbye to Anna, and went to stand in front of Makara. Even in the darkness, her cheeks reddened.

"Take care of yourself," he said. "I won't always be there to save you from crawlers."

Makara gave a small smile. "You have no idea what I am capable of, Jules."

Julian smiled, and turned back to his family. I was surprised at how sad Makara seemed to see him go.

"Come on," Ashton said, who had been quiet. "We should get going."

We turned back for *Gilgamesh*. After loading up, we lifted off, leaving New America behind. After the warmness of that community, the coldness of the *Gilgamesh* was a rather strange thing.

Chapter 24

We slept well into the next morning, hovering above the clouds. It was time for the next phase of our mission – going to Raider Bluff and speaking with Char.

Ashton dropped us off where *Odin* had been parked. The smaller spaceship was still there, looking as untouched as the day we had left it. It had been sitting there for a week, even though the sheer amount of events that had happened since then made it seem like months.

After bidding goodbye to Ashton and watching *Gilgamesh* disappear above the clouds, we boarded *Odin* once more. We had all of our provisions and supplies from Skyhome still. All that was left was to set course for Raider Bluff. It was time to meet with Char and tell him about our plan to resurrect the Angels. Samuel had already spoken with Makara about the plan, and he said that she was more than willing to try.

I sat up front with both Makara and Anna as the ship lifted off. Samuel decided to have another nap while he could snag one.

Once we were flying north, I decided to ask Makara a question.

"So what's going on between you and Julian?"

In the copilot's seat, Anna grinned.

"Nothing," Makara said, though her reddening face betrayed that answer. "He thinks he's hot stuff, but he has another think coming."

"Right," I said.

"I think it's good," Anna said. "It gives you someone who is your match."

"Like I wasn't?" I asked.

"You better watch yourself, buddy," Anna said.

"Yeah, what's going on between *you* two?" Makara asked. "You were getting kind of cozy on the beach."

"Look," Anna said, "we don't really have to talk about this."

"Why?" Makara asked. "You're curious about me, so why can't I be about you?"

"Point taken," Anna said.

I decided to change the subject. "So how do you feel about this Lost Angels thing?"

"I like it," Makara said. "I actually think it could work. Which is weird, because Sam and I disagree so often."

"Really?" Anna asked. "I don't ever see that."

I smiled. These girls had hated each other's guts just a couple months ago. Now, they were talking like best friends.

"Believe me," Makara said. "I don't say anything, but he is always just mission, mission, mission..."

Anna giggled. "Yeah, I guess that's true."

At that moment, Samuel walked onto the bridge. Everyone did their best to look busy.

"What's our ETA?"

"We're over northwestern Mexico, so just another hour or so," Makara said.

"Good. I want everyone suited and ready. We can land south of Bluff, a good distance away from the cliff and the road."

In a little over an hour, we were going to be back in Raider Bluff. It seemed so strange. Char hadn't seen *any* of us for two months. As far as he knew, we were all dead, and our mission had failed. We hadn't made contact with him the whole time we were in Skyhome. That whole time had been spent recovering and planning our next move.

"It'll be good to be back," Anna said.

"Yeah," Makara said. "This place is kind of like my home, in some strange way."

When we were close, Makara began to pilot the ship downward. "This whole 'New Angels' thing is a mess," she said.

"What do you mean?" I asked.

"I don't even know where to start with it. I need to talk to Char. He'll know what to do."

"Well," I said, "that's what we're here for, right? With us, you already have your first four recruits. Five, including Ashton. Six, if you count..."

"Don't mention that pig's name."

"Who, Julian?" I asked, baiting her.

Makara sighed, ignoring my comment. "I just hope Char doesn't see it as competition, you know?"

"Why would he?"

"I don't know. It's complicated."

"You'll be great," Samuel said. "Besides, you'll have us helping you."

She sighed. "I guess."

We burst through the red clouds that made their perpetual home above the Wasteland. It was strange to see that haunting familiarity and be comforted by it. We had come from a land of green, and were descending into a land of red. This was my home, barren as it was. It felt good to be coming back, even if this place tried to kill me at every turn.

Even as we reached five thousand feet, the air remained dusty. Visibility was near zero. A gust of wind blasted the side of the ship, jarring it. Lightning slashed ahead of us.

"Dust storm," Makara said.

"Can we still land?" I asked.

She nodded. "No reason we shouldn't. I'll just have to be careful. Bluff is right in front of us, but I can't see a damn thing."

The altimeter read one thousand feet. Still, I couldn't see the ground, much less the city ahead. There was only swirling red dust.

"Are you sure it's there?"

"I'm damn sure," Makara said.

"The coordinates check out," Anna said. "We're definitely in the right spot."

Five hundred feet. We continued to lower to the ground below. A few minutes later, we landed on the rocky, hard earth.

"Go out, or stay here?" I asked.

"Wait a minute," Samuel said, looking out the windshield.

"What is it?" Makara asked.

There was nothing out there we hadn't seen before – just the same tempest that we had flown through. The wind howled violently, and lightning forked the clouds above.

"Stay put for now," Samuel said. "I just have a feeling."

We didn't question Samuel. Instead, we waited on the bridge quietly. After a while, the storm began to let up. Before us, the shape of the mesa began to appear in the swirling eddies of dust.

"There it is," I said.

The shapes of buildings began to materialize. They were still hard to discern, but they were there.

"This is it," Samuel said. "Suit up and get your weapons ready. I'm not taking any chances."

"Wait."

At my voice, everyone stopped moving. The dust settled some more. That was Raider Bluff, alright. But something was off about it. I felt a creeping dread overtake me that I couldn't explain.

Despite the dust, the buildings couldn't be *that* pink. Or purple. I hoped it was my eyes playing tricks on me. But as the wind let up, and the dust settled for good, I saw that it wasn't a trick.

The buildings were covered with xenofungus. Many of them stood decrepit, and the walls had been shattered in several places. The walls that I had once thought so strong no longer protected the city. The Empire hadn't made it here first.

The xenovirus had.

"It's...gone..." Anna said.

"No..." Makara said.

It wasn't a "no" of disagreement – it was a "no" of disbelief. Raider Bluff was gone. It was all Blight. While we had been gone two months, somehow the virus had infiltrated what was going to be our chief ally in the Wasteland.

"Char..." Makara said.

She rushed off the bridge, leaving the rest of us to run after her.

"Makara, wait!" Samuel said.

She was out the door and into the Wasteland. The air was bitterly cold, harshly dry – worse than I could have ever imagined. I was still dressed for the south – but now, it was late December. Of course it was going to be cold.

Makara walked forward a few steps. She gazed at the lost city, her black hair whipping sideways in the wind. It was as if she believed walking forward could reverse time and return the city to its former state. Anna ran up to stand beside her, holding a hand to her eyes to keep the dust out.

I ran to join them. The fierce wind howled, throwing dust that threatened to obscure my vision

"We have to go up there," Makara said. "There might be survivors."

"Anyone who's up there is probably dead," I said. "Or...worse."

On the top of the incline leading to the city I could catch some movement, erupting out of Bluff at a run. There were at first dozens...then hundreds...then thousands. They came from the gates, running and screeching and screaming. There were crawlers, and the human forms of Howlers. Flyers shot out of the buildings, taking to the skies in clouds of thousands. And they were all heading this way.

"To the ship," Samuel said. "Now."

But an ungodly bellow stopped us in our tracks. Rising from the ruins of the town was the largest xenodragon we had seen yet, colossal in size and dwarfing every other one we had seen in Nova Roma. Those had just been grunts compared to this one. This dragon was the soul of Ragnarok itself.

No Raider had survived this attack.

As the monsters swarmed toward us in an unending tide, we ran back to the ship. The dragon did not chase us – it only watched, as if curious, as we lifted off into the air, as the crawlers occupied the space we had just vacated, jumping up into the air and snapping their jaws futilely at *Odin's* retracting landing struts. The flyers pecked at the ship's sides and windshield, their maddened white orbs disturbing, their lack of feathers revealing sickly pink flesh that dripped purple ooze.

Tears still in her eyes, Makara blasted upward, for the sky.

Once we were safely above the clouds, at an altitude of fifty thousand feet just to be sure, we didn't say anything. Char, the others...they were probably all dead. Many were probably Howlers.

I didn't want to ask, "What now?" There was no "now." Char had been a source of vision and wisdom for us before our journey to Bunker One. He was probably dead.

Makara held her head down on the dash, her shoulder shaking with sobs.

Samuel reached to turn on the transceiver. Makara grabbed his hand before he could pick it up.

"Not yet," she said, her voice shaky. "I have one more idea."

Samuel turned to her. "What do you mean?"

Makara sat straight, dried her tears, and steered *Odin* east.

"Where are we going?" Samuel asked.

"There is only one person I know who might be able to help," she said. "And one person only."

At first, I had no idea who she was talking about.

"He said there was a time where all would seem lost," Makara said. "He said to, at that moment, fly to the desert and seek those to whom injustice was dealt, and give them justice."

"The Wanderer said this," Samuel said. "But who are we going to see, Makara?"

"They will be first of the New Angels," Makara said. "This is where we begin."

"East takes us to the Great Blight," Samuel said, still confused.

"You mean Marcus," I said. "You're going to find the Exiles. They're in the Boundless, right?"

"Yes," Makara said. "They were kicked out of Raider Bluff, years ago, for going against the will of the Alpha. They wandered the desert for years. And Marcus was right. One day, Char was going to need them. We need them. If Char is anywhere, he's *there.*"

As we sped across the sky, I hoped that this wasn't a dead end. I thought of the Wanderer, and how each of the prophecies had so far come true. Lisa was told she would have to give her life. Samuel was told he must remain true to himself. Makara was told to seek help with the Exiles, if her interpretation was correct.

That left me and Anna. I knew what mine was. The Wanderer had told me that it all depended on me, somehow. That the mission would fail without me. For a moment, I remembered the Wanderer, and wondered just who he was, with his clouded, alien eyes that couldn't see one foot ahead of him but could somehow pierce the mists of the future. Had he been friend, or enemy? Would we ever see him again?

I didn't know what answers, or questions, awaited us in the Boundless, or among the Exiles. All any of us knew was that we had no other course. And Makara was the leader of the Lost Angels.

So all we could do was follow her.

About the Author

Kyle West is a science fiction author living in Oklahoma City. He is currently working on The Wasteland Chronicles series, of which there will be seven installments. Books 2, 3, and 4 are already available. Stay tuned for a preview of the fourth installment, *Revelation...*

Contact

kylewestwriter[at]gmail[dot]com

Revelation Preview

It's been three months since the fall of Bunker 108. In that time, I've survived Raiders, gangs, empires, cold, hunger, and monsters. By all rights, I should be dead. We all should be. It seems impossible that we aren't. Impossible that we are still fighting this.

I just wonder how much longer we can last.

The odds are stacked against us. At every turn, the xenovirus gets more deadly. The number of Blights in the Wasteland has tripled. The monsters it creates are more dangerous. Crawlers roam the dark, cold nights in packs, killing any they find. Anyone without a wall, without a home, is as good as dead.

The Great Blight has expanded one hundred miles further west over the past two months alone – a rate which will see the entire Wasteland covered by this time next year.

And, somehow, we are expected to stop all this. The four of us are expected to be the world's saviors. We are all too young for this job. I'm sixteen. Makara is nineteen, Samuel twenty-three, and Anna is seventeen. That's too much weight to rest on our shoulders – hell, too much weight for *anyone's* shoulders. Maybe, we aren't kids anymore. Responsibility is enough to make an adult of anyone.

As leader of the New Angels, Makara is now in charge of the group. Samuel still leads the mission against the Great Blight, but as far as building the group, Makara calls the shots. First on her agenda is finding the Exiles, Marcus's gang, somewhere in the Boundless. After we find them, they can lead us to the Raiders. Or at least, that's what we hope.

With the fall of Raider Bluff to the xenoswarm, we could only hope that'd been Char's thought process. Overrun by crawlers and Howlers and worse besides, we could only *hope* he had laid down his pride to seek the help of the brother he'd exiled over a decade before.

This is no longer a time for enmity and blood. The power of the Great Blight grows by the day, and the Great Dragon of Raider Bluff has yet to make his next move.

Yes – two months after we had left it, the Wasteland is a far more dangerous place. And the Wasteland is only the beginning. If we do not find some way to stop the Great Blight, the entire world will be swallowed by it.

With Raider Bluff gone, it makes sense for Vegas to be next on the Great Blight's list. That city is the closest to the Great Blight, and that's where all our roads lead – whether we are Angel, Exile, or Raider. With the alliance between Augustus of the Empire and Carin Black of Los Angeles, it's up to us to grab whoever is left and take the fight to Los Angeles – taking out Carin Black before Augustus can arrive with his legions – before the worst of winter is upon us.

But before we can do that, we have to find the Exiles. We have to find the Raiders.

It is our newest challenge. It is hard to tell whether this will be easier, or harder, than what we did in the Empire. Now back in the cold, bare reality of the Wasteland, I have a feeling it will be harder. Our mission is getting a bunch of people who don't like each other to work together. We have to convince them to leave the safety of their walls, strike out across the Wasteland in the dead of winter, and take out Black and the Reapers before Augustus arrives.

We have about two months to do it. Augustus's army is far – but it could be here in as soon as two months. Winter might help us, but we are planning for the worst. Our success as a group depends on being prepared for the worst. Augustus said he was going to be here in two months. We will take him at his word.

Even if such preparation seems impossible, we have to try. The entire world, literally, depends on it.

I would say it is a lot of pressure, but we are used to that by now. We are a well-honed team. We each know our strengths and weaknesses. We have two spaceships at our disposal, meaning we can jump between points quickly.

Even though we have new capabilities, so does the xenoswarm. The dragons are a game-changer that none of us could have predicted, and I'm sure they're not the last thing the Great Blight will throw at us.

First, we have to deal with the human opposition. Until everyone is standing together and on the same page, we can't make our attack on the Great Blight. We can't even protect ourselves from Augustus and Carin Black. If we do not unite, and unite soon, everything will fall.

And that's exactly what the Voice in Ragnarok Crater wants.

***

Makara was still flying. It was night, and *Odin* hummed all round us, sailing through the air at three hundred miles an hour. She stared ahead as if her willpower alone could pierce the veil of darkness cloaking the Boundless below. Everyone else was sleeping. Anna dozed in the copilot's chair, her head tilted to the side. Makara did nothing to wake her, taking the burden of both piloting and copiloting upon herself. It was very Makara-like.

Behind his sister, Samuel also slept. I was fighting my own battle with weariness, a battle I was sure to lose. It was two in the morning, and Makara had yet to cease her search for Marcus and the Exiles. This had been the story of the last three days, and still her reddened eyes scanned the desert floor with *Odin's* two

floodlights, revealing nothing but dune, hill, mesa, and the suː
pink of a patch of xenofungus. Periodically, Makara glanced at the
LCD, which displayed topography, speed, and *Odin's* location. We
were somewhere in central Arizona.

I felt it was all useless. This time-consuming search was eating
away at us all, and we could only take so much before it was time to
examine other options. Samuel had told Anna and me as much in
private earlier today. He dared not tell Makara; not yet. And with
each day that passed with no results, no clues, she became edgier.

She still believed the Wanderer had wanted her to search here,
when all seemed lost. And certainly, everything *did* seem lost. It was
the four of us, and Ashton, expecting to stop an entire army that
would soon be thundering its way north. And not only *that* army,
but the army of xenolife readying itself to strike from the east.
Everything depended on swelling our ranks, and all of us felt the
clock ticking.

With a curse, Makara leaned back in her chair. She sighed,
shutting her eyes. It was the first time she had broken her
concentration for hours. *Odin* flew on in a straight line, due east,
about a thousand feet above the surface.

I closed my own eyes. My conscious mind faded under the
weight of drowsiness. Makara's voice snapped me to attention.

"Let's call it a night."

She slammed the controls, the sudden sound doing nothing to
wake either Samuel or Anna. Out in the Wastes, both of them
would have been up in a heartbeat at the disturbance. But *Odin* was
a safe place, and there were allowances here that didn't exist on the
surface. Makara returned to the controls, angling the ship toward
the surface. Again, the change in trajectory did nothing to shake
either Samuel or Anna from their slumber. How I was still awake, I
didn't know. Even a week out of Nova Roma, I was exhausted from
the entire ordeal. Makara's side, which had been injured in the
Coleseo, was still tender, but healing. But our time in the Empire

had taken it out of all of us.

I would have thought sitting all day in a ship would be relaxing, but it wasn't. We had to stay alert, for either the Exiles, the Raiders, or the ever-present threat of the xenodragons. None of those had ambushed us – at least, not yet – but that didn't mean they wouldn't at some point.

Makara guided *Odin* down, toward the top of a mesa that rose above the desert floor, its massive shape shadowy in the darkness. The dunes below were discernable around the mesa, but just barely. Now that we were back in the Wasteland, the atmospheric dust from Ragnarok had returned. I was already missing the feel of the sun on my skin. The sunburns I had received while in Nova Roma were still peeling.

Odin hovered, giving a tiny lift as it alighted atop the mesa. Powering off the ship, Makara unstrapped herself from her seat and immediately left the cockpit. Anna and Samuel slept on, oblivious to the fact that we had stopped. Samuel snored lightly, his head leaning back against the headrest. Anna's head was still cocked to the side, a dribble of drool dripping from the corner of her mouth.

I touched her shoulder. "Hey. We've stopped."

Her eyes fluttered open. She gave a nod, wiped her mouth, and unstrapped herself from the seat. She stood, and we left Samuel where he was, walking down the corridor toward the bunks in the back. I knew Anna would prefer sleeping in her own bunk, and would have been upset if I had left her in the copilot's seat like that. Samuel, however, could probably sleep on a pile of rocks and not notice the difference.

When we got to the crew cabins, we were alone. Makara had appropriated the captain's quarters off the galley to herself.

"Sleep tight," I said, leaning in for a kiss.

She kissed me – not too enthusiastically, I must admit. She turned for her bunk, and I watched her lie down. Before she even covered herself with her blanket, her breathing became even with sleep. I'd always envied people with the ability to do that – fall asleep as if there *weren't* a million things wrong with the world.

I sighed, turning for my own cabin, which I shared with Samuel. I lay down on my bunk, closing my eyes. The hum of the ship, on low power, lulled me to sleep, a sleep none too fitful.

***

The next day I awoke early, stepped out of bed, and got dressed. I ducked out the doorway, went through the galley, and headed to the kitchen. The air was cool in *Odin's* metallic hull, automatic lights flashing on as I passed under them. I found the coffee pot and filled it with water, placing coffee grounds inside. Now back in civilization, I had the means to nurse my caffeine addiction with Skyhome's own brew.

As the water heated and filtered through the grounds, I went to the fridge, grabbed some fresh grapefruit, and opened the cabinet to get some granola, the latter sealed in a reusable, airtight bag. By the time I'd prepared my breakfast, the coffee was done. I'd made a whole pot, in case someone else wanted some later. The resources provided by Skyhome were almost as good as what I'd had back in Bunker 108.

I grabbed both my food and coffee, and walked to the table in the galley. I sat, the first steaming sip of coffee warming me up. The stuff was like an elixir. Though Makara and Anna liked to sleep until the last possible moment before we left (in fact, Makara usually just rolled out of bed and headed straight to the pilot seat), I liked to be up an hour earlier than everyone else to have some alone time. It was great to have the entire ship to myself, to be alone with my thoughts, my food, my coffee.

After downing the last of my coffee and finishing off my grapefruit and granola, I got up and headed for the blast door. I pressed the button. The door slid open, letting in a rush of frigid, dry wind. I stepped outside, ignoring the extreme cold. It was winter now, and it showed in every way imaginable. The darkness was near absolute, and though I could not see it, I knew the cliff's edge was just a few feet away from the edge of the boarding ramp. Nevertheless, I stood on the ramp, weathering the harsh wind as it buffeted against me. I peered into the sky, trying to discern where the moon was. On the western sky, there was a milky glow of cloud. Such was the effect of the meteor fallout – we all might as well have been in a cave deep in the heart of the Earth.

I took out my digital watch, and lighted it up. I went to the temperature tab. It was minus nineteen Celsius. Two below zero Fahrenheit.

"Yeah," I said. "Time to go back inside."

I entered *Odin*, the door shutting behind me. The ship's interior, once cool, now felt warm by comparison, tingling my skin. To my surprise, Samuel sat at the table, a cup of coffee in hand. His handgun was partially disassembled, its parts lying neatly at the table's center. He was brushing the action of the handgun. I noticed several other guns sitting on the table corner.

"Put yours in line, if you like," Samuel said.

After two months of heavy use, my Beretta was probably much in need of a cleaning. I set the gun down, removed the magazine, and checked the barrel to make sure it was empty.

"You can use an AR, right?" Samuel asked.

I nodded. "It's been a while since I've used one, but yeah. Chan, the CSO of Bunker 108, had everyone trained on a variety of things."

"Good. I'm thinking of having everyone diversify a bit. We're seeing a lot of action, and there are points where it would be useful to have a rifle. We have an entire armory on *Odin* that is hardly getting any use, except when we need to restock on ammo."

"If you give me some time to practice, I'm sure it'll come back quickly."

"You'll have to show me a few things too," Samuel said. "I've always wanted to fire one of those things."

"Will do."

Samuel moved on to Makara's handgun. His movements were deft, methodical. Within moments he had the essential parts disassembled and was already brushing the interior with the cleaning solvent.

"What's our next move?" I asked.

"We keep going, until we find the Exiles."

"I mean, if we *can't* find them. It's been three days, after all." I hesitated a moment. "You said it yourself, yesterday. If we can't find them..."

"We're all here because Makara believes the Wanderer told her to find the Exiles," he said. "And until we do, I don't think she's going to want to move on."

"I want to know what that guy's *exact* wording was. Maybe she's just interpreting it wrong."

"I've interpreted *nothing* wrong."

Makara glared at me from the doorway to the captain's quarters. I hadn't heard her come in.

"I know that's what you believe," I said. "But..."

"Alex..." Samuel said, low. "Careful."

Makara was still staring daggers at me. She walked up to the table and placed a hand on its edge. She looked at me, her green eyes blazing.

"We *will* find them. And what the Wanderer said...it's between me and him. Got it?"

"Yeah. Sure."

Makara walked off to the kitchen. I heard the sounds of her digging in the fridge and filling a cup with coffee.

"What's up with her?"

"She's just stressed," Samuel said. "Don't take it personally."

From the kitchen came the sound of Makara cursing about something. Apparently, she had burned herself.

"You're up early," Samuel called.

"A lot to do," she called back. "Today's the big day. We're going to find them. I feel it."

"I hope so," I said, low enough so that Makara wouldn't hear.

Makara returned to the table with two slices of cantaloupe, toast, and coffee. She sat down, her eyes red, dark underlines set deeper than ever.

Makara dug into her cantaloupe, as if her mission were to get it down as quickly as possible rather than enjoy it. While she ate, Samuel finished cleaning the last handgun, which happened to be Makara's. Anna's saw so little use that it probably didn't even need a tune-up. After putting the brush and solvent away in the kit on the table, Samuel closed the kit, then slid the gun over to Makara.

While Makara finished her food, Anna walked in. Dreary-eyed, she looked at all of us before heading for the kitchen.

"Well," Makara said, standing up, "I'm going to fire up the engine. Figured we'd make a sweep a little closer to the Great Blight today."

"Not until we've exhausted every other option," Samuel said.

Makara frowned. "It's the biggest chunk of land we haven't surveyed yet. Trust me, if any of those *things* come flying at us, I can handle it."

"I don't see how anyone could survive being that close to the Great Blight," I said. "Even the Exiles. It would make sense for them to be further away."

"Well, no one asked you. I just have a gut feeling about this that I want to follow." She stood, leaving her dirty plate on the table for me to clean. "We'll be in the air in five minutes."

Makara headed for the cockpit, just as Anna sat down next to me with her breakfast.

"Hey," I said.

"What's up?" She started to eat.

"Try to be up in the cockpit in five," Samuel said, rising to go. He left Anna and me at the table.

"I had this random thought this morning," Anna said.

"What?"

"You know that toothpaste we use, the minty one?"

I paused. "Yes?"

"Well, where the hell does it come from?"

I frowned. "Skyhome?"

"Yeah, I know *that*. Back when I lived on the surface, you were lucky to find anything salvaging, and most of the time it would be so old that it was like brushing your teeth with caulk. Mom and I would always use ashes from our fires mixed with water."

"Ash and water? I would have never thought of that."

"It's because you're from a Bunker. What did *you* guys do for toothpaste?"

"I don't know. We just always seemed to have it. How it's made is probably in the archive, somewhere. Or maybe they stocked up enough to last for a long time."

She shrugged. "I guess it will always be a mystery, huh?"

She went back to her food. Like Makara, Anna favored cantaloupe.

"I'll have to remember the ash and water thing. Might come in handy."

The ship began to hum as the fusion drive warmed up. Within minutes, we would be in the air.

Anna finished the last of her food. I touched her shoulder, causing her to pause mid-bite.

"Come on, let's go up front."

After she swallowed the rest of her food, we left the table and the dirty dishes behind.

***

It was midmorning, and we had been searching three hours. The long, pink border of the Great Blight crawled north to south on the ship's right side. Just seeing that field of blaring pink, orange, and purple was unsettling. The xenofungus coated the desert floor, climbed over rocks, stretched over plains, slithered up mountains. The eastern sun cast a red, fiery light on the alien growth, setting its colors aflame. Swarms of creatures – probably birds – flew in tornado-like clouds, for the time being ignoring our presence.

It was like staring at the surface of an alien planet. And I guessed, for all intents and purposes, it *was* an alien planet. *This* was what we were fighting. Seeing all that alien growth was depressing.

We followed the line of the Great Blight until it started veering northwest. As the minutes passed and we continued our search, the Great Blight's border turned even *more* toward the west. The Great Blight stretched not only to the east, but also endlessly to the north.

"Was all this here before?" Makara asked.

We stood in silence seeing the fields touch the far horizon. We had never been this far north before, so maybe it had always been like this. Or maybe it had only recently expanded in this direction. It gave me a sense that time was definitely running out.

"I don't know," Samuel said. "Keep following the border, toward the west. That'll put us closer to Vegas in a couple of hours."

We followed the ground at a low altitude of about a thousand feet – high enough to be safe, yet low enough to easily see anything, or anyone, below. The Great Blight persisted in its westward crawl, sliding past our field of view. A purple lake glimmered far to the north, making me think that it was filled with purple goo rather than water. The xenoviral flora stood thick along its alien shoreline in a tangle of webbed growth.

The comm on the ship's dash began to beep, lighting red.

"Did anyone check in with Ashton last night?" Makara asked.

We all looked at each other. We were supposed to update Ashton once a day on how things were going.

"I forgot," Samuel said. "Put it on speaker."

Makara answered the call. "Yeah?"

"Give me your update from yesterday," Ashton said.

"Nothing to report, really," Makara said, angling the ship as the Great Blight's border started heading due west. "Did some more recon on the coordinates I sent you. We found nothing but dust."

"Makara, if you can't find anything soon..."

"We will," Makara said, interrupting. "I feel it in my bones."

"Feeling has nothing to do with it," Ashton said. "We are on a limited timetable, and I can't have you guys wasting time searching for a needle in a haystack."

"I understand that," Makara said. "But I know Char. If he went anywhere, it would have been to his brother."

"Even though he *hates* him?" Anna asked from the copilot's seat.

"I need you on my side, Anna," Makara said.

"I'm allowed my own opinion," Anna said. "Maybe Ashton is right."

"Alright," Makara said, annoyed, "if not the Exiles, who do we go to?"

No one said anything.

"Well, there's Vegas," I said. "There are the northern Bunkers, 76 and 88..."

"Have you tried calling those Bunkers, Ashton?" Samuel asked.

"Repeatedly. I'm getting nothing. On 76, the line is going through, only...no one is answering."

"That's not a good sign," Makara said.

"What about Bunker 88?" I asked.

"Nothing," Ashton said. "It's safe to assume they are both offline, though at some point, you guys will still have to check it out yourselves. That is, if we have time. With what we're facing from Augustus and the xenovirus, we need every ally we can get."

"So, what about Vegas?" Samuel asked. "Why not just go there first?"

"Did you not learn from the Empire?" Makara asked. "If Char and Marcus back us up, we'll be bargaining from a position of power. We'll have hundreds at our back from the get-go. The Vegas Gangs will be more willing to listen to us."

"Good luck getting those two to work together," Anna said.

"They *will* work together," Makara said.

"I hope you're right, Makara," Ashton said. "Because this is your last day. I *cannot* allow you to waste any more time on this exercise."

"It's *not* an exercise," she said. "It's a necessity. I'm not allowing us to walk into Vegas with our pants down. From what I've heard, it's just as bad as L.A."

"That remains to be seen," Ashton said.

"How's your project coming, Ashton?" Samuel asked.

"I've finished one of the two wavelength monitors. The one Makara and I dropped earlier is still functioning, so getting these two done will help us triangulate the Voice's exact point of origin. Although I'm missing a few parts that I will have to find down on the surface."

"Where are they?" Samuel asked.

There was a pause. "Bunker Six."

Bunker Six. It was just a hop from Bunker One, toward the north. Like Bunker One, it had fallen in the xenoswarm's first major attack on humanity. That place was going to be thick with crawlers, if our time at Bunker One was any indication.

"Ashton, it's too dangerous," Makara said.

"I can handle myself," Ashton said. "I've gotten in and out of Bunker One half a dozen times over the years. What makes you think it will be different with Bunker Six? If the dock doors are still functional, getting in will be easy. My preliminary scans show that the Bunker's empty. No waves coming from that area, so the Voice is focused on something else. In fact..."

Ashton paused a moment.

"What is it?" I asked.

"Just give me a second." Once again, Ashton was quiet. I could hear the clacking of keys from his computer. "The Voice seems to be focused on where you guys are right now. Lots of waves coming in your direction."

That didn't sound good.

"Well, we have visual on the Great Blight right now," Samuel said. "It looks clear."

"Still, be on the lookout," Ashton said. "Something fishy is going on. Like Makara said...don't get caught with your pants down."

"So, you're *really* going into Bunker Six?" I asked.

"I have to, kid. In fact, I'm going as soon as this call is over. With the Voice focused elsewhere, it might be my best time to get in. The parts I need aren't too far from the hangar." Ashton cleared his throat. "Sorry. Anyway, another thing we might add to our to-do list is liberating *Perseus* and *Orion.*"

"The other two ships?" Anna asked.

"That's right. That's further in the future, but if we have four ships at our disposal, and more trained pilots, it will give the New Angels flexibility. It will also give us an edge in any upcoming battles we have to fight."

Battles. Yes, there would be those, soon. But those battles were months away. Augustus was coming for us, and would have troops in the Wasteland as soon as he possibly could. That could be two months – that is, if the Wasteland winter didn't stop him first. Ashton had mentioned that fact on one of his radio calls a couple days ago. For now, it looked as though his legions were still coming. When they got here, we had to be ready to pull out all the stops.

"Wait," Makara said. "I think I'm seeing something."

At the top of the ridge to the west was a swarming movement. It took me a moment to discern the distant shapes.

"Crawlers," I said. "I wonder what they're after."

As Makara sped up and we drew closer, we could see more clearly. Crawlers surrounded a large group of people whose discarded bikes formed a perimeter around them.

"Ashton, we have contact," Makara said. "The Exiles need our help."

"Go get 'em, kid."

Ashton cut out, as we zoomed in close.

***

Find the rest of *Revelation* on Amazon.

Glossary

10,000, The: This refers to the 10,000 citizens who were selected in 2029 to enter Bunker One. This group included the best America had to offer, people who were masters in the fields of science, engineering, medicine, and security. President Garland and all the U.S. Congress, as well as essential staff and their families, were chosen.

Alpha: "Alpha" is the title given to the recognized head of the Raiders. In the beginning, it was merely a titular role that only had as much power as the Alpha was able to enforce. But as Raider Bluff grew in size and complexity, the Alpha took on a more meaningful role. Typically, Alphas do not remain so for long – they are assassinated by rivals who rise to take their place. In some years, there can be as many as four Alphas – though powerful Alphas, like Char, can reign for many years.

Batts: Batts, or batteries, are the currency of the Wasteland and the Empire. They are accepted anywhere that the Empire's caravans reach. It is unknown *how* batteries were first seen as currency, but it is rumored that Augustus himself instigated the policy. Using them as currency makes sense: batteries are small, portable, and durable, and have the intrinsic quality of being useful. Rechargeable batteries (called "chargers") are even more prized, and solar batteries (called "solars," or "sols") are the most useful and prized of all.

Behemoth: The Behemoth is a great monstrosity in the Wasteland – a giant creature, either humanoid or reptilian, or sometimes a mixture of the two, that can reach heights of ten feet or greater. They are bipedal, powerful, and can keep pace with a moving vehicle. All but the most powerful of guns are useless against the Behemoth's armored hide.

Black Reapers, The: The Black Reapers are a powerful, violent gang, based in Los Angeles. They are led by Warlord Carin Black. They keep thousands of slaves, using them to serve their post-apocalyptic empire. They usurped the Lost Angels in 2055, and have been ruling there ever since.

Black Files, The: The Black Files are the mysterious collected research on the xenovirus, located in Bunker One. They were authored principally by Dr. Cornelius Ashton, Chief Scientist of Bunker One.

Blights: Blights are infestations of xenofungus and the xenolife they support. They are typically small, but the bigger ones can cover large tracts of land. As a general rule of thumb, the larger the Blight, the more complicated and dangerous the ecosystem it maintains. The largest known Blight is the Great Blight – which covers a large portion of the central United States. Its center is Ragnarok Crater.

Boundless, The: The Boundless is an incredibly dry part of the Wasteland, ravaged by canyons and dust storms, situated in what used to be Arizona and New Mexico. Very little can survive in the Boundless, and no one is known to have ever crossed it.

Bunker 40: Bunker 40 is located on the outer fringes of the Great Blight in Arizona. It is hidden beneath a top secret research facility, a vestige of the Old World. Many aircraft were stationed at Bunker 40 before it fell, sometime in the late 2050s.

Bunker 108: Bunker 108 is located in the San Bernardino Mountains about one hundred miles east of Los Angeles. It is the birthplace of Alex Keener.

Bunker 114: Bunker 114 is a medical research installation built about fifty miles northwest of Bunker 108. Built beneath Cold Mountain, Bunker 114 is small. After the fall of Bunker One, Bunker 114, like Bunker 108 to the southeast, became a main center of xenoviral research. An outbreak of the human strain of the xenovirus caused the Bunker to fall in 2060. Bunker 108's fall followed soon thereafter.

Bunker One: Bunker One was the main headquarters of the Post-Ragnarok United States government. It fell in 2048 to a swarm of crawlers that overran its defenses. Bunker One had berths for ten thousand people, making it many times over the most populous Bunker. Its inhabitants included President Garland, the U.S. Senate and House of Representatives, essential government staff, and security forces, along with the skilled people needed to maintain it. Also, dozens of brilliant scientists and specialists lived and worked there, including engineers, doctors, and technicians. The very wealthy were also allowed berths for helping to finance the Bunker Program. Bunker One is the location of the Black Files, authored by Dr. Cornelius Ashton.

Bunker Six: Bunker Six is a large installation located north of Bunker One, within driving distance. It houses the S-Class spaceships constructed during the Dark Decade – including *Gilgamesh*, the capital ship, and three smaller cruisers – *Odin*, *Perseus*, and *Orion*. While *Gilgamesh* and *Odin* are under Cornelius Ashton's care, *Perseus* and *Orion* are still locked inside the fallen Bunker.

Bunker Program, The: The United States and Canadian governments pooled resources to establish 144 Bunkers in Twelve Sectors throughout their territory. The Bunkers were the backup in case the Guardian Missions failed. When the Guardian Missions *did* fail, the Bunker Program kicked into full gear. The Bunkers were designed to save all critical government personnel and citizenry, along with anyone who could provide the finances to construct them. The Bunkers were designed to last indefinitely, using hydroponics to grow food. The Bunkers ran on fusion power, which had been made efficient by the early 2020s. The plan was that, when the dust settled, Bunker residents could reemerge and rebuild. Most Bunkers fell, however, for various reasons – including critical systems failures, mutinies, and attacks by outsiders (see **Wastelanders**). By the year 2060, only four Bunkers were left.

Chaos Years, The: The Chaos Years refer to the ten years following the impact of Ragnarok. These dark years signified the great die-off of most forms of life, including humans. Most deaths occurred due to starvation. With mass global cooling, crops could not grow in climates too far from the tropics. What crops *would* grow produced a yield far too paltry to feed the population that existed. This led to a period of violence unknown in all of human history. The Chaos Years signify the complete breakdown of the Old World's remaining infrastructures – including food production, economies, power grids, and the industrial complex – all of which led to the deaths of billions of people.

Coleseo Imperio: *El Coleseo Imperio*, translated as the Imperial Coliseum, is a circular, three-tiered stone arena rising from the center of the city of Nova Roma, the capital of the Nova Roma Empire. It is used to host gladiatorial games in the tradition of ancient Rome, and serves as the chief sport of the Empire. Slaves and convicts are forced to fight in death matches, which serves the dual purpose of entertaining the masses while getting rid of prisoners and slaves who would otherwise be, in the Empire's eyes, liabilities. Many festivals, and even ritual sacrifices, take place on the arena floor.

Crawlers: Crawlers are dangerous, highly mobile monsters spawned by Ragnarok. Their origin is unclear, but they share many characteristics of Earth animals – mostly those reptilian in nature. Crawlers are sleek and fast, and can leap through the air at very high speeds. Typically, crawlers attack in groups, and behave as if of one mind. One crawler will, without hesitation, sacrifice itself in order to reach its prey. Crawlers are especially dangerous when gathered in high numbers – at which point there is not much one can do but run. Crawlers can be killed, their weak points being their belly and their three eyes.

Dark Decade, The: The Dark Decade lasted from 2020-2030, from the time of the first discovery of Ragnarok, to the time of its impact. It is not called the Dark Decade because the world descended into madness immediately upon the discovery of Ragnarok by astronomer Neil Weinstein – that only happened in 2028, with the failure of *Messiah,* the third and last of the Guardian Missions. In the United States and other industrialized nations, life proceeded in an almost normal fashion. There were plenty of good reasons to believe that Ragnarok could be stopped, especially when given ten years. But as the Guardian Missions failed, one by one, the order of the world quickly disintegrated.

With the failure of the Guardian Mission *Archangel* in 2024, a series of wars engulfed the world. As what some were calling World War III embroiled the planet, the U.S. and several of its European allies, and Canada, continued to work on stopping Ragnarok. When the second Guardian Mission, *Reckoning,* failed, an economic depression swept the world. But none of this compared to the madness that followed upon the failure of the third and final Guardian, *Messiah,* in 2028. As societies broke down, martial law was enforced. President Garland was appointed dictator of the United States with absolute authority. By 2029, several states had broken off from the Union.

In the last quarter of 2030, an odd silence hung over the world, as if it had grown weary of living. The President, all essential governmental staff and military, the Senate and House of Representatives, along with scientists, engineers, and the talented and the wealthy, entered the 144 Bunkers established by the Bunker Program. Outraged, the tens of millions of people who did not get an invitation found the Bunker locations, demanding to be let in. The military took action when necessary.

Then, on December 3, 2030, Ragnarok fell, crashing into the border of Wyoming and Nebraska, forming a crater one hundred miles wide. The world left the Dark Decade, and entered the Chaos Years.

Exiles, The: The Exiles are led by a man named Marcus, brother of Alpha Char. The Exiles were once Raiders, but were exiled from Raider Bluff in 2048. Raider Bluff faced a rival city, known as Rivertown, on the Colorado River. A faction led by Char wanted to destroy Rivertown by blowing up Hoover Dam far to the north. Marcus and his faction opposed this. The two brothers fought, and in his rage, Marcus threw Char into a nearby fireplace, giving him the severe burns on his face that Char would live with for the rest of his life. For this attack, the Alpha at the time exiled Marcus – but in solidarity, many Raiders left to join him. For the next twelve years, the exiled Raiders wandered the Boundless, barred from ever returning farther west than Raider Bluff. The Exiles at first sought to found a new city somewhere in the eastern United States, but the Great Blight barred their path. Over the next several years, they hired themselves as mercenaries to the growing Nova Roma Empire. Now, they wander the Wastes, Marcus awaiting the day when his brother calls upon him for help – which he is sure Char will do.

Flyers: Flyers are birds infected with the xenovirus. They fly in large swarms of a hundred or more. They are only common around large Blights, or within the Great Blight itself. The high metabolism of flyers means they cannot venture far from xenofungus, their main source of food. They are highly dangerous, and cannot be fought easily, because they fly in such large numbers.

Gilgamesh: Gilgamesh is an S-Class Capital Spaceship constructed by the United States during the Dark Decade. It holds room for twelve crewmen, thirteen counting the captain. Its fuselage is mostly made of carbon nanotubes – incredibly lightweight, and many, many times stronger than steel. It is powered by a prototypical miniature fusion reactor, using deuterium and tritium as fuel. Its design is described as insect-like in appearance, for invisibility to radar. The ship contains a bridge, armory, conference room, galley, wardroom, two lavatories, a clinic, and twelve bunks for crew in two separate dorms. A modest captain's quarters can be reached from the wardroom, complete with its own lavatory. Within the wardroom is access to a spacious cargo bay, where supplies, and even a vehicle as large as a Recon, can be stored. The Recon can be driven off the ship's wide boarding ramp when grounded (this capability is the main difference between *Odin* and *Gilgamesh*...in addition to the cargo bay boarding ramp, *Gilgamesh* also contains a passenger's boarding ramp on the side, that also leads into the wardroom). The porthole has a retractable rope ladder that is good for up to five hundred feet. *Gilgamesh* has a short wingspan, but receives most of its lift from the four thrusters situated aft, thrusters that have a wide arc of rotation that allows the ship to fly in almost any direction. Two more thrusters are situated fore, allowing the ship to hover. The ship can go weeks without needing to refuel. As far as combat capabilities, *Gilgamesh* was primarily constructed as a reconnaissance and transport vessel. That said, it has twin machine gun turrets that open from beneath the ship. When grounded, it is supported by three struts, one in front, two in back.

Great Blight, The: The Great Blight is the largest xenofungal infestation in the world, its point of origin being Ragnarok Crater on the Great Plains in eastern Wyoming and western Nebraska. Unlike other Blights, the Great Blight is massive. From 2040-2060, it began to rapidly expand outside Ragnarok Crater at an alarming rate, moving as much as a quarter mile each day (meaning the stretching of the xenofungus could actually be discerned with the naked eye). Any and all life was conquered, killed, or acquired into the Great Blight's xenoparasitic network. Here, the first monsters were created. Animals would become ensnared in sticky pools of purple goo, and their DNA absorbed and preserved. The Great Blights, obeying some sort of consciousness, would then mix and match the DNA of varying species, tweaking and mutating the genes until, from the same pools it had acquired the DNA, it would give birth to new life forms, designed only to spread the Blight and kill whoever, or whatever, opposed that spreading. As time went on and the Xeno invasion became more sophisticated, the Great Blight's capabilities became advanced enough to direct the evolution of xenolife itself, leading to the creation of the xenovirus, meaning it could infect species far outside of the Blight – including, eventually, humans.

Guardian Missions: The Guardian Missions were humanity's attempts to intercept and alter the course of Ragnarok during the Dark Decade. There were three, and in the order they were launched, they were called *Archangel, Reckoning,* and *Messiah* (all three of which were also the names of the ships launched). Each mission had a reason for failing. *Archangel* is reported to have crashed into Ragnarok, in 2024. In 2026, *Reckoning* somehow got off-course, losing contact with Earth in the process. In 2028 *Messiah* successfully landed and attached its payload of rockets to the surface of Ragnarok in order to alter its course from Earth. However, the rockets failed before they had time to do their work. The failure of the Guardian Missions kicked the Bunker Program into overdrive.

Howlers: Howlers are the newest known threat posed by the xenovirus. They are human xenolife, and they behave very much like zombies. They attack with sheer numbers, using their bodies as weapons. A bite from a Howler is enough to infect the victim with the human strain of the xenovirus. Post-infection, it takes anywhere from a few minutes to a few hours for a corpse to reanimate into the dreaded Howler. Worse, upon death, Howlers somehow explode, raining purple goo on anyone within range. Even if a little bit of goo enters the victim's bloodstream, he or she is as good as dead, cursed to become a Howler within a matter of minutes or hours. How the explosion occurs, no one knows – it is surmised that the xenovirus itself creates some sort of agent that reacts violently with water or some other fluid present within the Howlers. There is also reason to believe that certain Howlers become Behemoths, as was the case with Kari in Bunker 114.

Hydra: A powerful spawning of the xenovirus, the Hydra has only been seen deep in the heart of Bunker One. It contains three heads mounted on three stalk-like necks. It is covered in thick scales that serve as armor. It has a powerful tail that it can swing, from the end of which juts a long, cruel spike. It is likely an evolved, more deadly form of the crawler.

Ice Lands, The: Frozen in a perpetual blanket of ice and snow, the northern and southern latitudes of the planet are completely unlivable. In the Wasteland, at least, they are referred to as the Ice Lands. Under a blanket of meteor fallout, extreme global cooling was instigated in 2030. While the glaciers are only now experiencing rapid regrowth, they will advance for centuries to come until the fallout has dissipated enough to produce a warmer climate. In the Wasteland, 45 degrees north marks the beginning of what is considered the Ice Lands.

L.A. Gangland: L.A. Gangland means a much different thing than it did Pre-Ragnarok. In the ruins of Los Angeles, there are dozens of gangs vying for control, but by 2060, the most powerful is the Black Reapers, who usurped that title from the Lost Angels.

Lost Angels, The: The Lost Angels were post-apocalyptic L.A.'s first super gang. From the year 2050 until 2055, they reigned supreme in the city, led by a charismatic figure named Dark Raine. The Angels were different from other gangs – they valued individual freedom and abhorred slavery. Under the Angels' rule, Los Angeles prospered. The Angels were eventually usurped in 2056 by a gang called the Black Reapers, led by a man named Carin Black.

Nova Roma: Nova Roma is the capital of the Nova Roma Empire. It existed Pre-Ragnarok as a small town situated in an idyllic valley, flanked on three sides by green mountains. This town was also home to Augustus's palatial mansion – and it was around this mansion that the city that would one day rule the Empire had its beginnings. Over thirty years, as the Empire gained wealth and power under Augustus's rule, Nova Roma grew from a small village into a mighty city with a population numbering in the tens of thousands. Using knowledge of ancient construction techniques found in American Bunkers, Augustus employed talented engineers and thousands of slaves to build the city from the ground up. Inspired by the architecture of ancient Rome, some of the most notable construction projects in Nova Roma include the *Coleseo Imperio,* the Senate House, the Grand Forum, and Central Square. An aqueduct carries water over the city walls from the Sierra Madre Mountains north of the city. The city grows larger each passing year, so much so that shantytowns have overflowed its walls, attracted by the city's vast wealth.

Nova Roma Empire, The: The Nova Roma Empire (also known as the "Empire") is a collection of allied city-states that are ruled from Nova Roma, its capital in what was formerly the Mexican state of Guerrero. The Empire began as the territory of a Mexican drug cartel named the Legion. Through the use of brutal force, they kept security within their borders even as other governments fell.

Following the impact of Ragnarok, many millions of Americans fled south to escape the cold, dry climate that permeated northern latitudes. Mexico still remained warm, especially southern Mexico, and new global wind currents caused by Ragnarok kept Mexico clearer of meteor fallout than other areas of the world. At the close of the Chaos Years, Mexico was far more populous than the United States. Many city-states formed in the former republic, but most developed west of the Sierra Madre Mountains. Language clashes between native Mexicans and migrant Americans produced new dialects of both Spanish and English. Though racial tensions exist in the Empire, as Americans' descendants are the minority within it, Americans and their descendants are protected under law and are entitled to the same rights – at least in theory. The reality is, most refugees that entered Imperial territory were American – and most refugees ended up as slaves.

Of the hundreds of city-states that formed in Mexico, one was called Nova Roma, located inland in a temperate valley not too far east of Acapulco. Under the direction of the man styling himself as Augustus Imperator, formerly known as Miguel Santos, lord of the Legion drug cartel, the city of Nova Roma allied with neighboring city-states. Incorporating both Ancient Roman governmental values and Aztec mythology, the Empire expanded through either the conquest or annexation of rival city-states. By 2060, the Empire had hundreds of cities in its thrall, stretching from Oaxaca in the southeast all the way to Jalisco in the northwest. The Empire had also formed colonies as far north as Sonora, even founding a city called Colossus at the mouth of the Colorado River, intended to be the provincial capital from which the Empire hoped to rule California and the Mojave.

Because of its size and power, the Empire is difficult to control. Except for its center, ruled out of Nova Roma, most of the city-states are autonomous and are only required to pay tribute and soldiers when called for during the Empire's wars. In the wake of the Empire's rapid conquests, Augustus developed the Imperial Road System in order to facilitate trade and communication, mostly done by horse. In an effort to create a unifying culture for the Empire, Emperor Augustus instigated a representative government, where all of Nova Roma's provinces have representation in the Imperial Senate. Augustus encouraged a universal religion based on Aztec mythology, whose gods are placed alongside the saints of Catholicism in the Imperial Pantheon. Augustus also instigated gladiatorial games, ordering that arenas be built in every major settlement of his Empire. This included the construction of dozens of arenas, including *El Coleseo Imperio* in Nova Roma itself, a large arena which, while not as splendid as the original Coliseum in Old Rome, is still quite impressive. The *Coleseo* can seat ten thousand people. By 2060, Augustus had accomplished what might have taken a century to establish otherwise.

Oasis: Oasis is a settlement located in the Wasteland, about halfway between Los Angeles and Raider Bluff. It has a population of one thousand, and is built around the banks of the oasis for which it is named. The oasis did not exist Pre-Ragnarok, but was formed by tapping an underground aquifer. Elder Ohlan rules Oasis with a strong hand. He is the brother of Dark Raine, and it is whispered that he might have had a hand in his death.

***Odin*:** *Odin* is an S-Class Cruiser Spaceship built by the U.S. during the Dark Decade. It is one of four, the other being *Gilgamesh,* the capital ship, and the other two being *Perseus* and *Orion,* cruisers with the same specs as *Odin.* Though *Odin's* capabilities are not as impressive as *Gilgamesh's, Odin* is still very functional. It contains berths for eight crew, nine counting the captain. It has a cockpit, armory, wardroom, galley, two dorms, one lavatory, and the fusion drive in the aft. A cargo bay can be reached from either outside the ship or within the wardroom. Unlike *Gilgamesh,* it is not spacious enough to store a Recon. It contains a single machine gun turret that can open up from the ship's bottom. *Odin,* in addition to being faster than *Gilgamesh,* also gets better fuel efficiency. It can go months without needing to refuel.

Praetorians, The: The Praetorians are the most elite of the Empire's soldiers. There are one hundred total, and they are the personal bodyguard of Emperor Augustus. They carry a long spear, tower shield, and gladius. They wear a long, purple cape, steel armor, and a white jaguar headdress, complete with purple plume. They are also trained in the use of guns.

Raider Bluff: Raider Bluff is the only known settlement of the raiders. It is built northeast of what used to be Needles, California, on top of a three-tiered mesa. Though the raiders are a mobile group, even they need a place to rest during the harsh Wasteland winter. Merchants, women, and servants followed the Raider men, setting up shop on the mesa, giving birth to Raider Bluff sometime in the early 2040s. From the top of the Bluff rules the Alpha, the strongest recognized leader of the Raiders. A new Alpha rises only when he is able to wrest control from the old one.

Ragnarok: Ragnarok was the name given the meteor that crashed into Earth on December 3, 2030. It was about three miles long, and two miles wide. It was discovered by astronomer Neil Weinstein, in 2019. It is not known *what* caused Ragnarok to come hurtling toward Earth, or how it eluded detection for so long – but that answer was revealed when the Black Files came to light. Ragnarok was the first phase of the invasion planned by the Xenos, the race of aliens attempting to conquer Earth. Implanted within Ragnarok was the xenovirus – the seed for all alien genetic life that was to destroy, acquire, and replace Earth life. The day the Xenos arrive, according to the Black Files, is called "Xenofall." The time of their eventual arrival is completely unknown.

Ragnarok Crater: Ragnarok Crater is the site of impact of the meteor Ragnarok. It is located on the border of Wyoming and Nebraska, and is about one hundred miles wide with walls eight miles tall. It's the center of the Great Blight, and it is also the origin of the Voice, the consciousness that directs the behavior of all xenolife.

Recon: A Recon is an all-terrain rover that is powered by hydrogen. It is designed for speedy recon missions across the Wastes, and was developed by the United States military during the Dark Decade. It is composed of a cab in front, and a large cargo bay in the back. Mounted on top of the cargo bay is a turret with 360-degree rotation, accessible by a ladder and a porthole. The turret can be manned and fired while the Recon is on the go.

Skyhome: Skyhome is a three-ringed, self-sufficient space station constructed by the United States during the Dark Decade, designed to house two hundred and fifty people. Like the Bunkers, it contains its own power, hydroponics, and water reclamation system designed to keep the station going as long as possible. Skyhome was never actually occupied until 2048, after the falls of both Bunker One and Bunker Six. Cornelius Ashton assumed control of the station, along with survivors from both Bunkers, in order to continue his research on the xenovirus which had destroyed his entire life.

Voice, The: The Voice is the name given to the collective consciousness of all xenolife. It exists in Ragnarok Crater – whether or not it has a corporeal form is unknown. However, it is agreed by Dr. Ashton and Samuel that the Voice controls xenolife using sound waves and vibrations within xenofungus. The Voice also sends sound waves that can be detected by xenolife while off the xenofungus. The Voice gives the entire Xeno invasion sentience, and is a piece of evidence pointing to an advanced alien race that is trying to conquer Earth.

Wanderer, The: A blind prophet who wanders the Wasteland.

Wastelanders: Wastelanders are surface dwellers, specifically ones that live in the southwestern United States. The term is broad – it can be as specific as to mean only someone who is forced to wander, scavenge, or raid for sustenance, or Wastelander can mean anyone who lives on the surface Post-Ragnarok, regardless of location or circumstances. Wastelanders are feared by Bunker dwellers, as they have been the number one reason for Bunkers failing.

Wasteland, The: The Wasteland is a large tract of land comprised of Southern California and the adjacent areas of the Western United States. It extends from the San Bernardino Mountains in the west, to the Rockies in the east (and in later years, the Great Blight), and from the northern border of Nova Roma on the south, to the Ice Lands to the north (which is about the same latitude as Sacramento, California). The Wasteland is characterized by a cold, extremely dry climate. Rainfall each year is little to none, two to four inches being about average. Little can survive the Wasteland, meaning that all life has clung to limited water supplies. Major population centers include Raider Bluff, along the Colorado River; Oasis, supplied by a body of water of the same name; and Last Town, a trading post that sprung up along I-10 between Los Angeles and the Mojave. Whenever the Wasteland is referred to, it is generally not referred to in its entire scope. It is mainly used to reference what was once the Mojave Desert.

Xenofall: Xenofall is the day of reckoning – when the Xenos finally arrive on Earth to claim it as their own. No one knows when that day is – whether it is in one year, ten years, or a thousand. It is feared that, when Xenofall *does* come, humans and all resistance will have been long gone.

Xenofungus: Xenofungus is a slimy, sticky fungus that is colored pink, orange, or purple (and sometimes all three), that infests large tracts of land and serves as the chief food source of all xenolife. It forms the basis of the Blights, and without xenofungus, xenolife could not exist. The fungus, while hostile to Earth life, facilitates the growth, development, and expansion of xenolife. It is nutrient-rich, and contains complicated compounds and proteins that are poison to Earth life, but ambrosia for xenolife. It is tough, resilient, resistant to fire, dryness, and cold – and if it isn't somehow stopped, one day xenofungus will cover the entire world.

Xenolife: Any form of life that is infected with the xenovirus.

Xenovirus: The xenovirus is an agent that acquires genes, adding them to its vast collection. It then mixes and matches the genes under its control to create something completely new, whether a plant, animal, bacteria, etc. There are thousands of strains of the xenovirus, maybe even millions, but most are completely undocumented. While the underlying core of each strain is the same, the strains are specific to each species it infects. Failed strains completely drop out of existence, but the successful ones live on. The xenovirus was first noted by Dr. Cornelius Ashton of Bunker One. His collected research on the xenovirus was compiled in the Black Files, which were lost in the fall of Bunker One in 2048.

Also by Kyle West

The Wasteland Chronicles
Apocalypse
Origins
Evolution
Revelation

Watch for more at kylewestwriter.wordpress.com.

Made in the USA
Lexington, KY
04 March 2014